THE THANE'S DAUGHTER

JOHN J. SPEARMAN

OTHER BOOKS BY THIS AUTHOR

The Halberd Series
Gallantry in Action
In Harm's Way
True Allegiance
Surrender Demand

The Pike Series
Pike's Potential
Pike's Passage
Pike's Progress
Pike's Purpose

The FitzDuncan Series
FitzDuncan
FitzDuncan's Alchemy
FitzDuncan's Enlightenment
FitzDuncan's Fortune
FitzDuncan's Gambit
FitzDuncan's Hope
FitzDuncan's Inheritance
FitzDuncan's Navy
FitzDuncan's Peril
FitzDuncan's Beginning

The Perseverance Andrews Series
The Defense of the Commonwealth
The Courage of the Commonwealth
The Resolve of the Commonwealth

Mercenary Navy Series
Rawlins' Redemption
Swiftsure Ascendant
Tenuous Defense

Burden Series
Burden

Orion Spur Series
Misfortune's Favorite
The Scourge of the Scyllans
Fondness for Adversity
Defender's Awakening
Deceptive Betrayal

PANTHEON

Major Gods

- Sky and heavens: **Zoryn** (male)
- Earth: **Teryssa** (female)
- Sea: **Marivelle** (female)
- Death: **Thalorix** (male)

Lesser Gods

- Fertility: **Vyran** (male)
- Romance and sexual pleasure: **Lysmera** (female)
- War: **Kravyna** (female)
- Commerce, travel, thievery: **Sylvaris** (male)
- Wisdom: **Eldryne** (female)
- Literature and arts: **Calithra** (female)
- Health and medicine: **Vionelle** (female)
- Smiths and manufacturing: **Korath** (male)
- Luck and fortune: **Serethyn** (female)

CALENDAR

Zorynth: Begins at Winter Solstice, lasts 31 days
Calithran: 30 days
Lysmeran: 30 days
Teryssan: Begins at Vernal Equinox, lasts 31 days.
Vyranth: lasts 30 days
Kravynth: lasts 31 days.
Vionelleth: Begins at Summer Solstice, lasts 31 days.
Sylvarith: lasts 30 days.
Marivelleth: lasts 30 days.
Serethyan: Begins at Autumnal Equinox, lasts 31 days.
Eldrynan: lasts 30 days.
Korathan: lasts 30 days.

1

It was three days until the end of Vionelleth. The solstice was four weeks past, and we were in the midst of the hottest days of the summer. I was sitting by the window, hoping for a breeze. The smells of the city—some pleasant, like food cooking, others not, like sewage fermenting in the heat—wafted into my flat.

The bell on my door at the bottom of the stairs next to the milliner's shop tinkled. I was not expecting anyone, so my ears pricked up, and I looked for my sword. Before I rose out of my chair, I heard someone call out.

"Hello?" a voice asked from below. "Is this where I would find Dexter Falk?"

"Who wants to know?" I yelled back.

The man did not answer. I could hear him puffing up the steps. He knocked on my door.

"I asked who you were, friend?" I stated, although my use of the word friend was tinged with menace.

By now, I was next to the door. My sword was in my hand. From the sound of the labored breathing, however, I did not think a threat was waiting on the other side.

"My name is Louis Ugarte," he said, "and I am looking for Dexter Falk. I would like to hire him."

"Then, welcome, friend," I said in a much friendlier tone than before.

His name seemed vaguely familiar. I tucked my sword behind the door so he would not see it, then undid the bolt and swung the door in. A short, fat man, his face streaming with sweat, stood there. His caftan-style robe, made of linen, was of the highest quality. He was clearly a prosperous man, unused to physical activity, such as climbing stairs on a hot day.

"Come in. May I offer you some refreshment? Though I only have water, I'm afraid."

"Some water would be welcome," he said as he shuffled over to the chair in front of the window where I had just been sitting.

As I went to pour him a cup of water, I saw that he was fanning himself with his hands. He gave up on that and wiped his face with his sleeve. I handed him the cup and pulled a chair over so we could talk.

"I am indeed Dexter Falk. How may I be of service, Mister Ugarte?"

"I am the head of a large merchant concern. Perhaps you've heard of us?"

"Ugarte Trading," I said, figuring out why his name triggered something earlier. "Yes, I have. What seems to be the problem, sir?"

I figured a little sucking up was called for. Ugarte Trading specialized in luxury goods. Mr. Ugarte was undoubtedly a rich man. Clients like him do not come along too often. "Sir" was a concession to his status. I didn't much like being deferential ordinarily.

"My first spice shipment of the season has gone missing," he said.

"Missing? You mean someone stole it?"

"Yes," he replied glumly.

"Tell me more."

"One of our ships collected the first cargo of the season from the Kryyder Islands. As is the usual custom, they sailed to Lenoa, on the other side of the isthmus. Following the usual procedure, the goods were loaded onto wagons and joined a caravan that would bring them here. They never arrived. The rest of that caravan made it, but not my wagons. When I had my people ask what happened, they heard as many different answers as people they spoke to."

"You paid the customary donative at the temple of Sylvaris in Lenoa?"

"Of course. I'm no fool., Well, I didn't, but my people did. I'd cut their balls off if they didn't."

The Kryyder Islands were on the eastern side of the continent of South Langjord, just south of the equator. Rather than sailing around the southern tip of the continent, a long and perilous route due to the storms that seemed never to leave the vicinity of Cape Veer, it was safer and cheaper to deliver the material to Lenoa, in the Midonese Republic. The material would then join a caravan for the 150-mile journey across the isthmus to Tallesin, the capital of the kingdom of Thetlaria, where we now were.

Sylvaris was the god of commerce, travel, and thievery. The donative I mentioned was, in reality, a bribe or, if you prefer, a toll. The priests of Sylvaris headed all the trading guilds and were also supposed to keep banditry on the caravan route under control. If you paid the demanded fee, your goods were supposed to arrive safely. If you did not, you took your chances.

"You're sure of this?"

"My man in Lenoa, Ferrare, has been with me for years. I trust him."

"How much would the donative have been?"

"Two percent of the value of the shipment, as usual, so around two thousand guilders."

"Two thousand guilders?" I asked, somewhat stunned. "For that much, the temple should have sent a half-dozen of the priests-militant along."

The priests-militant were acolytes, not yet fully consecrated into the holy orders. They were armed guards as well as holy men. Their mission was to patrol the main cargo routes as a sort of extranational police force.

Sometimes they traveled with caravans, but often they roamed free. Their relationship with the bandit groups in a particular area was ambiguous. Sylvaris was the god of thieves, after all, as well as of merchants.

The priests-militant kept the brigands in check without eliminating them. Shipments whose owners had paid the donative were off-limits. Their crates would be marked by seals attached by a temple priest. Not all merchants paid, and individual travelers were often assessed a small "toll" for passing through certain areas.

"According to Ferrare, they claimed they had none to spare."

"You've spoken to the priests here in Tallesin?"

"I have. They claimed at first that they must not have received my donative. Then, they claimed that my goods were never part of the caravan. I sent a person to my man in Lenoa to collect the receipts, but he is now long overdue. I fear that he has been waylaid."

"Waylaid? Or if Ferrare absconded with the funds he was supposed to provide as a donative, he might have killed the one you sent. In fact, Ferrare might have been given a healthy bribe by someone who wanted your wagons. Spices are expensive and easily sold."

"I suppose it's possible," Ugarte admitted.

"And you would like to hire me to do what?"

"I want my two dozen wagons back. Or if Ferrare is behind this, track him down and bring him to me."

"How long has it been since the caravan arrived?"

"Five … no, six weeks ago now."

"Mr. Ugarte, I do not think it will be possible for me to find and return the goods," I said. "Too much time has elapsed. They have surely already been sold. Would you be satisfied with the value of the shipment? If I am successful in tracking down who was responsible, I might be able to do that for you."

"If it's Ferrare, I was serious when I said I would cut his balls off," he said with a frown. "My customers are already upset because I failed to deliver the orders they placed. I have needed to return their deposits to them, and still, they are unhappy."

"Could one of your competitors have arranged this?"

"That's always possible."

"If I learn that it was one of the other trading houses, how would you like me to handle it? Would you like me to give you the opportunity to present what I find to the traders' guild?"

"The guild would do nothing," Ugarte snarled. "I can do more damage by word of mouth. Get the money, I suppose."

"When is your next shipment due to arrive in Lenoa?"

"Roughly a week, Marivelle, wind and tide permitting."

"It seems to me that safeguarding the incoming shipment should take precedence over the one already lost," I said. "I will need to leave immediately in order to reach Lenoa in time to meet it."

"I was planning on hiring soldiers to accompany the next shipment."

"You know the priests of Sylvaris will not allow your soldiers to travel with their caravan. Your people would need to travel on their own. And which soldiers would you hire?"

"My man in Lenoa, Ferrare, says there are sell-swords in Lenoa, available for a fee."

"In my experience, the type of sell-swords available in Lenoa would be more likely to have participated in the theft of the previous shipment than to prevent any losses."

"What would you do instead?"

"Arrange to join the caravan as a wagoneer."

"But you're only one man, Mr. Falk. What can you do?"

"Against a group of armed men, probably not much," I admitted. "I would, however, be able to track them and learn who is responsible. Even if the caravan is not attacked, I will probably find out a great deal from the other wagoneers. I only wish there were more time. Whether your man in Lenoa is involved, the priests of Sylvaris in Lenoa are certainly mixed up in this, and I would like to find out more."

"You'll take my problem on, then?" Ugarte asked.

"Well, Mr. Ugarte, that depends on whether you're willing to pay my rates. I charge ten guilders a day, plus expenses. The expenses, especially in this situation, could end up totaling far more than my fees. For most of the larger disbursements, such as bribes, I will not be able to furnish a receipt. You will need to take my word for it."

"You were recommended to me as being an honest man, Mr. Falk."

"Such pride as I possess is reserved for my reputation," I replied.

"Ten guilders a day is a lot of money, with no guarantee of results."

Ugarte was not wrong. The average annual earnings for a skilled tradesman in my country, Thetlaria, might come to three hundred guilders. A month of steady work would earn me that much. My clients came and went, but I generally worked enough to clear five times that. I suppose I was rich compared to most, but I hadn't bothered to count it for a couple of years. It was enough that the wolf was comfortably far from my door.

"I'm sorry, Mr. Ugarte," I said as I began to rise from my seat. "You're a trader and used to negotiating prices. My fee is my fee. I am the one who runs the risk of bodily injury or worse. My talents and skills are unique. You are welcome to try to find someone else who—"

"Please sit down, Mr. Falk," he pleaded. "You are correct. I am a trader, and haggling is in my nature. I meant no offense. Ten guilders a day, it is. The people with whom I spoke about this problem told me that you were the one man in Thetlaria who could unravel this problem for me."

What I did not tell Ugarte was that he had no hope whatsoever of besting me in any sort of negotiation. In fact, if he tried, he would end up paying me more than ten guilders a day. You see, I am one of the rare people in the world touched by one of the gods—in my case, Sylvaris. One of my many god-given talents was the ability to wear down an adversary in any discussion of financial terms.

It had been many years since I last engaged in haggling. I found it boring, and as a result, I stick to a firm line regarding my fees and expenses. It saves time and energy for both parties.

"Just to be sure, Mr. Ugarte, when I submit the accounting of my expenses, there will be no adjustment."

"I understand."

"To reach Lenoa and return with the caravan will consume more than two weeks. If you wish to employ me, I will need a hundred and fifty guilders to start. When I return to Tallesin, I will present you with a list of my expenses to that point and a progress report. You will reimburse me for those expenses and for any days beyond the initial fifteen that I spend. I hope by then that we will have some firm idea of the scope of what has happened and what it will take to resolve the matter. Do you understand?"

"I do, Mr. Falk. I did not bring that much money with me today, but if you come with me to my offices, I can provide it."

"That will be fine," I said. "I can then use the rest of the day to prepare for leaving in the morning to reach Lenoa."

"You'll start right away?"

"To meet your second shipment in Lenoa, and arrange to be hired on as a wagoneer for the caravan, I need to leave immediately. I hope I am not too late. That would make things far more difficult and awkward."

I ushered Ugarte from my flat ahead of me. Before leaving, I buckled my sword on my hip, then followed him downstairs. An open carriage was waiting.

We drove to his offices near the harbor front. He unlocked the door, and we went inside. Ugarte crossed to a large safe. Using a key that had been around his neck, he unlocked it and withdrew a tray containing guilders stacked in neat rows. He counted out a hundred and fifty and put them in a leather pouch for me. After returning the tray to the safe, he closed and locked it.

"My driver will be taking me home now," he said. "Would you like us to return you to your flat?"

"Please."

They delivered me back to my flat. I needed to prepare for a lengthy journey away. After unlocking my door, I went to the spare room. Inside were wardrobes containing clothing for almost any occasion.

I found the armoire that contained the sort of attire I would need to pose as a wagoneer. Having found what I wanted, I pulled them out. I would only bring one change of clothes. They would fit easily in one of my saddlebags. I found them and stuffed the clothing in. In the same spot where I kept my saddlebags were two blankets. I rolled them up.

My sword was too fine a piece for my character. I found a long knife that I could hide in my boot. That was the sort of weapon one would expect a wagoneer to have. I didn't like leaving my sword behind. It gave me a certain comfort when I had it on my hip. I was good with all sorts of blades, though. The knife I would carry should see me through any trouble I thought I might encounter. If it wasn't enough, I would be better off running away.

I grabbed a small kettle and some utensils. If I happened upon a caravan, I could probably buy a meal from them (if they wouldn't feed me for free), but I needed to be prepared to fend for myself. That also meant buying supplies.

I then headed to the money changers in the market square in front of my flat. I gave the man five guilders and asked for small denominations—quadrans, mostly, and a few florins—half in Thetlarian coin, and half in similar small Midonese specie. A guilder (made of gold) was worth twenty-four silver florins. It took sixteen quadrans, our bronze coin, to equal a florin. The Midonese used different names, but the values of their coinage were close. Their version of the bronze coin, however, was twelve to a silver. I put the change they gave me in a travel-worn leather pouch.

From the money changer, I went to the livery stable. It was a bit of a walk, and not terribly enjoyable on such a hot day. I arranged to rent a mule for the journey to Lenoa. Because there was regular traffic between Tallesin and Lenoa, they were willing to have me leave the animal with their stable in Lenoa upon my arrival. It would be convenient, as I would use the same outfit to hire a wagon and pair of mules for the return trip.

I would return to the livery in the morning, get the animal, ride back to my flat and load my gear, then head across the isthmus. During the journey, I would allow my beard to grow. By the time I arrived in Lenoa, I would look the part of an itinerant wagon driver—and probably smell like one, too.

On my way back to my flat, I pondered Mr. Ugarte's problem. The simplest answer was usually the solution to the riddle. His man, Ferrare, was probably heavily involved. The priests of Sylvaris were likely caught up in it as well.

Still, it was ten guilders a day, and I didn't have anything else going on at the moment. A couple of weeks, maybe three, and I'd be finished. Then I would wait for my next client.

In the market in front of my flat, I bought dried vegetables, some salted meat, and some dried fruit. That would fill my other saddle bag. I asked for a jute sack to carry everything in. I figured I could use the sack to hold my kettle and utensils.

2

The following morning, I woke after a poor night's sleep due to the heat. I dressed and headed to the livery. They provided me with a mule—Sara—and tack for her.

Why a mule and not a horse? In my experience, mules were hardier, not as finicky about their feed, and required less water. The trail across the isthmus had some rough patches, and a mule was generally better at navigating difficult terrain.

Sara and I rode back to my flat. I tied her next to the water trough two doors down while I went to collect my things. She waited patiently while I loaded everything on her. I then went to the well in the middle of the square and filled my waterskins.

We set off. By the time the full heat of the day came, we would be out of the city. That would make things more bearable.

We were in luck and encountered a caravan heading east. They were carrying huge bales of wool. The sheepy smell didn't bother me, and they agreed to feed me without charge, as long as I contributed some of my store of food to theirs. That was an easy decision to make. They didn't ask for all of it—only half. The man who did their cooking was talented—far more so than I. They spoke Midonese, in which I was fluent.

It was the third night of the journey when I noticed that one of the drivers was a woman. She disguised herself well. Being tall and broad-shouldered helped, and she kept her hair tucked under her floppy-brimmed felt hat. She kept it pulled down low, hiding her face. She wore the same sort of clothes as the rest of us, and they were loose, obscuring her figure. It was only when I saw her at the edge of the firelight, taking off her hat and shaking her long, straw-colored hair out, that I realized.

The next day, I tried to get a better look, but she did not make it easy. She kept to herself, and the few times she spoke, she pitched her voice low. The other members of the group must have known she was a woman, but she still tried to hide it.

On a couple of occasions, I was able to see her face. Though smudged in a couple of spots, I could tell she possessed fine features. I would describe her as "handsome" rather than "pretty." Her jawline was too bold for prettiness, and her skin was tanned instead of a fashionable pale, but I found her quite attractive.

It started to rain that afternoon, although rain is an understatement. Zoryn poured down buckets upon us. We had not yet reached the top of the Fullan pass, and the track became a rushing torrent. The leader of the group pulled everyone off the path to a small rise.

"I hoped to clear the pass today," he announced, "but Zoryn has other ideas. Set up camp, and we'll continue tomorrow, weather permitting."

I stayed close to the woman. After unhitching her mules from her wagon, she hobbled them. She then grabbed her bindle of belongings and crawled under the wagon for shelter.

I'd hobbled Sara as well so she couldn't wander too far, then set out the canvas bucket. With this rain, I wouldn't need to go fill it. The rain would do it for me in no time. For a moment, I stood there, my saddlebags over my shoulder and my blankets under my arm, just getting soaked. The rain was cold, and it felt great at first.

"C'mon you," she growled. "You've been giving me the side-eye all damned day. Get out of the wet, you fool. Just to warn you, don't try anything."

"Thank you," I replied, and tossed my things under the wagon before unsaddling Sara and bringing the tack in with me. "And why shouldn't I try anything?"

"Because these people are my friends, and if I don't kill you, they certainly will."

That answered one of my questions, at least. They all knew who she was. Her being female was known and accepted.

"So, what's your problem with me?" she asked.

"Curiosity, mainly."

"What's a girl like me doing in a place like this?" she asked with a sarcastic tone.

"It *is* unusual," I replied. "You answered one of my questions already, though. I was wondering if the others knew you were a woman."

"They do, and if you look around, you'll see that a number of them are watching closely to see if you're going to cause me trouble."

"They're friends, then, and good ones to have if they look out for you. I could say you have nothing to worry about as far as I'm concerned, but I know actions speak louder than words."

I arranged my saddle so I could lean against it. I faced her from as far away as I could and still say out of the rain. Putting my hands behind my head, I stretched out. She seemed to relax slightly upon seeing me do that, pulling off her hat and letting her long hair fall down.

"So, who are you, and why are you traveling to Lenoa?" she asked.

"My name is Dexter Falk, but my business is my own," I replied good-naturedly. "Who are you and what's a woman like you doing in a place like this?"

"I'll give you my name as freely as you provided yours: Agatha Voss. As far as why I'm here, I'll keep that to myself for now."

"It's a pleasure to make your acquaintance, Miss Voss."

"Mrs. Voss."

"My apologies. I did not see a ring."

"Hocked it over a year ago to buy this wagon and these mules," she said. "And that's all you get for now."

"Fair enough, ma'am. If I could trouble you with one more question?"

"Depends on what it is."

"Does anyone in the group have some soap? Zoryn has sent this marvelous rainstorm, and, although it's a bit chilly, it also strikes me as a perfect opportunity to rinse away the sweat and grime of the last few days."

"I do. Are you going to strip off in front of me and wash?"

"That was my plan."

"You do this sort of thing often with women you've just met?"

"Never before, actually, and you bringing it up makes me feel a little bit self-conscious, but not enough to persuade me that I wouldn't enjoy being clean."

"Go ahead, then," she said with an amused snort, after reaching into her bindle and retrieving a cake of soap wrapped in a small rough cloth.

I took the soap and set it down. It took some wriggling to peel off my wet clothes, but I thought I managed it without looking too awkward. I took the clothes from my saddle bag and gave them a sniff. They could use some freshening up as well. I tossed all of my clothing out into the rain, then crawled after it with soap and cloth in hand.

After arranging my clothes to hang from the edge of the wagon, where the rain might wash them clean, I began to lather myself up. Agatha had rolled over to get a better view of me, lying on her stomach with her chin in her hands. She was watching with interest.

To be fair, I've been told by other women that they find me attractive. I'm two inches over six feet tall and fit. There are a few scars on my body here and there, reminders of past adventures. My hair is down to my collarbone and sandy brown. I have light blue eyes.

I tried to pretend I was uninterested in her scrutiny of me. Once a part of me decided to react to her presence, however, I turned my back on her. Her voice, coming from right behind me, startled me a couple of minutes later.

"I'll take the soap now, Mr. Falk," she said quietly.

I turned to face her. She was standing naked in front of me. Her figure was slender but possessed curves in all the proper places. I could not see her breasts, as her wet hair covered them. She was not tan everywhere—just her face and hands. The darker tone of the skin of her face made her blue eyes seem all the brighter.

"Turn around," she ordered.

When I did, I felt her begin to wash my back vigorously. She slapped me on the butt to let me know when she was finished. I turned to face her. She was busy soaping herself up, but I saw a mischievous glint in her eye and a hint of a smile. Beyond her, I could see that she had arranged her clothing on the side of the wagon next to mine.

"May I return the favor?" I asked.

She handed me the soap and the washing cloth and turned, pulling her hair out of the way. I started at her shoulders. I could feel the muscles beneath her skin. She leaned into my touch slightly. A woman's naked back and shoulders I find to be highly arousing on the right person. I found this view of Agatha spectacular.

Tempted though I was to reach around and cup her breasts, I did not. I got as far as the dimples of Lysmera on her lower back, then felt I should stop. Reaching around, I handed her back the soap and cloth. She took them without a word.

All of my clothing was drenched. Piece by piece, I wrung each out. By the time I finished, I noticed that other members of the group were following the example Agatha and I set. There was some good-natured hooting at one another. Several of them were looking over at us. I could not read their expressions. Curious? Jealous? Concerned? I couldn't tell through the pouring rain.

I wrung my garments out again. There was a small shovel tied onto Agatha's wagon. We were parked sideways on a slight slope. I took the shovel and quickly levered a small trench in the sod on the uphill slope where the water was streaming off the wagon, and continued the slit in the turf down along each side.

"What are you doing?" she asked.

"If it keeps raining like this, which I think it will, now the water will not run down under the wagon. It will follow the path I just made, so we will be drier."

"Huh. Good idea. Now figure out what we're going to wear. "

"Our blankets."

She shrugged in acceptance, then bent over to crawl back under the wagon. The view from my angle was exquisite. I waited for her to arrange herself before following. She was wrapped in one of her blankets. Although mine were somewhat damp, I did the same with one. They were of thin wool and would still be warm.

Given the bales that were on the wagon and my blankets, the smell of wet wool was everywhere. In a way, it reminded me of the dog we had when I was a boy. The memory brought a smile to my face.

"What's got you so happy?" she asked.

I told her about "Woof," a black-and-white dog that showed up at our farm when I was three. He was of indeterminate breed—a mutt—and a stray. My mother fed him, and he stayed with us until he died. He was my boon companion in many youthful adventures.

"Woof?" Not the most imaginative name for a dog."

"I was three."

"Where was this?" she asked.

"My father's farm, in the Duchy of Chiftel."

"That's way up in North Langjord, isn't it? You don't have a northern accent. You speak Midonese like a native."

"Thank you. Languages come easily to me. As far as the farm, between the rocks in the fields and the short growing season, farming is a hardscrabble existence in Chiftel."

"Is that why you're here? Your farm failed?"

"Oh, no," I replied. "My younger brother took the farm. He's managing well enough—working his ass off, I'm sure, and loving every minute of it."

"Your younger brother?"

"I never felt the least desire to follow in my father's footsteps," I said. "He was a good man, and there was never ill feeling between us, but when the time came, the three of us talked and decided my future lay elsewhere."

"What about your mother?"

"She died a few years before that."

"I'm sorry."

"Thank you. It was more than a decade ago."

"So, you set off to do—what?" Agatha asked.

"Nuh uh, ma'am," I said. "You don't get any more out of me until you provide a little bit in return."

"I shared my soap and washing cloth with you," she countered.

I shook my head.

"I let you wash my back," she then said.

"A memory I will treasure to the end of my days," I replied, "but you benefitted as well."

"I'll think about it," she said with a sigh.

Agatha then rearranged the blanket around herself and lay down. I did the same, resting my head against my saddle. We listened to the rain continue to cascade down.

- 15 -

3

"There is no more Mr. Voss," she said quietly, not quite an hour later. "He's in the afterworld, same as your mother, but not in the same realm, I figure."

I didn't know what to say, but I wanted to hear more, so I replied with a simple, "Hmm."

"It was an arranged marriage. My family comes from property in Swardle."

The kingdom of Swardle occupies a broad plain in South Langjord—a plain known as the cortaderia. I knew enough about the country to understand what she meant when she said her family came from property. They probably owned a vast tract of land on which they raised cattle.

"You'll notice that I said property, and not means," she added. "My marriage to Abner Voss was supposed to provide the *means* to restore the family fortune.

"The year I turned twenty, my father borrowed the last bit of credit anyone would extend to him to prepare for my introduction to society at the feast honoring the Celestial Ascendance in Corwig, the capital of Swardle. For six months, I was allowed to do no work, so the calluses on my hands would disappear, and I was not allowed out during the day, so my skin would remain fashionably pale. That evening, I was dressed in a beautiful white gown and presented along with other nobly born twenty-year-old girls. The entire purpose of the exercise was to find a husband. In our case, one who could pay off the family's debts—some of which dated back to my great-grandfather.

"You see, my father was—is—the Thane of Hessel. We are one of the oldest landed families in Swardle. We were also bankrupt, thanks to the misdeeds of my grandfather and his father before him. I was the last best hope the family had of avoiding the necessity of selling land which had been in the family for hundreds and hundreds of years. My brother would have ended up with nothing but a name that once meant something.

"Like a good daughter, I accepted my fate. Although I would have greatly preferred managing the herds on the cortaderia to being a merchant's wife, I allowed myself to be sold to the highest bidder—Voss. He met with my father the next morning and arranged to pay the family's debts in full. I married Voss that afternoon, wearing the beautiful dress from the previous evening.

"Voss was a pig. He raped me that night after he knocked me nearly unconscious. I told him that if he ever touched me again, I would slice his dick off and kept a knife under my pillow. That didn't stop him. Three times, he had his men come and beat me, then tie me up. Voss would go first, then allow his men to take their reward."

"That's horrible!" I blurted without thinking.

"Although he presented himself as a successful merchant, his real business was smuggling. You name it, his ships would carry it, including people—slaves, usually children kidnapped from their parents. He would take them across the sea to Molutia, where they still allow such barbaric practices. In the entire time I knew him, Voss did only one decent thing—paid off my family's debts."

"How did you escape?" I asked.

"Good word—escape," she commented. "It was not quite a year since our marriage when he came after me one night—drunk. He would have needed to be in order to think he would be able to overpower me by himself. We grappled, and he fell down the stairs, breaking his neck."

"And then?"

"That's the funny thing," she said. "The servants hated him as much as I did. They helped me dispose of the body. When anyone asked, we explained that he was out of the city on business. That worked for months. Meanwhile, I took over his company. I quit smuggling and focused on legitimate trade. I got away with it for three months."

"Then what happened?"

"The man for whom Voss smuggled children came calling. While I pretended to be acting on my husband's behalf, I learned where the children were being held. I contacted the Garda, and they raided the warehouse, freeing the children and returning them to their parents.

"Unfortunately, someone in the Garda told Oderic, the kidnapper, that I was the source of the information. I needed to disappear, so I did."

"And now you're a wagon driver?"

"Bartell leads this caravan," she explained. "His daughter was one of the children I freed. He found me before Oderic did and gave me a job. I've been traveling back and forth across the isthmus for the last four years."

"Have you tried to contact your family?"

"I sent them a letter to inform them that I was safe and well four years ago. There was no way I could tell them where I was—not that the post would have an easy job of finding me—for fear that Oderic would find out. When we arrive at Lenoa, I stay with the wagons. I only go into the city with the group to deliver a load and pick up the next. So, that's my story. Your turn."

"I help people solve problems."

"That's it?" she said, after waiting for me to elaborate.

"Mhm."

"I spill my guts and you give me that?"

"It's what I do," I said with a shrug.

"How did you get the scars I saw?"

"Helping people solve their problems."

"Oh, come on!" she whined.

"I also enjoy a reputation for being discreet," I said with a wry smile.

"So, what takes you across the isthmus? Solving a problem for someone?"

"Exactly."

"What sort of problem?"

Figuring that Agatha might be able to help me, I decided to tell her, although I left names out of it. Her anger with me lessened as I continued. She listened with great interest, nodding at certain points.

"Thank you," she said when I finished. "I can see why you might be reticent about sharing other things you have done."

"You're an intelligent woman. What do you think is going on here?"

"The merchant's person in Lenoa is probably in it up to his neck," she said. "I think he not only pocketed the donative he was supposed to pay the priests but also accepted a pay-off from the person who hijacked the goods. If it's not him, then the priests of Sylvaris are behind it."

"Meaning?"

"Meaning he paid the donative, and they will deny it. They accepted a reward from the hijacker for tipping him off or might even be involved themselves."

"Involved themselves? They robbed the caravan?"

"It's possible."

"That would be earthshaking," I said. "The Temple of Sylvaris is darned particular about safeguarding their reputation. The last time a priest was caught doing something remotely like that, they made a public spectacle out of his torture and death."

"When?"

"A few decades ago," I said. "I wasn't alive then, but I heard about it."

"What did they do to him?"

"Are you sure you want to know?"

"I asked, didn't I?"

"He was dragged, racked, and gutted."

"Which means?"

"He was dragged behind a horse by his heels from the prison to the place of execution. Once he arrived, they put him on the rack, and dislocated all of his major joints, pausing and reviving him whenever he fainted. Then they started with the knives, and that's all I will say about it. Such things are not meant for a lady's ears."

"I'm no lady," she protested. "I ceased to be one when my father sold me. I went along with it willingly. That makes me a whore."

"Agatha, you are no whore," I said quietly.

"A whore sells her body," she replied sharply. "As I did. I understood the deal my father made. None of us knew that Voss was a monster. Even if he had been a reasonable man, it doesn't change what I did."

"I don't see a whore," I said. "I see a brave young woman who willingly sacrificed her own happiness to save her family. Your brother and your father owe you a debt that they can never repay—a debt not measured by money. That

Voss turned out to be a deviant only makes your action more heroic. You said you sold your wedding ring. Do you have no other assets? What about Voss's accounts?"

"I did not have the opportunity to visit the banks," she said. "Oderic would have found me if I did. I did send them letters, indicating that I would be traveling, possibly for several years, and would meet with them upon my return. I also engaged a solicitor to make sure my interests were protected."

"You trust him?"

"I do."

"That, Agatha, was extremely clever of you. Do you have the last statements?"

"If I do, they're in a safe place."

"Good for you."

It was then that I decided that I would kill Oderic if I encountered him in the course of my current project. I usually tried to avoid bloodshed if I could, but I wanted to free Agatha and would make an exception for him. Her story was the truth. Don't ask me how I knew, but I was certain.

"It's getting late," she commented. "And I don't think anyone will try to cook. Do you have anything to eat?"

"I have some jerky and dried fruit."

"Enough for two?"

"If you are one of the two," I responded flirtatiously.

"Good. I'm hungry. Can we eat?"

Turning around, I rummaged through my saddlebags. I found the pouches with the food and withdrew them. She took a hank of jerky and started to chew on it after I offered it to her.

"Ever seen a 'lady' gnaw on jerky before, Mr. Falk?"

"There's a first time for everything," I replied. "And I would also say that your surroundings do not change your character. One favor I would ask?"

She tilted her head in response, indicating I should make my request.

"We've shared a shower, and now food. I would say that we're on our way to becoming friends. Would you please call me Dexter? If we grow closer, Dex."

"Very well," she said with a dramatic sigh. "And you may call me Lady Agatha."

"What?"

"You're so convinced I'm some great lady, and you're just a soil-scratching farmer's son from the gods only know where, so I think Lady Agatha is appropriate," she said, her eye twinkling. "But if we become friends, you may call me … Lady Agatha."

She started to laugh. Her laugh was delightful. She was laughing so hard at her own jest that she fell over on her side, clutching her ribs. Her jocularity infected me, and I began to chuckle as well.

"Hoo!" she breathed once she recovered. "I haven't laughed that hard since last winter when I saw Pedro slip on the ice and fall on his ass."

"Yes, Lady Agatha," I replied, causing her to start all over again.

When she recovered, she went back to gnawing on the strip of dried beef. Teasing me, she mm-ed and ah-ed, smacking her lips as though it was a gourmet meal. When she finished, she held out her hand.

"Yes, Lady Agatha?"

"What will you serve me for dessert?"

"Dried apple slices, dried cherries, or raisins. You'll be pleased to know that the cherries have already been pitted."

"That's too bad. I would show you how ladylike I can be while spitting cherry stones."

"Some other time, then, Lady Agatha."

By now, darkness was falling. It had been dark before due to the storm, but now it was obvious the sun was going down behind the unbroken clouds. The temperature also started to fall.

Wrapped in our blankets, we both stretched out to sleep. Even I was feeling the greater chill in the air. Before I could suggest to Agatha that we cuddle to share blankets and warmth, she changed position. She turned herself around and tucked herself up to me, with her back to my front. We broke apart so I could rearrange the blankets. I put the driest one beneath us. Agatha had wrapped herself in one like a cocoon, so I put the other two on top of us. She tucked back into me, then clutched my left arm and drew it over herself, holding it to where her tummy was covered by her blanket.

She fell asleep quickly. I did not. I was all too conscious of holding an attractive woman in my arms, even though she was securely bundled up.

4

Sometime in the middle of the night, I sensed the rain had stopped. I disengaged myself as gently as I could, trying not to disturb Agatha. I crawled out from under the wagon and, working by feel, wrung out our clothing again. With any luck, it would be mostly dry by morning.

When I returned to my previous spot, Agatha murmured something. She squirmed herself right into me. Once again, she found my arm and pulled it over her.

I awoke before she did. The day was dawning clear and crisp. Cooler temperatures followed in the storm's wake. Our clothing was mostly dry, so I dressed quickly. I gathered some of her things and tossed them under the wagon.

When I bent down to see if she was awake, I was treated to the sight of her pulling her blouse over her head. The blanket she had wrapped around herself was on the ground, and I saw the glint of a knife blade. She must have hidden it under her blanket the night before.

Agatha caught me looking at her once her blouse settled on her shoulders. She merely rolled her eyes, then lay back, lifted her hips, and pulled on her underclothes, then her trousers. I'd seen everything she had to offer the day before when we washed, but it was still a delightful view.

She threw the blankets out to me, then crawled out herself. We could smell the smoke of a cookfire and headed for it. A small group was already gathered. Bartell, the leader of the group, motioned for me to join him a few paces away from everyone.

"If you hurt her in any way, I will kill you," he growled softly, looking into my eyes fiercely.

"If she herself doesn't kill me first," I replied quietly.

His glare softened, and a smile crept onto the corners of his mouth.

"You have been kind enough to allow me to ride with you, Bartell," I added. "You've shared your food freely and asked little in return. I have no intention of harming you, her, or anyone in your group."

"I welcomed you to join us because I see that you are a hard man, Falk," he said. "I paid the expected donative in Tallesin before we left, but I've heard that it may no longer be the guarantee of a safe journey as it used to be. Having someone like you in our group seemed to be an additional measure of defense against untoward things befalling us."

"Really?" I asked. "Have caravans been attacked?"

"Only one that I know of," Bartlett replied, "but one is enough—too many, actually."

"What did you hear?"

"On the Lenoa side of the pass, bandits stopped a group heading for Tallesin. They took only the wagons belonging to a particular merchant and left the others untouched. Not only that, but they paid off the other drivers, asking them to make up stories about what happened."

"Interesting," I said. "What was in the wagons they stole?"

"Spices—very valuable. Worth a whale of a lot more than the crap we're carrying."

"Did the merchant pay the donative before the goods set out?"

"I hope not," Bartlett replied. "That would make things easier to swallow. If he did, and the priests allowed the theft to take place anyway, then it means trouble for all of us."

"It would be pretty stupid not to pay," I said.

"Nevertheless, people do stupid things all the time," Bartlett cracked.

"That, they do," I agreed with a smile.

"Be good to Miss Hessel," Bartlett warned, becoming serious again. "Do not bother her. Let her decide if she wants you around."

"Miss Hessel? She said her name was Voss. And I take your warning seriously."

"Voss," he spat. "When Thalorix weighed his life, the obsidian pan might have broken the god's toe; it dropped so hard."

I laughed at Bartlett's remark. Thalorix is the god of the afterlife. He judges all souls, weighing out their good and evil with his scale. A person's good deeds are placed in the ivory pan, and his bad, in one made of obsidian.

"Miss Hessel is too good a person to be tainted with that man's name," Bartlett added.

"She told me a little about it last night."

"Then she must trust you," Bartlett said. "I don't understand why. You look a little bit too hard-bitten for me to pour my heart out to, but then again, you probably know how to keep a secret."

"I'll take that as a compliment."

"I guess you could," he said with a shrug. "The porridge should be ready, and I'm starving. Let's eat, shall we?"

I went back to my saddlebags and retrieved my bowl and spoon. On the way, I checked on Sara. She seemed perfectly happy, unbothered by the rain the day before. Her canvas bucket was half full, so she did not need water.

I ate by myself. Agatha was sitting with others by the time I returned, and I did not wish to presume anything. When I finished, I rinsed out my bowl with water someone had collected from a nearby stream and returned to Sara.

After a brief grooming, I saddled her and put my things away in my saddlebags. Agatha hitched her two mules to her wagon while I was busy. We finished at nearly the same time.

"Why didn't you eat with me?" she asked.

"It felt like I would be intruding."

"Huh."

When we set off, I didn't pay any closer attention to Agatha on the ride than the days before. Less, actually, since my curiosity was somewhat sated about her. At dinner that evening, she patted the ground next to her, indicating I should join her.

"You'll be sleeping with me again tonight," she said, making it a statement and not a question.

"If you wish, Lady Agatha. Will your knife be joining us again as well?"

"Huh. You saw that, did you? Yes, the knife will be with us."

"Fine with me. I just don't want either of us to roll over onto it by accident."

"Don't worry. I keep it clutched in my dainty ladylike hand."

"Your hands would be ladylike without the calluses," I said, taking one and examining it, "but not dainty. They are the hands of a strong and capable woman, which you are. I would not want them any softer."

"Your silver tongue will not land you between my thighs, Mr. Falk."

"Thank you for letting me know. That was not my immediate intent. It was meant to be a compliment. I just want to say that I think you are an impressive person, Lady Agatha."

"Not your immediate intent? When do you plan to bed me, then?"

"Technically, we 'bedded' last night."

"You know what I mean."

"If it happens, I would welcome it," I said. "But, given your past experience, I suspect it will be some time before you have any interest in paying homage to Lysmera in that way."

"You are a silver-tongued devil. 'Paying homage to Lysmera'? That's just a fancy way of saying 'screwing' isn't it?"

"Indeed. And if you decide you would like to do that with me, please let me know. We men can be a bit thick-headed, and I am no exception. Subtle hints will not be enough."

"I'll keep that in mind."

"Thank you."

I slept with Agatha in my arms every night for the remainder of the journey. Nothing more than that. There was no kissing, caressing, or other form of intimacy. She seemed to take comfort in it. Though her lithe body and sharp wit attracted me more than a little, I tamped down my frustration.

As far as I knew, Agatha's experience with men was limited to Voss. What she suffered was the opposite of a loving and respectful relationship. I wanted to show her that not all men were pigs, even if I never benefited from it.

Don't mistake me for an altruist. I simply know the difference between right and wrong. I strive to do what I consider to be right. It's easier to look at yourself in the mirror that way.

When we reached the outskirts of Lenoa. I separated from the group, thanking Bartlett for allowing me to travel with them. When I went to say goodbye to Agatha, she looked around to see if anyone was watching, then darted toward me and kissed my cheek quickly. It made me blush.

I rode into the city, toward the harbor front, looking for Ugarte's warehouse. It wasn't the biggest I saw, but its location was advantageous, next to one of the wharves. The hour of siesta was over, and I figured I would find Ferrare before I did anything else.

He was in, and the clerk immediately ushered me back to his office. Ferrare looked very similar to his employer—short, fat, and balding. When he saw my workmanlike clothing, the smile faded quickly from his face.

"Ugarte sent me," I announced.

Fear took over his expression. He started to stand as I slid into the chair opposite his desk. Before he could begin, I held up my hand to silence him.

"Mr. Ugarte told me to cut your balls off and feed them to you," I said calmly as I withdrew the long knife from my boot.

"But it was not me!" he protested as I started to clean my fingernails with the tip of my blade. "You should know that. I gave the receipts to Melton."

"Who is Melton?"

"A man from Tallesin who works for Ugarte there. He arrived three weeks ago. I had been expecting him ever since I heard what happened to the caravan. He said Mr. Ugarte worried that I did not pay the donative to the priests, but I did. I gave Melton the receipts."

"Melton never returned to Tallesin."

"Oh, no," he moaned. "Sir, let Thalorix be my witness! I paid the donative. Melton took the receipts, but I can show you the books with the entry for the expense."

"What do the priests say?"

"At first, they tried to deny that I paid the donative. When I returned with the receipts, they claimed they had confused me with someone else, and, of course, I had paid, it had just slipped their mind. Then I asked, if I had paid, why was my shipment—and only my goods out of the whole wagon train—stolen? They had no answer to that, but said they sent people to look into the theft."

"Did you believe them?"

"Well, that's the thing with the head priest of Sylvaris here in Lenoa," he complained, holding his palms up. "When you speak with him, he makes perfect sense. You feel like a fool for even asking such a stupid question. But after you leave, you realize that what sounded reasonable when you heard it from his lips is only a half-truth at best."

"Sit down, Mr. Ferrare," I instructed. "I will not cut your balls off right now."

I believed Ferrare. As an accomplished liar myself, I am pretty good at spotting the attempts of others to hide the truth. Ferrare was clearly terrified by me. His story was by no means clever enough. A good liar would have had a more intricate tale, and it would absolve him of blame.

Ferrare's explanation did not. He did not have the receipts. The man who did was missing (and, I was thinking, probably dead). Hearing his story, any reasonable person would continue to assume Ferrare was involved.

The one thing he said that convinced me he was not to blame was his description of the head priest. As I mentioned earlier in my narrative, I am god-touched by Sylvaris. When the god wishes, I can convince people that black is white.

I can summon the abilities he has granted me, but I cannot safely rely on them. The special skills Sylvaris lends me often desert me in moments of crisis, forcing me to rely solely on my native talents. The priests with whom I studied when I learned I was god-touched told me that is his way; he is the biggest prankster of all the gods after all. I have heard that those who are god-touched by other members of the pantheon can trust their abilities. When they call upon them, they can use them until their supply of asomatous energy is drained. Anyway, from Ferrare's story, the head priest seemed to possess some of the same ability I had, but not to the same degree.

"Mr. Ferrare, when do you expect the next shipment?"

"I received word not long before you arrived that the ship will arrive with the morning tide."

"Then I will ask you for a favor. I crossed with a caravan, led by a man named Bartlett. Give the shipment to him. He will allow me to travel with them on the return to Tallesin. I will go collect him and bring him here."

"I've already made arrangements with a man named Molsen."

"Let me go speak with Bartlett. Then we will visit the temple of Sylvaris and pay the donative. You will ask for two receipts. I will take one back to Mr. Ugarte. You will keep the other in your safe."

5

"I know of Bartlett, but I have never done business with him," Ferrare said. "We have used the same caravan masters for years."

"Contract with him for this shipment," I said.

"He may have his return to Tallesin already booked. That's the way these things work."

"Right. Let me ask anyway. If he is unavailable, perhaps he can recommend someone. The only thing I know is that you should not do business with the outfit that lost that last shipment. I also need to know who they are," I said. "I need to question them. They allowed themselves to be paid off. According to Mr. Ugarte, every man told a different story upon their return. The drivers of the wagons containing your goods went with the bandits. I'm willing to wager that they have reappeared somewhere. With the next shipment ready, my time is limited, as I will need to accompany it back to Tallesin. If nothing happens along the way, I will probably need to return to Lenoa in order to dig into this further. In addition, I must speak to the head priest at the temple of Sylvaris."

"The man in charge of the caravan that lost the last cargo is named Serdlik. He has not shown his face in Lenoa since. As far as the temple, I can take you when I pay the donative," Ferrare said. "You should have Bartlett come talk with me first. If he can take the shipment, the temple will need to know whose caravan I will be using."

"I'll go fetch him now," I said. "How many wagons do you anticipate needing?"

"Two dozen, give or take."

Bartlett was surprised to see me so soon. When I told him I wanted him to carry Ugarte's next shipment. He frowned. I did not expect that reaction.

"What's the problem?"

"I am already committed for the return trip to Tallesin," he said. "To add Ugarte's wagons would make the group too large to manage, plus I don't think I can find that many on such short notice. On the one hand, it's a shame, because I have been trying to get his business for years. On the other, Ugarte's goods were stolen a few weeks back, and I don't ever wish for trouble."

"Is there anyone you would recommend?"

"No one in particular, except I would warn you away from Serdlik. He's the one who let Ugarte's—"

"As I have learned," I said. "According to Ugarte's man here, Serdlik has not been seen in Lenoa since. He has already arranged for a man named Molsen—"

"Molsen is good—reliable, like me. I will go see Ugarte's local manager tomorrow," Bartlett said. "We have a wait of at least two days before our next cargo arrives, according to the agent. Perhaps there will be an opportunity in the future."

When I returned to Ferrare, he seemed relieved not to need to make new arrangements. He promised he would give Bartlett a fair chance to earn some business. Ferrare then asked if I still wanted to go to the temple with him.

"Of course," I replied.

"Good. I will feel safer. Carrying chests of gold through the streets makes me nervous."

"The temple makes you pay in coin?" I asked, slightly incredulous. "I would insist on using a bank draft."

"That's the way things used to be," Ferrare said, "until the leadership of the temple changed last year. The new head priest insists on cash."

"I would refuse. You deal in high-value merchandise. How much is this shipment worth?"

"A hundred thousand dinars, give or take," Ferrare said.

The dinar was the Midonese equivalent of the Thetlarian guilder. Both coins weighed the same and were made of the same quality gold. The difference was only in the design stamped onto them.

"And the expected donative is still two percent?"

"Yes."

"Ridiculous. You can't demand that people supply that much cash. It's an invitation to disaster."

"Tell that to the head priest," Ferrare said with a shrug.

"When the first shipment was stolen, he tried to deny that you paid the donative, didn't he?"

"He did. When I returned and produced the receipt, he apologized and said it must have slipped his mind."

"And what was his response to the news of the theft?"

"He expressed great unhappiness and consternation."

"As well he should. Priests have been defrocked for smaller losses. My word, for a donative of two thousand dinars, he should have sent a half-dozen of the priests-militant along with the caravan. I would have demanded it."

"The previous head priest usually did. This one claimed he had no men to spare. I'm sorry," Ferrare moaned. "If you don't think I'm crooked, you must think I'm a complete imbecile who has never done business before. All I can say is that, when you are speaking with him, everything he says seems perfectly agreeable. It's only later, when you have a chance to think, that you realize you approved something that is totally unsatisfactory."

"How did this priest come to be in charge?"

"I'm not exactly sure. It happened in the month of Zorynth, I think—in midwinter, certainly—when there was no ship traffic due to the weather. When I went to the temple to make arrangements for the upcoming season, he was in charge. I asked about his predecessor and don't remember what the new man said."

"What about the other priests?"

"That's another thing," Ferrare explained. "I didn't recognize any of the priests. They were all new. And, forgive me, Sylvaris, but I must speak the truth," Ferrare said, looking to the heavens with his palms upraised, "the new people are quite thuggish, in my opinion."

The more I learned, the more convinced I was that Ferrare was in the clear. All signs were pointing to the head priest. I would travel with the shipment back to Tallesin, but the answers to Ugarte's problem were probably here in Lenoa. That would add at least two more weeks for me to travel back and forth. At ten guilders a day, Ugarte might complain, but if I saw his current shipment safely to Tallesin, he could not whine too much.

Ferrare had a wagon brought around. His workers brought two small wooden chests, each containing a thousand dinars. Despite their lack of size, the chests were heavy.

Ferrare climbed heavily up onto the wagon and grasped the reins. He gestured for me to join him. Two of the warehouse workers climbed onto the back and sat with their legs hanging over. I noticed both of them had cudgels that they laid flat in the bed, out of sight.

We set off through the streets of Lenoa to the temple. I'd been here a handful of times and remembered the way. The city had not changed much since my last visit.

"When we reach the temple, come in with me," Ferrare said. "I would like your assessment of the head priest."

We arrived and pulled up in front of the marble edifice. Ferrare passed me the reins and asked me to tie the mules up to a post there. Our two men slid the chests out and followed Ferrare up the steps. There were two men dressed as priests-militant who stood at the entrance to the temple.

Even from the street, I could tell that these were no acolytes. These two were goons, with the broken noses, mashed ears, and swollen knuckles to prove it. The steps themselves were dirty. That was unthinkable. Temples were usually spotless, inside and out. Another thing stood out—I usually felt the touch of the god's numen when at a temple. There was nothing here.

They stopped Ferrare, making him stand in the hot sun. One of them whistled over his shoulder, and another bruiser appeared. The one who whistled merely jerked his head at Ferrare, and the man he summoned disappeared into the temple.

It was a good long wait before anything happened. Finally, the door opened, and a man dressed in the fine robes of a head priest of Sylvaris appeared. One look at him told me the man was as crooked as a soft nail in hard wood. I couldn't put my finger on exactly why, but something about him made the hair on the back of my neck tingle.

His hair was black, except for a shocking white streak on the left side. He was sharp-featured, and his skull was narrow. His eyes were set close together.

He was all smiles for Ferrare at first. His expression hardened when he caught sight of me. He only dropped his happy face for an instant, but I saw it. He gestured for his men to take the chests.

"Mr. Ferrare, how good to see you," the man gushed. "Here to pay the donative, I see. Sylvaris will be happy to know you have not lost faith, despite the unfortunate circumstances surrounding your last shipment."

This man was no more a head priest than I was. He was a gangster, through and through. I decided to provoke him to see how he would respond. Drawing on my connection with Sylvaris, I pitched my voice in the most persuasive tone.

"You'll be sending some of the priests-militant this trip to make sure nothing happens, won't you?"

"Of course," he answered before he had a chance to think.

Then, he gritted his teeth, realizing that I had employed a trick on him. He recognized what I did because he possessed some of the same ability, though only a faint shadow. He gave me a steely look. Before he replied, he paused just long enough for me to realize that whatever came from his mouth next would be a lie.

"Except, I fear, that all of the priests-militant are currently on the road," he said, ignoring Ferrare and addressing me directly. "Perhaps you will encounter them on the way to Tallesin."

"Yes, perhaps," I replied, my tone of voice clearly indicating I knew he was lying. "In any event, we need two copies of the receipt for the donative."

"Two?"

"Yes. I will be accompanying the shipment back to Tallesin and will take one with me. Mr. Ferrare will keep the other here. You will send a priest to affix the seals to the crates tomorrow morning?"

"Yes, someone will be over first thing. Who are you, may I ask?"

"The man whom Ugarte hired to find his stolen goods. I will find them, you know. And everyone who played a part in their disappearance will be brought to justice. Surely you would support me in my mission? After all, if a shipment of as much value as Mr. Ugarte's can disappear on the road to Tallesin, nothing is safe. People would no longer pay donatives for protection, and you would be replaced."

Ferrare probably couldn't read the man's expression, but I could. I had just threatened him. It suddenly became clear to me that he was never appointed as the priest of this temple. He arrived during the off-season and probably killed the previous man and his staff. If the temple hierarchy learned of his usurpation, his days would be numbered.

"Yes, we all want to find the people responsible," he replied.

His words said one thing, his eyes another. I knew for certain that the caravan would be attacked. Even more, I knew that he wanted me dead, for fear that I would ruin his scheme.

"Oh, I already have a solid idea of who was behind it," I said, looking him dead in the eye. "It's only a question of gathering the evidence to ensure a proper conviction. We wouldn't want to take the law into our own hands. The receipts, please?"

The man narrowed his eyes. I thought he might object for a moment. Then he turned and went into the temple.

After more minutes in the hot sun, he reappeared. He handed two pieces of paper to Ferrare, not to me. I insisted on looking over Ferrare's shoulder to make sure they were accurate. The man's handwriting was childlike, but legible. These receipts would hold up in any court.

"Good day to you, *Your Eminence*," I said, stressing the usual honorific to let him know that I was aware he was a fake.

I helped Ferrare climb into the wagon when we returned to it. We turned around and headed back to the harbor. Ferrare had a curious look on his face.

"What just happened back there?" he asked.

"I can say that the man Melton is certainly dead."

"What? How do you know?"

"I just do, Mr. Ferrare. It is also certain that this so-called head priest was involved in the loss of the earlier shipment. This shipment will also come under attack. He wants me dead as well."

"Should we hire some men?"

"I'm told the kind of men available for hire here in Lenoa are the type of men who work for him. Don't worry, Mr. Ferrare. I will make sure the shipment reaches Tallesin."

"But you're only one man."

"Yes, but I'm a hard man to kill."

6

I left Ferrare at the warehouse and went to replenish my meager stock of traveling food for the return journey. Not far away was an inn, and I handed Sara off to the groom there. It was extra for a hot bath and for having my clothing laundered, but I happily paid the charge. Both were overdue. I had not washed myself or my things since the rainstorm near the top of the pass.

The inn catered to working men. Rooms were small and the furnishings minimal. The sheets were clean, however, and the bed comfortable enough, even though I shared the room with three others. Dinner was a fish stew, the main ingredients of which had probably been swimming that morning.

The general bustle at daybreak woke me. People were already up and about. A quick breakfast, and I returned to Ugarte's warehouse.

The ship with his goods had arrived on the incoming tide a couple of hours before. Ferrare introduced me to Molsen, the wagon master, explaining that I would be accompanying them back to Tallesin. The goods were already loaded. We were waiting for the priests to arrive and affix their seals to the crates. While we were waiting, I asked Molsen if he knew the wagon drivers well.

"All of them have been with me for at least a year, except one. One of my regulars was delayed by a day in reaching Lenoa—broken wheel. Another wagon master, Bartlett, recommended the new one to me."

"Oh? I just came from Tallesin with Bartlett. Show me the driver. I'm sure I know him."

Molsen led me down the line of waiting wagons. We were still a few dozen paces away, but I recognized Agatha. This gave me deeply mixed feelings.

On the one hand, I was delighted to see her again. On the other, this promised to be a perilous trip. I did not want her to face any danger. I stopped well short of her and tugged at Molsen's sleeve.

"Mr. Molsen, did Ferrare tell you about our interaction with the temple yesterday?"

"He did and said I should expect trouble."

"That's putting it mildly," I said. "I fully expect we will be attacked along the way. Is there anyone else you can find to take this woman's place?"

"You know her, eh? Unfortunately, to replace her at this late hour? Impossible. I scrambled all day yesterday to find her and pry her away from Bartlett. Don't worry, though. My regulars are all capable and trustworthy men. I'm not like Serdlick, either. Whoever stole the last shipment paid him and his men off, I'm sure of it. My people won't go so easily. Besides, brigands just want the goods and to run away. She shouldn't be in any greater danger than the rest of us."

"Mr. Ferrare told me that the leadership of the temple here changed over the winter. What do you know about it?"

"I know that Sylvaris looks out for merchants, travelers, and thieves," Molsen replied, "but the man who took over the temple is a hard-bitten criminal if ever I saw one. Most places, they use the threat of bandits to keep the donatives coming. Folks who don't pay get hit. The ones who do, stay safe. The temples are supposed to pay off the brigands to keep them from violating the trust, and the priests-militant step in if any of them forget. Based on what happened last time, we should have at least a half-dozen priests-militant with us, but Ferrare said the head priest made some excuse. He also said you irritated the man. On purpose?"

"Aye."

"Why?"

"The whole situation is rotten. I could see that from the moment we approached the temple. If the guards out front were priests-militant, then I'm Zoryn. I think this 'head priest' took the temple by force and killed his predecessor. The order hasn't figured it out yet."

"I agree. What do you think his plan is?"

"The man in charge is collecting the donatives but not administering the other duties of the temple. He'll keep doing this until he gets caught. Ugarte's last shipment was too lucrative for him to keep his hands off, so he didn't. And, after our interaction yesterday, he'll be sending some of his thugs after this caravan."

"I don't like that you stirred up trouble that my people will need to face."

"Molsen, I do not want any of your people to get hurt. If the bandits show up in force, let them take the wagons, but not your people. I'll give you the receipt for the donative. You can apply at the temple in Tallesin for them to reimburse you for new wagons."

"And what will you do?"

"I'll follow them and see where they go and what they do."

"What if it's a smaller group—like the priests-militant who should be guarding this shipment?"

"Then I would appreciate the support of your people. Don't kill them, though. Let them live and leave them behind. I can follow them and see who else is involved."

"That could be dangerous."

"It's how I earn my living."

"You've done this sort of thing before?"

"Once or twice."

"Well, I'll wish you luck if it comes to pass," Molsen said, then turned away.

I waited for him to leave the area, then proceeded toward Agatha. She was sitting on the bench of her wagon, her lips drawn tight. As I approached, she nodded slightly.

"Don't get me wrong," I said quietly, "I am delighted to see you, but why did Bartlett send you? He should know this will be dangerous."

"He didn't send me. I demanded to come," she said tersely.

"You are a formidable woman, Lady Agatha. I already knew that, but this is another reminder."

"You shouldn't need reminding."

"Can I at least get you to promise me that you'll try to stay out of harm's way?"

She looked at me and laughed harshly in response.

I could not help but chuckle. Shaking my head, I patted her leg. She put her hand on it and held it there for a moment, then released it when we heard commotion at the entrance to the warehouse.

The "priests" had arrived to affix the seals to the crates, proving that the donative had been paid. I say "priests," but these were brutes just like the ones I saw at the temple doors the day before. They were rude and obnoxious, ordering the wagon drivers around. On top of that, they were clumsy and sloppy in the way they fastened the seals.

In my experience, this was a job normally given to acolytes, under the supervision of a single priest. If he saw them do a shoddy job, he would make them do it over. I suspected this temple had no acolytes under the current management. These thugs never learned how to attach the seals correctly, nor did they seem to care that their work was half-assed.

When they finished, Molsen called out for everyone to set off. We left the warehouse and proceeded along the street, heading for the gate on the road to Tallesin. The priests watched us pass. None of them wished us a safe journey, as was customary. I took note of their faces, as I had a feeling I might see some of them again in a few days.

We rode a short distance out of the city walls and met up with the rest of Molsen's caravan. There were another three dozen wagons, already loaded and waiting for us. Molsen took the lead, riding ahead on his mule, and our group fell in behind the others.

That night, after dinner, Lady Agatha crooked her finger at me. Under her wagon, she had already spread a blanket. She crawled to it when I approached.

"Am I spending the night with you, Lady Agatha?" I asked, bending over to speak to her.

"Yes. To keep me warm. Plus, I don't know these people. There might be brigands among them. You must defend my honor."

"Let me get my blankets then."

"Hurry back."

When I returned, I brought my saddle with me, tucking it under the wagon away from where Agatha was lying. Crossing to her, I arranged the blankets over us. Agatha scooched herself to fit her back against my chest. She pulled my arm over her and fell asleep within minutes. I, on the other hand, was not so fortunate.

The situation with the temple of Sylvaris bothered me. I had never heard of a temple of any of the gods being taken over like this. Cleaning up the mess was not my problem. Getting Ugarte's goods safely to Tallesin was.

A thief would know where to attack the caravan. Another day's journey from our current location, we would encounter the north-south road that wended its way along the foothills of the mountain range that bisected the isthmus. From there, the bandits could head north to the Kholl Pass, which would also deliver them to Tallesin.

The Kholl Pass served northern trade, primarily foodstuffs and livestock from the port of Dropan, as the Fullan Pass and Lenoa did for the southern continent. Of course, the bandits might not head to Tallesin. From the Kholl Pass, they could also aim for Eudus. It would take them an additional twelve days, but the spices they planned to steal would command an even higher price there, making the additional time spent on the road well worth the trouble.

That was probably what the thieves did with Ugarte's first shipment. Arriving in Tallesin with Ugarte's stolen goods would have raised questions. The spice trade primarily went through Tallesin. Merchants in Eudus would have seen the opportunity the thieves presented to obtain these spices at a lower cost than someone like Ugarte would charge. They would happily ignore any evidence that the goods had been stolen.

Once I had this worked out in my mind, I was able to relax. The bandits would not hit us tonight. They would wait until the wee hours of the next, striking at a time guaranteed to cause the maximum of confusion and panic.

When I woke, I realized that Agatha was no longer sleeping. Her breath was different. She was clasping my hand to her breast in an intimate manner. It was quite pleasurable, though as soon as she sensed I was awake, she lifted my hand away. Her action was not one of anger. It seemed to me more that she realized the moment had ended. She twisted around to look in my eyes.

"Time to begin the day, Mr. Falk."

"Yes, Lady Agatha. Thank you for keeping me safe in the night."

"You're welcome," she replied, then rolled away from me and crawled out from under the wagon.

I followed after I gathered our blankets. Once out from under, I handed hers to her and began folding my own. Along with my saddle, I took them to where Sara was hobbled.

After dumping them there, I went to where everyone was forming up for breakfast. A bowl of porridge with raisins to start the day, and then we would be breaking camp. I looked for Molsen and crossed to him when I found him.

"I think we should expect some unwanted company tonight," I said.

"I was thinking the same thing," he responded. "How many, do you think?"

"Around a dozen, I'll venture. No more than twenty."

"That's nothing to worry about, then."

"I wouldn't go that far," I replied. "They'll be armed and armored, equipped like priests-militant—except they killed the real ones last winter, I'm guessing."

"You don't want us to fight them off?"

"They'll arrive in the middle of the night. Yes, we will outnumber them, but they will have swords. Your people have knives and cudgels. We might be able to take down a few, but they'll kill a lot more of us."

"So, we … what? Surrender?"

"That would be the wisest choice."

"If they have only twenty at most, how will they take all of Ugarte's wagons?"

"They will attempt to convince some of your people to join them, with promises of a big reward when they reach Eudus."

"Except the reward will actually be paid with cold steel and not gold or silver, once they get near Eudus," Molsen commented.

"Exactly."

"Most of my people are trustworthy. There are a few who might be tempted. I'll talk to them. Do you plan to just let the bandits go?"

"Oh, no," I said. "I'm going to trail them all the way to Eudus and make sure the whole scheme gets uncovered. The leadership at the temple of Sylvaris will be extremely unhappy to learn what is going on in Lenoa."

7

"What was that all about?" Agatha asked later.

I told her what I discussed with Molsen. She looked at me with narrowed eyes. It was clear she did not approve of what I intended to do.

"You plan to simply let them go?"

"I do."

"What happens when they catch you following them?"

"They won't."

"How can you be so sure?"

"I'm rather good at this."

"So you say."

"Lady Agatha," I stated, "this is how I earn my living. Beyond that, it irritates me to a great degree that these bastards have taken over the temple of Sylvaris in Lenoa."

"It's not your problem."

"Except it is," I countered lamely. "Mister Ugarte, whose spices we are carrying, has hired me to solve this problem."

"And you would die for him?"

"Lady Agatha, I won't die. Trust me. I really am good at this. They won't have any idea that I am following them."

"I should go with you."

"Absolutely not, Lady Agatha. I know you are an extremely capable woman, but you have no experience with a situation like this. You would get me caught and put us both in danger. Please?"

Her facial expression softened at the word "please." She responded a moment later with a "harumph," and then turned her eyes away from me. I didn't know whether I convinced her. Time would tell.

"By the way, Lady Agatha, have you ever met Oderic?"

"Never formally introduced, if that's what you mean, but I've seen him."

"Does he have black hair, with a white streak?"

"Yes. Why?"

"I met him at the temple. He is claiming to be the head priest."

"He's no more a priest of Sylvaris than I am," Agatha scoffed.

"I know."

We met another caravan heading toward Lenoa at midday. Molsen met with its leader, and they exchanged information. I waited close by to eavesdrop. The incoming caravan had seen nothing of note.

More interesting was the discussion regarding the temple of Sylvaris in Lenoa. Both caravan masters were aware that something was not right. Molsen agreed that he would visit the temple in Tallesin and make a report.

The rest of the day passed uneventfully. We camped near the intersection of the north-south road that crossed our path. When the group gathered to share the evening meal, Molsen asked for their attention.

"Mr. Falk here believes we will have some visitors in the middle of the night," he announced, "just as happened to Serdlick a few weeks back. They'll be after the spices—the most valuable things we have. We'll let them take whatever wagons they want, but none of us will go with them. They won't have the numbers to force the issue."

"Then why don't we fight them off, if they don't have the numbers?" someone asked.

"Because they will be armed and armored, I suspect," I replied, "and would be able to kill quite a few of us before we were able to overwhelm them. There's no point in anyone dying over this. Molsen has a copy of the receipt from the temple of Sylvaris in Lenoa. If they take your wagons and animals, the temple in Tallesin will make good."

"How many do you expect?"

"No more than twenty," I answered. "They won't be able to take all the wagons loaded with spice if none of you agree to go with them. Don't fall for their promise to reward you if you agree to join them. The only compensation you will receive will be a dagger between your ribs when they reach Eudus."

"This isn't right," one complained. "The donative has been paid. All the crates are marked with seals."

"Sloppy-ass job on the seals," one commented.

"Something is wrong with the temple in Lenoa," I said. "Molsen will be informing the folks in Tallesin what we suspect."

"Molsen? What about you?"

"I plan on following the bandits we're expecting and will track them to Eudus. Once they arrive, I'll let the temple there know what's going on."

"So, sleep lightly," Molsen added. "They'll wait until the middle of the night. Wake up quickly, and don't do anything that will get you, or anyone else, killed."

"I don't want you to go by yourself," Agatha said later when the stars came out and we were wrapped by our blankets under her wagon.

"It warms my heart that you want to help me, Lady Agatha," I said, "but I'll be safer on my own. You'll have to trust me. I promise I will come find you when this is over to reassure you that I survived."

"You promise?"

"Yes, I do. And if you really want to help me, you can do some things in Tallesin for me."

"Such as?"

"Make sure Mr. Ugarte and Molsen meet. Please tell Mr. Ugarte that Ferrare, his man in Lenoa, is honest and not the problem. Molsen will go to the temple of Sylvaris to present the receipt from the temple in Lenoa, in order to be reimbursed for the wagons the bandits will take. You need to make sure the priests understand that I suspect the bandits will take the spices to Eudus. They should send some priests-militant to meet us there."

"What if they don't listen to me?"

"Lady Agatha," I said reprovingly. "You are a great and forceful lady. I am sure they will listen to you. If, for some reason, they do not, use my name. I am known to the priests."

"How are you known to them?"

"I have provided assistance to them from time to time. You should also have Mr. Ugarte take you to my flat. You can stay there until I return to the city."

"Doing what?"

"Entertaining yourself, Lady Agatha. My flat is above the millinery shop in Gund Square. Miss Katherine, who owns the shop, will open the door for you. In one of my wardrobes, you will find a money pouch, concealed in a false bottom. There will be enough in it to keep you comfortably until I make it back."

"Why would you do this for me?"

"Because you accepted the burden the gods placed upon you and have endured hardship without complaint. If there is anyone who deserves my help, it is you."

In the light of the half-moon reaching under the wagon, I could see her blue eyes seeking mine. The camp around us was settling in for the night. There were muffled, quiet conversations, a faint crackle from one of the fires, and the sounds of the mules shifting in their sleep. Agatha reached out and put her hand on my cheek. Her fingers were rough, but her touch was gentle.

"You're a fool," she whispered with a hint of wonderment in her voice. "A romantic one, but a fool nonetheless."

"Perhaps," I murmured back, reaching up to capture her hand and press it to my lips. "But I have a gift for making it work out for the best in the end."

She leaned in, and her lips brushed mine. Our kiss, tentative at first, soon deepened. I had not intended to escalate matters with her. Her previous experience with her husband had been horrible. I resolved to move no further than she wished.

Her lips grew more urgent, and she threw her leg over me, holding my head in her hands. I wrapped my arms around her gently. She began a slow, sinuous writhing atop me.

No words were spoken. Talk would have ruined the moment. Somehow, our clothes were moved aside. She traced the lines of the scars on my body, remembering where they were from when I took advantage of the rain on our previous trip. We found ourselves making tender, quiet love, moving slowly, sighing, and gasping quietly.

Agatha stayed above me, relaxing fully when we finished. I held her gently as she lay her head upon my chest, pulling up a blanket to cover us from the growing night chill. For a few hours, I forgot about troubles with temples and thieves.

A shout from one of the people on watch woke us both. Agatha rolled off me quickly. I scrambled to put my clothing back together. The bandits had arrived, and it was time for me to go.

"Don't get yourself killed, Dexter Falk," she whispered, using my given name for the first time, then kissed me gently.

"I won't, Lady Agatha," I said, pecking her nose with my lips. "Please do as I asked. Go to Tallesin. I will get there as soon as I can."

I woke Sara and saddled her quickly in the dark once she gained her feet. Molsen had just arrived to talk to the leader of the bandits. The bandit was wearing armor that looked exactly like that worn by the priests-militant, though showing signs of poor maintenance. I stayed in the shadows, listening. One of the gifts of Sylvaris is the ability to be difficult to notice. I cannot be invisible, but I can make myself hard to spot. I did so now.

"The donative was paid. You can see the seals on the crates," Molsen said.

"I don't give a rat's ass about any damned donative," a man snarled.

I recognized the voice. When he turned and spat, the torchlight illuminated his face. He was one of the men from the temple in Lenoa.

"There are two dozen wagons loaded with spices. We'll be taking them with us."

"If you're going to ignore the rules of the road," Molsen said, "fine. Take the bloody wagons. They're not worth dying for. My people stay behind, though."

"The wagoneers come with us."

"Not a chance," Molsen answered calmly. "You have … what? A dozen and a half men? Sure, you could kill some of us if you try to force the issue, but you would end up just as dead. You can have the wagons, but none of my people."

The rest of the camp was awake by now and gathered just outside the range of the light from the torch Molsen was holding. The leader of the bandits sensed he was surrounded. He tried to stare Molsen down, but Molsen just looked coolly back at him.

"Any of you want to join us?" the bandit called out. "Whatever he's paying you, we'll double it."

Complete silence greeted his offer. No one even murmured. I could see the gleam of drawn knives in the flickering torchlight.

"No one?" the bandit called out. "We'll pay you a full share when we reach Eudus—in gold. You won't have to work for years."

No one stepped forward.

"Go on, then," Molsen said when no one responded. "Take what you came for and be gone."

The bandit whistled, and more of his men came into the light.

"Get some torches and separate the wagons we want from the others," the man said. "You'll each need to take one."

"Boss, we'll have to leave some behind."

"Then leave the least valuable ones."

"How the hell am I supposed to know that?"

"Just quit carping and get to it."

None of Molsen's people lifted a finger to help the bandits. I stayed well out of sight. It took almost an hour, but finally, the bandit crew pulled away.

After meeting briefly with Molsen and reminding him to show the receipt to Ugarte and then take it to the temple in order to recover the cost of the lost wagons and animals, I set off on foot after the bandits. I knew where they were headed—they said as much. There was no point in following too closely.

8

It was easy to follow the bandits. I could smell the saddle sores on their horses. It gave me another reason to detest them. The horses were destriers—warhorses—bred to carry armored men, trained to withstand the tumult of battle. These men were thugs and had no idea of how to care for their mounts, not knowing that each one was worth at least five hundred guilders.

They were in no great hurry, either. Only a few miles up the track, well before dawn, they called a halt. Once they lit a fire, I led Sara well around where they stopped, trusting that they would not be able to see us.

Sara and I would stay just in front of them. All eighteen of the bandits were driving wagons, so they would not be scouting ahead. Once they committed to the Kholl Pass, Sara and I would head to Eudus and alert the temple of Sylvaris. If Molsen and Agatha did the same in Tallesin, it was probable that they would be able to muster enough priests-militant to capture these bandits.

We kept a safe distance, moving through the scrub. The half-moon provided enough light to enable us to navigate quietly. Sara, bless her heart, was more sure-footed than I, picking her way along without difficulty. I, on the other hand, stumbled a few times when my foot encountered an unexpected rock or declivity.

When we were an hour further down the track, I headed off to the side. I unsaddled Sara and hobbled her so she couldn't run off, then rested my head. The rising sun's rays snapped me out of the light slumber I allowed myself. I saddled Sara again and returned to the road.

As I suspected, we heard the bandits approach well before they came into sight. Sara and I could hear them bitching to one another, complaining about needing to drive the wagons. These were not disciplined professionals of any ilk. From what I observed at the temple and in the shadows the night before, they were the kind of men whose size and cruelty always gave them an advantage—brutes, in other words. Seaports were full of men like them. They'd never given anyone an honest day's work. They were supremely confident that they would encounter no difficulty on their journey.

I mounted Sara, and we set off, pulling ahead to where we could no longer hear them. We reached the crossroads, and I headed west toward the pass. There was a copse of trees on a small hill to the north. From there, I could confirm that the group was heading for the pass and still make my escape unseen on the other side of the rise.

Sara and I settled in the shade. I loosened her girth and allowed her to wander around, grazing on the sparse grass while I helped myself to a bite of jerky. The sun was climbing higher, and the morning air was growing humid. This side of the isthmus tended to be somewhat steamy at this time of year.

It wasn't long before we heard the rumble of the approaching wagons, and the men carrying on, complaining about the heat, the flies, the hard benches on the wagons—you name it. There were eighteen, as I figured the night before. I could see the intact seals on some of the crates glinting in the sun, a mockery of the protection they were supposed to provide.

The leader halted the group. He stood and gestured toward Kholl Pass to the west. I couldn't make out all of his words, but he was obviously telling them which way to go. I did hear him reference "Eudus."

That confirmed my thinking. Eudus was slightly closer to here than Tallesin, and fewer questions would be asked about where their loads came from. As long as the price was right, no one would care. Having intact seals would also help convince a buyer that the cargo was legitimate.

They set off on the western track. I tightened up the saddle and led Sara down the far side of the rise. Reaching the track, I mounted, and we headed toward the pass.

It was a two-day ride to the top of the pass from there. I would stay within reach of the bandits today, just to make sure they didn't change their minds.

Tomorrow, Sara and I would ride for Eudus and alert the temple of the problems we had encountered.

The heat was oppressive, but Sara didn't seem to mind. We stopped for water but kept a steady pace as the track climbed and began to wind through increasingly rough terrain. When the sun began to dip behind the hills ahead of us, I stopped.

After tying Sara to a tree off the path, I headed back down the trail on foot. Once again, I smelled them and heard them before I could see them. They had already called a halt for the day. I snuck close enough to ascertain that all eighteen wagons were there, then crept away.

Rejoining Sara, we continued westward as the light faded. Once the sun was no longer visible, I pulled us off the path toward a nearby stream. After Sara drank her fill, I unsaddled her and gave her a quick grooming. When that was done, I filled a feedbag with oats and let her munch.

While gnawing on my own dinner of jerky and dried fruit, I thought back to Agatha. What happened the night before was something I hoped for but did not expect to happen so quickly. She was an admirable woman with unmatched strength of character. I meant what I had said to her. If she waited for me in Tallesin, I would help her reclaim her life. We would find Oderic the slaver and eliminate him, freeing her to return to the plains she loved.

Unfortunately, I had a job to do for Mr. Ugarte first, and a mess to clean up regarding the temple in Lenoa. I stretched out, resting my head against the saddle, facing east. The morning sun would wake me.

When it did, I headed back down to where the bandits were. Only a few of them were awake and moving. That was all I needed to see. I returned to Sara, saddled her, and we headed west toward Eudus.

We neared the top of the pass with a few hours of daylight remaining. Just on the other side, a man came out of the rocks to the side of the trail and stood in the middle of the path, his hand on the hilt of a sizeable knife. I pulled Sara up short of him.

"That's as far as you go," he said, "without paying the toll."

"Unless you have twenty more men hiding in the rocks, I have something more valuable to offer than money," I replied as charmingly as possible.

"Nothing is more valuable than money."

"Really? What about your life?"

"You're joking. We've been watching you approach. There isn't anyone else with you."

"We, eh? And where are your brave companions?"

Two more men stepped out of hiding. They were scruffy, with the rawboned look of men who spent their time in the hills, living an uncertain existence, preying on travelers, and staying away from the priests-militant. One had his knife drawn, and he smiled with yellow teeth. The other held a nasty-looking club made from knotty wood. They stood to either side of the first man.

"Three of you, then. You must like your odds," I said as I slid from the saddle. "I feel it's only fair to warn you that I am exceptionally skilled, and would be happy to prove it to you, but you would end up dead, and I really don't want to have to go to the effort to bury your bodies. Or, I can give you a warning that will save your lives both today and tomorrow."

As I said this, I tapped into my connection to Sylvaris, hoping to use the gift of persuasion he often granted me. From the softening of their expressions, my words were having an effect. They looked at one another uncertainly.

"What's the information, friend?" the leader asked.

"Beyond my warning that I can kill you where you stand, tomorrow, a group of eighteen well-armed bandits will be coming through. They aren't the type to give you any sort of warning. Besides that, I'm willing to give you each a florin to leave me alone and let me go on my way."

"A florin? Make it two each, and we'll let you pass," the leader said.

"I'm sorry, a florin is all I can spare, and I'll have to give it to you in quadrans."

"Midonese or Thetlarian?" he asked.

That was when I knew I won this exchange. When Sylvaris was with me, I could convince anyone of anything. I could sense my connection to the god was active from the way the hair on the back of my neck tingled.

"I'll give you as many Midonese as I have," I offered.

"Let's see it."

I retrieved my money pouch and started counting out the coins. The way I tipped the contents out, none of my silver coins appeared, only the bronze. Several of them spilled to the ground, and I bent quickly to pick them up. It was obvious that I would not have enough to give each of them a florin's worth.

"You're as bad off as we are," the leader said, interrupting me as I started to count.

"Worse," said the one with yellow teeth.

"Keep your money, mister," the leader said. "And be on your way. We'll take your warning about those behind you to heart."

"Well, thank you," I said. "I'm delighted you chose to listen to reason. As I mentioned, I don't have the time to bury the three of you properly, and I don't wish to offend Thalorix."

"Keep dreaming, friend," the leader said. "You showed us that you can't afford the toll. Don't push your luck."

The three of them moved off the path. I mounted Sara again, and we set off. Within minutes, the trail twisted and I could no longer see the place where they stopped me.

Sara and I continued until the sun was about to set. The path from the top of the pass traveled next to a stream, so water was not a problem. I unsaddled her and quickly groomed her. After she drank her fill of water, I fed her, then tied her with a long lead to a tree.

I did not expect any trouble. Sara and I made much better time than the bandits and their slow wagons. We would reach Eudus at least two days before the bandits. The problem then would be to convince the head priest of the need to muster the priests-militant.

Sara was up with the sun, and that woke me. We set off immediately and soon encountered a caravan heading toward the pass. I went to speak with the leader.

"You in charge?" I asked.

"Ayuh. Dan Labitie. And you are?"

"Dexter Falk. In another day, you will encounter a group of eighteen wagons heading down from the pass. The wagons were hijacked from a caravan heading through the Fullan Pass to Tallesin."

"Didn't the idiots pay the donative?"

"Oh, they did. The problem is, the bandits are linked to the temple of Sylvaris in Lenoa. I'm riding to Eudus to let the temple folks know that they have a mess to clean up."

"Are my people in any danger?" Labitie asked.

"Not unless what you're carrying is more valuable than the spices they stole. Are you heading for Dropan or Lenoa?"

"Dropan."

"I can't speak to what's happening there. If you were heading to Lenoa, I would warn you to keep your distance from the temple of Sylvaris."

"What's your part in all this?"

"Ugarte hired me to investigate why his first shipment of the season went missing. This is the second."

"You're not doing the greatest job of protecting his interests, are you, Mr. Falk?"

"I'm only one man, and the temple folks have a much greater interest in solving this problem than I do. In the process, they'll make my client whole. He paid the donatives. You'll see the seals on the crates."

"That's bad," Labitie said, then spat—a common superstitious gesture to prevent bad luck of the same sort from finding you.

"I agree. Just keep your distance from these folks. You'll recognize the type of men they are."

"Rough trade?"

"Exactly."

"We'll be on our guard then. Thanks, Falk. Good luck in Eudus. The temple there is well-tended."

"I know. I've been there a time or two."

We parted ways. After midday, dark clouds rolled in from the west. We could smell the rain before we reached it. There was a grove of fir trees nearby, and I guided Sara to them.

The rain came cold and in sheets—a typical summer storm. I took advantage of the opportunity to wash my clothes and myself while it lasted. In less than an hour, the rain stopped, though the clouds remained overhead.

With all my clothes wet, I decided we'd traveled far enough for the day. I tended to Sara and sat on a blanket spread across a soft bed of pine needles. My last thoughts that evening were of Agatha.

9

Two and a half days later, we rode into the city of Eudus. After the storm, the weather had been beautiful—perfect midsummer days under a brilliant blue sky. We traveled through rolling fields, full of crops—a testament to the bond between Teryssa, the goddess of the earth, and Vyran, the god of fertility.

Once in the city, I headed straight to the temple. Along the way, we dodged the bustle of the city streets. Eudus was a fair-sized city, not as big or prosperous as Tallesin, but still an important hub of commerce and industry.

The temple of Sylvaris here showed evidence of the city's prosperity. It was fronted with gleaming marble columns. Unlike what I saw in Lenoa, the grounds were spotless. Two acolytes in robes stood by the huge entrance doors. I dismounted and tied Sara to a post.

"How may I be of service?" the one on the left asked when I reached the top of the steps.

"I'm afraid I need to speak with the head priest."

"May I ask why?"

"It is an important yet delicate matter," I said in a kindly tone. "If he wishes for you to know, that will be for him to decide."

"Your name, good sir?"

"Dexter Falk. He will remember me."

"Very well, sir. If you will wait here."

He disappeared inside, his robes swishing as he turned. The other acolyte eyed me with mild curiosity. I leaned against one of the columns, staying in the shade.

Unlike the temple in Lenoa, I felt the faint presence of asomatous energy linked to Sylvaris—the presence of his numen. It had been absent in Lenoa. It was a sort of refreshment for my soul, making me feel healthier in a non-physical manner.

"The head priest will see you now, Mr. Falk. If you will please come with me," the acolyte said when he returned, even giving me a small bow of his head.

The head priest, Rafe Jobson, had clearly admitted to knowing me, as well he should. Even better, he must have indicated to the acolyte that I was someone of importance. That wasn't necessarily true, though it may have been in this case.

We passed into the cool interior of the building. Hangings from the beams in the high ceiling showed Sylvaris in some of his customary roles—a spectral figure whispering in a merchant's ear and another of him guiding a weary traveler. The scent of incense—enough to notice but not so much as to overwhelm—filled the air. We reached the door of the priest's office, and the acolyte knocked. Hearing a grunt from inside, he opened it and stood aside.

Jobson was rising from behind his desk as I entered. He was tall and spare, with gray hair and hawklike features above a neatly trimmed beard. Crossing to me, he extended his hand in greeting.

"Dexter Falk," he said. "How long has it been? Three years? Four? Since the affair with the forged seals in Thagnar?"

"Four years, Rafe. And you still owe me for that one."

"I haven't forgotten, Dex, but you did that for Sylvaris as much as for any of his earthly attendants."

"Which is why I have never pestered you about it," I said with a smile.

"You look road weary. Wine? Or business?"

"You'd better give me the wine. I'm afraid you won't be in such a kindly mood when we finish."

"That bad, eh?"

"Worse."

"Then I'd better pour."

After he handed me a glass of belly-warming ecclesiastical port, I started telling him what I had learned, beginning with Ugarte's visit to me. Rafe's face grew darker as I continued. He managed to remain silent until I finished.

"By the shadows!" Rafe muttered darkly, clearly holding back anger. "The priest in Lenoa was a good man and a friend. I don't think I've ever heard of thieves attacking a temple like this. This is far worse than forged seals, Dex. Sylvaris himself might approve of that sort of trickery, but murder and dishonoring his name? We must not allow this to stand."

"I'm glad to hear you say so."

"You will help us clean up this mess," he stated.

"On one condition."

"Which is?"

"You must have your priests-militant intercept the group heading down from Kholl Pass and return the stolen wagons to Tallesin. The temple must also reimburse Ugarte for the first stolen shipment—based on the market value of the contents in Tallesin. By doing so, you solidify my reputation. Do those things, and I will assist in restoring the temple in Lenoa."

"We don't usually compensate victims—"

"In this case, you must. Ugarte's man acted in good faith and paid a sizeable donative in coin."

"In coin?"

"Yes. Two thousand guilders."

"By all the heavenly beings!" Jobson muttered.

"It is not just my reputation that needs to be bolstered, but the temple's."

"Yes, I can see that."

"Ugarte's man in Lenoa can provide you with the manifest of the materials in the first shipment."

"Fine. I agree. But first, we have these men approaching. I can only muster ten of the priests-militant on short notice. The rest are out in the field."

"Ten should be enough. I will play a part as well if you'll lend me a blade. We're not going to face skilled men. These are dockside thugs. Chances are they will try to run for it."

"As bullies do."

"Once we deal with this lot, I must return to Tallesin and inform Mr. Ugarte of what I have learned. Once I have done that, I will be free to return to Lenoa. Once there, I must ask for another favor."

"Which is?"

"I need to find a man named Oderic. It's possible he is the one behind the usurpation of the temple. I have a score to settle with him on behalf of someone I care about."

"Information is easy," Jobson replied. "No other assistance?"

"I plan to kill the man," I said calmly. "The temple should maintain its distance."

"Understood," Jobson said.

I was relieved that he did not try to dissuade me. He knew me well enough to understand that I had my reasons and that they were probably valid. His silence did not mean he approved—only that he would not get in my way.

"I'll need to enlist the aid of the temple in Tallesin to help clean up Lenoa anyway," Jobson said. "Ned Wilbur there will be happy to help. I'm somewhat surprised he hasn't heard anything about the situation in Lenoa."

"He may have heard rumors and dismissed them as people's usual bitching about the donatives," I suggested.

"That's entirely possible. As far as this man Oderic, I will leave him to you, unless he is the one behind the violation of our order. If that is the case, he belongs to us."

"I understand. Your punishment will be far worse than mine. When can you muster the priests-militant?"

"Before the end of the day. Will that be soon enough?"

"If we can set out in the morning, we should meet them in plenty of time."

"Where are you staying?"

"I just arrived and came straight here, Rafe."

"Then let us offer you lodging for the night. I can even have the acolytes prepare a bath for you and take care of your mount."

"She's just a rented mule, but she deserves a little pampering."

"Consider it done."

Cleaned and refreshed, I joined Rafe and the others for dinner. The ten priests-militant were assembled, and their captain wanted to know what we would be facing. Rafe asked me to explain what I knew about the situation in Lenoa for the benefit of everyone.

"So, common criminals, then?" the captain asked.

"Exactly," I said. "They won't be mounted, not that it would make much difference. They aren't very comfortable in the saddle, from what I've seen. I doubt they have much skill with weapons either."

"Bully boys," one of the men commented.

"Just so," I said.

"Try to capture them," Rafe suggested. "I know it will be far easier to kill them, but if we take them alive, we can make examples."

I repressed a shudder. The punishments meted out by the temple of Sylvaris were harsh. Bandits who ignored the seals on crates marking a protected shipment were typically branded on the cheek just beside the nose. Its placement was such that it could not be hidden. It marked the man for the rest of his life.

That didn't necessarily end his career. Along the waterfront of any major harbor, you would find brutes bearing the crossed keys, the sigil of Sylvaris, upside-down, marking them as men who infringed on the tenets of the god of thievery. Any normal person would stay well clear of them, but there was always a need for men with strong backs, weak minds, and a penchant for cruelty. Their time would come when Thalorix judged them and found them wanting.

When we finished the meal, I headed to the temple proper. As I entered, I felt the subtle influence of asomatous energy. Despite my links to the god, I was not a particularly observant worshipper, but I wanted to make sure that he understood I was serious right now.

I prayed to him that Agatha would reach Tallesin safely and be waiting for me when I arrived. She deserved a chance at the life she sacrificed for her family, and I would do my best to help her. I asked for nothing beyond that.

Over the years, I've found it best not to ask Sylvaris for any personal boons. Of all the gods, he is renowned for his sense of humor. There have been times when his gift of persuasion has deserted me in a moment of need, making it necessary for me to extricate myself from dangerous circumstances by physical means.

You may ask how I know this is deliberate on his part. It is because I have sensed his amusement. Fortunately, the skill I have with a blade has never failed me in a moment of need.

Perhaps he gets bored. That explanation makes the most sense to me. Still, I am not resentful. With his help, I have found an interesting way to make a living. My life is seldom dull.

- 60 -

10

In the morning, an acolyte woke me. I dressed and joined the group for breakfast. When we finished, I found Sara already saddled and waiting.

We set off, heading to the eastern gate of the city. I did not anticipate we would encounter the bandits today. Based on the sluggish pace I had observed, we would not run into them until the following day.

Rafe booked us into an inn for the night. The innkeeper was curious, seeing us obviously engaged in temple business, but knew enough not to pry. We would have rebuffed his questions.

Compared to our quarry, we would be much better fed and well rested when we met up with them. It would not be enough to generate any sympathy from me. These thugs would get what they deserved.

We set off early the next day. Just after midday, we saw the line of wagons approaching from Kholl Pass. I rode ahead with Rafe to ascertain that they were the same ones. When we drew close enough to determine that they were, we halted. Rafe gestured for the priests-militant to join us.

We were on an open plain, with the grain growing waist high. The men in the wagon train could see us approaching. It was only when we drew closer that they realized it was a group of priests-militant. We could see the moment it registered with them.

I think the leader hoped to bluff his way past us. That plan was ruined when half of his men jumped from their wagons and started to run, not even pausing to untie the unhappy destriers tied to the back of the wagons. Seeing that, the others did the same.

"So much for a fight," Rafe said dryly. "It will just be like rounding up stray cattle."

"Only not as difficult," I commented.

The priests-militant rode out and tracked down every one of the bandits. When they caught up with one, they prodded him with their short lances to head back to the wagons. After they gathered the last of them, Rafe instructed them to resume driving the wagons toward Eudus. I recognized the leader of the group.

"Why should we?" he asked.

"It makes little difference to me," Rafe replied with a shrug. "I'll be happy to kill you all and leave you for the vultures and crows."

"Then who will drive your wagons?"

"There's a village only a few hours ahead. I'm sure I can find some folks to help us. You want to die first? Just say the word."

The leader looked around at his men. From their fearful expressions, he could tell he would have no support from them. He spat at Rafe's feet but then climbed back onto a wagon.

When we reached the village a couple of hours later, the same man tried to bolt. He made it no more than fifty paces before one of the priests-militant whacked him in the back of the head with the flat of his sword. The priests trussed him up securely and threw him on the wagon; then one of them took the reins after tying his horse to the rear of it.

As the day started to fade, we called a halt. The priests-militant made our prisoners remove all their clothing and tied their feet and hands. By now, their leader had regained consciousness, but the priests left him bound and helpless.

The priests were especially upset by the condition of the destriers the prisoners had stolen. They took out their anger on their captives, cuffing and kicking them at the slightest provocation. I found it hard to blame them. Mistreating magnificent animals the way they did, even out of ignorance, was inexcusable.

Rafe went and questioned the man later. They were far enough from the rest of us that I could not hear what was said, but it was clear from the tone of the man's words that he did not want to answer. Rafe was persistent, and the man was clearly growing increasingly uncomfortable from how he was tied up.

Eventually, he started to talk, probably because Rafe promised to loosen his bindings. Of course, Rafe had no intention of doing any such thing. After he got the information he sought, he struck the man in the head with the pommel of his sword, knocking him out again.

"Did you learn anything useful?" I asked when Rafe returned to our group.

"I did, but you're not going to like it."

"And why is that?"

"Because the man Oderic, whom you seek, is the ringleader of what has happened at the temple in Lenoa. We will exact our retribution as the god demands. You will be welcome to observe, of course. I can even offer privileged seating."

Privileged seating to watch a man being dragged, racked, and gutted—I had no desire to see that, no matter how much the man might deserve it. Rafe's eyes held a look of sadness. I sensed he didn't look forward to the punishment either.

"What happened?" I asked.

"As you suspected, he arrived in the winter with a gang of brutes, asking for asylum. The head priest took them in and was slaughtered in his sleep for his kindness. As each of the priests-militant returned to the temple on their usual schedule, this Oderic ambushed them, one by one."

"That's pretty much what I guessed."

"It's much worse than that, Dex. Hijacking Ugarte's last two shipments was not the most lucrative venture Oderic engaged in. He has been using the temple to hide slaves—boys and girls mostly."

"That's disgusting."

"It's desecration of the worst sort," Rafe said sadly. "When we get our hands on Oderic, the full penalty will be extracted."

"I think I will pass on your kind offer of preferential seating."

"If only I could as well," Rafe said. "When I was an acolyte, I observed a similar punishment. It was part of the training. I hoped never to see it again. Unfortunately, Ned Wilbur and I will need to preside."

"When will you move against him?"

"As soon as possible. Grint, the man I questioned, indicated that Oderic suspected he might soon overstay his welcome in Lenoa. He has around thirty men in the temple with him. I think tomorrow, you and I will best be served by heading for Tallesin, while the captain takes this lot to Eudus and makes sure they pay the penalty. He will make arrangements for these wagons to go to Tallesin to Ugarte. As soon as that is done, he will gather more of the priests-militant and ride for Lenoa."

"And you?" I asked, looking beyond Rafe to the rest of the group.

The priests-militant were divided into three groups. One set of four was keeping watch over the captive bandits, bound, naked, and miserable, far from the fire. The other six were ringed around a campfire. Grint, the leader Rafe interrogated, was still out cold, now tied to a wagon wheel, his head slumped on his chest.

"I'll ride with you to Tallesin. Ned Wilbur will need a couple of days to gather his priests-militant, and my captain will follow from Eudus and meet us there. We can't wait too long."

"Good. I will need a day or two in Tallesin. I owe Ugarte an update—let him know his shipment will arrive soon and collect the money he owes me for the additional days I've spent and expenses I've incurred. The livery will want to know about Sara. I'll need to bring them current, and I have other business to attend to."

"This other business … the woman you mentioned?"

"Yes—I hope. I asked her to wait at my place in Tallesin. She's strong-willed and independent, so who knows if she'll be there. If she is, she will be very interested in what you plan to do with Oderic."

We turned in for the night not long after. The priests-militant were keeping watch over the prisoners. Even so, I slept lightly, keeping my long knife in my hand.

Dawn broke crisp and clear—the promise of a beautiful summer day. Zoryn's sky was an unblemished blue. We broke camp quickly. I mounted Sara, and Rafe mounted his gelding, and we turned to the south toward Tallesin while the priests-militant continued west to Eudus with the wagons.

"Ned Wilbur can muster twenty men easily. My captain will bring a similar number. None of the temples are built for defense, so we will get in easily. We will have the advantage of numbers."

"And skill," I said.

By now, Agatha would have arrived in Tallesin. I hoped she went to my flat and found the stash of guilders in the false bottom of the wardrobe. I meant for her to use the money to buy clothing more suitable than the rough garb of a wagoneer. If I had my way, I would dress her befitting her station—a proud lady of the cortaderia. I doubted she would be so extravagant. She might be reticent, thinking that the money she discovered was my life's savings. It wasn't even a tenth part.

Rafe and I made good time, encountering groups heading north to Eudus and passing others on the way to Tallesin. We stopped at an inn in a tidy village that night. In the morning, we set off at first light. As the day faded, we saw the buildings of Tallesin rise from the horizon.

Entering the city, Rafe headed for the temple. I rode with him and then continued on my way to the livery where I obtained Sara. The proprietor was slightly grumpy that I had been much longer than initially anticipated but seemed to brighten up when I paid his requested charges without complaint.

"She's been a good girl," I said. "If she's still available, I will be heading back to Lenoa in a couple of days. I would like to take her again, if I could."

"It looks like you treated her well," the stableman said. "And your money is certainly good. I can make sure she's still here for the next three days, for an additional two quadrans."

"Money well spent," I said, handing him the coins.

"We'll see you soon, then, Mr. Falk."

I set off for my flat with my saddlebags and bedroll. It was a great pleasure to see a light in the window when I arrived outside the milliner's shop below my rooms. When I opened the door at the bottom of the stairs leading up to my rooms, I called out to Agatha to let her know it was me. Then I climbed up.

"It's Dex," I said from outside, in case she hadn't heard me from the bottom of the stairs, then opened the door.

Agatha stood there in one of my tunics. It was far too large on her, almost like a short dress. Her straw-colored hair was gathered in a loose ponytail. There was a strange gleam in her eye. For a moment, she stood still, then she suddenly launched herself at me. I staggered backward, slamming the door shut behind me.

"I've been so worried," she gasped in between hungry, almost feverish, kisses.

I learned that my tunic was the only thing she was wearing. Her scent was intoxicating. She was demanding, finding a way to undo my belt. We paid homage to Lysmera right there, with her in my arms, against the wall.

When we finished, we collapsed to the floor, with her still in my arms, lying on top of me. I brushed a stray lock of hair from her face to look in her eyes. She lifted her head and smiled.

"I'm hungry now," she said. "You have no food in this place. Take me and feed me, Dex."

"You should get dressed first," I suggested.

"I suppose so," she said with a laugh as she raised herself off me. "Wait here. I'll be ready in a minute."

Agatha went into my bedroom. I stood and pulled my trousers up, tying my belt. My sword was still behind the door where I left it. I buckled it on, its familiar weight a comfort.

Agatha did not take long. We went to the closest inn. As we walked, Agatha reached for my hand and held it. Such a simple gesture, but one she would not have made ten days earlier. It warmed my heart.

The innkeeper knew me and ushered us into the dining room without delay. Once we were seated, he brought us wine and bread. Once we'd had a nibble and a sip, Agatha told me she had been to the temple with Molsen, and they had also called on Mr. Ugarte. Ugarte wanted to see me when I arrived.

I told Agatha everything I'd learned about the temple in Lenoa and Oderic's role. Her face darkened. She waited for me to finish.

"I'm going with you," she stated firmly.

"Of course."

"Huh. I expected a fight."

"Nope. He prolonged the ruin of your life. If you want, I can obtain preferential seating for you to see his punishment."

"Just to know that he will suffer is enough. I don't need to see it."

11

Sleeping in my comfortable bed with Agatha in my arms was blissful. I hated to get up, especially with her draped atop me and my nose buried in her hair. Unfortunately, nature called. I did my best to slide out from under and disturb her as little as possible, but she woke.

We dressed, then set off, with our first stop at a bakery to grab something to eat. After that, we headed for Ugarte's office. It was busier than on my last visit. The clerk at the front desk retrieved Ugarte, who came out with an uncertain expression, clearly wanting to hear good news from me.

"Hello again, Miss Mountjoy," he said to Agatha. "Mr. Falk."

I raised my eyebrows at his greeting to her. When we met, she had used the name of her dead husband. I did not know her maiden name until now.

"The remainder of the wagons from the second shipment will be arriving from Eudus in a few days," I said. "The temple will make good the loss of your first shipment. They will want to see the manifest in Lenoa but have promised me that they will pay full market value—at Tallesin prices."

Ugarte's eyes widened, and relief washed across his face. He gestured for us to follow him into his office. After we entered, he bade us sit while he closed the door.

"I'm somewhat surprised the temple has agreed to these terms," he said. "I would expect them to try to pay me what the shipment would be worth in Lenoa, which is far less."

"The situation in Lenoa is a stain on the god's reputation," I said. "They cannot allow that to linger. The quicker they can restore order, the better, and that includes making you whole."

"What about the thieves?"

"Those who hijacked the recent shipment will be dealt with in Eudus. The ringleader is in Lenoa, and the priests-militant will deal with him, most unpleasantly."

"I see. And my man in Lenoa?"

"Ferrare is an honest man. He gave the receipts for the first shipment to Melton."

"That's who I sent. What happened to him?"

"I suspect he's dead, sir."

"You've earned your fee, Mr. Falk," he said as he relaxed upon hearing the worst was behind him. "How much do I owe you?"

I took out my small pad with the notes I kept. The cost of renting Sara, the food I'd bought, and my traveling expenses were all jotted down. I added up the total in my head.

"You paid for fifteen days up front. It has been another fifteen, plus my expenses. Two hundred guilders, sir."

"A bargain at twice the amount," Ugarte said. "I won't pay you that, but I will hand over three hundred, as a symbol of my gratitude."

"Thank you, sir."

Ugarte counted out the money and put it in a small chest for me. Three hundred of the gold coins were too big for a money pouch. When he finished, he handed me the box and stood.

"Thank you, Mr. Falk. I will spread word of your excellent assistance."

"Thank you, Mr. Ugarte," I replied, and headed out of his office, with Agatha right next to me.

"Three hundred guilders!" she hissed quietly. "There were only fifty in the pouch I found. You're rich!"

I chuckled as I shifted the box under my arm. When we reached the street, Agatha had taken my hand again. This need for contact was something new. I liked it but wondered what was driving it.

"I suppose I am, compared to most."

"Then where is it? Your flat is nothing special. Your clothes, too. Why not live a more comfortable life?"

"Because I still need to work for a living. And a flashy appearance would present the wrong image. Plus, it would draw unwelcome attention from troublesome people looking for a quick and easy score."

"I don't think you're easy, or quick," Agatha said with loaded meaning, her blue eyes flashing with her secret joke.

"Thank you, Lady Agatha," I said with a smirk. "We need to return to my flat now. I don't like carrying this much money around. Then, to the temple of Sylvaris. The head priest from Eudus rode with me. He and the man in charge of the temple here in Tallesin will be planning what they will do in Lenoa."

We returned to my flat. When we climbed upstairs, I pried up one of the floorboards and put the chest with the coins there. Agatha looked over my shoulder and saw other, larger chests in the same spot. I found a pouch and checked it, making sure it held more than twenty guilders. When I straightened up, she was looking at me oddly.

"How much money do you have, Dex?"

"I've never bothered to count it," I answered truthfully. "Plenty, I suppose."

"From the little I saw just now, you could live a comfortable life and never work again, especially with how modestly you keep yourself."

"Perhaps. I don't think about it. Besides, a life of leisure would seem unbearably long. The boredom would send me to an early grave."

After refastening the floorboard, we headed for the temple. An acolyte met us and recognized me. He took us inside, explaining that the head priest was expecting me.

Rafe Jobson and Ned Wilbur were standing next to a table, with some sort of drawing on it. They looked up when we entered. I introduced them to Agatha, who curtsied for them—a polite and graceful gesture that should not have surprised me, but did.

"Dex," Ned said, "Rafe and I have been reviewing the layout of the temple in Lenoa. We don't anticipate any difficulties. There aren't any places these bastards can fortify and hole up."

"How many men can you muster?" I asked.

"Seventeen on short notice. Rafe's men should arrive tonight. We'll set off in the morning with what numbers we have."

"What if they threaten their captives?" I asked, mindful that there might be children present, kidnapped and headed for a life of slavery.

"We've been discussing that," Rafe said. "That's where we might need your assistance. Someone who can slip in, quick and quiet, and get the children out."

"Children?" Agatha gasped.

"The man who took over the temple has been using it to house captives he plans to sell as slaves," Rafe said. "Didn't Dex tell you?"

"I hadn't gotten around to it yet," I mumbled.

"There can be no worse desecration of the temple than that," Ned said. "The punishment demanded by Sylvaris is grisly and disgusting, but in this case, it will be well-deserved."

"Why didn't you tell me that Oderic was using the temple for his slaving?" Agatha demanded angrily after we left.

"I wasn't keeping it from you," I said. "Other things seemed more important. There is nothing we can do about it at the moment anyway."

"I suppose that's true," she replied after she calmed down. "But those poor children…"

"Perhaps that is the part you must play once we deal with Oderic," I said. "Helping the children return to their families."

Agatha stopped abruptly, yanking her hand away from mine. Her blue eyes sparkled with fury. I took a step back before she erupted.

"You think I'm some cringing violet? A useless piece of baggage who will only get in the way? I have news for you, Dexter Falk. I've—"

"Whoa, Lady Agatha, whoa!" I said, clasping her upper arms lightly. "That's not what I meant at all. You're tough as nails—I know this first-hand, remember? I'm sure you can handle yourself in a fight. That's not the issue."

"Then what is?" she demanded, her arms crossed over her chest.

"The children will be frightened. Oderic's men might try to use them as shields or bargaining chips. We need to get them to safety as quickly and quietly as possible. Who do you think these children will find less scary? Who will they be more likely to listen to? Priests-militant in the same sort of armor they've seen the thugs wearing, or a woman? I think you give us the best chance of getting as many of them as possible out of harm's way. Will you consider it?"

Agatha's expression and posture did not relax a bit, yet I could tell she was considering what I said. Her jaw clenched, then relaxed. She realized I wasn't trying to sideline her—that I sincerely believed she would be more effective in convincing the children to follow her.

"You might be right," she said finally, not admitting defeat, but acknowledging that my point was valid.

"The children have been through hell. Snatched from the street, beaten, starved—with the threat of being sent over the sea to a life of slavery hanging over them. We need to send someone to them whom they will trust on sight, not another armored brute. The quicker we get them out of the place, the better it will be for all of us."

"I want to see Oderic's face when he realizes it's all over for him," she said, disappointedly.

"You might not be able to. I realize how much it means, but I really think you are the best hope we have of getting the children out of the way fast."

She frowned but uncrossed her arms. The furrow in the middle of her forehead disappeared as she relaxed her expression. I stepped closer to her and looked into her eyes.

"Agatha Mountjoy, they say that living well is the best revenge. Think of yourself on your horse, out on the cortaderia, then weigh that against what you might miss seeing. Which will fill your soul more satisfyingly?"

She stared into my eyes for a long moment. The hustle and bustle of Tallesin continued around us—the creaking of carts, the distant ring of a blacksmith's hammer, a street vendor overheard haggling with a customer. At length, she sighed and clasped my hand again.

"Yes. Living well would be the best revenge. But don't think I'm agreeing to this out of any fear of combat. I'm only willing to do it because of the expediency. You're right—the children will be more willing to follow a woman. But if I encounter any of Oderic's men … I'll show them what a lady of the cortaderia can do with a knife—I'll geld them."

"And if they knew you were coming, they would be smart to already be seeking passage as far away as possible."

"Where are we going now?" she asked as I led her by the hand down the street.

"To the livery. I need to let them know I'll be taking Sara again in the morning, and we need to make arrangements for a mount for you."

"Molsen owes me for the wagon and mule the bandits—"

"Which are on the way from Eudus. They will not be here until after we leave. I doubt you will return to Tallesin anytime soon, so—"

"Why wouldn't I?"

"Because after we clean up the mess in Lenoa, and you regain access to your late husband's accounts, I intend for you to return to your family. If you would like, I can dispose of your wagon and mule when I return to Tallesin. How much did you pay for them? I can give you the money today. We'll leave word for Molsen to sell them and get the money from him the next time we see him."

"Why are you doing this?"

"I told you already."

"No one is this generous without expecting something in return."

"What more can you offer me that you haven't already given?"

That silenced her protests for the moment. I could tell she was chewing that over. We continued on the way to the livery.

"Fine," she said at last. "But don't think you can order me around."

"I would only attempt that if I wanted to be publicly humiliated."

"And if we're going to Lenoa, I want my own mount. I will not ride double."

"I had not planned on asking you to do that."

"A horse, not a mule."

"Of course. And no sway-backed nag."

"Then I'll take you up on your offer to give me the money for my mule and wagon. I'll use that to buy a horse and tack."

"We'll need to stop by my flat again. I don't have the coin on me to buy a horse."

12

"How much will I need?"

"Fifty guilders," she said. "That's about what my wagon and the mule are worth. And if I can't find a decent horse for fifty guilders, then the market in Tallesin is entirely populated by bandits and thieves."

I pried up the floorboard and found a larger, sturdier money pouch. After making sure I had at least fifty guilders in it, I put the board back down. Agatha had been watching me the entire time.

"We'll stop at the livery first and let the man know I'll be taking Sara again in the morning."

'Why don't you have your own mount?" she asked. "You can clearly afford it."

"I only need one occasionally," I said. "Rarely when I'm in the city. It just doesn't seem fair to the animal if I'm going to ignore it most of the time."

"That's a good point."

At the livery, I informed the proprietor of my plans, and we would likely be away for a month. We negotiated a fair price, and I paid it without argument. Then Agatha and I headed for the horse market.

When we arrived, it was clear she was in her element. We went from vendor to vendor. Agatha examined what they had to offer and asked what they were charging for each one. At each stop, she checked their legs and feet, inspected their eyes and mouth, felt their backs, and asked to see them move.

"Well?" I asked when we finished. "Any that look promising?"

"The bay gelding from the third man we visited is the best of the lot. I just need to convince him to lower his price."

"Would you like my help?"

Agatha gave me a scornful look. She was not angry, though. Her expression was more one of amusement.

"While you were growing up on your hardscabble farm, I was going with my father to livestock traders. Remember, we didn't have much money, so I learned to strike a deal. Watch and learn," she said smugly.

"Fine. I'll just stand there with my arms crossed, backing your play."

"Good."

We circled back to the man with the bay. He had a sun-leathered face and a bushy gray mustache at odds with the black hair peeking out from under his hat. When he saw Agatha approaching, he straightened up from where he had been slouching against a post.

The bay stood patiently, tethered to a rail. Its reddish-brown coat gleamed in the sun. To me, it seemed like a solid choice.

"Good sir," she greeted him as she strode up.

I was fascinated. In just a few strides, the wagoneer had disappeared. Despite her clothing, her bearing was erect and confident. I realized she truly was a thane's daughter.

"I've been thinking about this bay of yours," she said.

"Aye?"

"He's a fine mount, no doubt, but not worth the seventy guilders you said you wanted for him."

"And why not?" the man said defensively. "He's sound as a bell."

Agatha stepped close to the horse and ran her hand along his flank. She bent and lifted his foreleg. The bay shifted slightly but did not resist.

"He needs shoes. I'll need to take him to a farrier right away. The condition of the shoes means you cleaned him up for market, but he's had hard use recently. And this scar, here?"

She pointed.

"That's from an old saddle sore. I'm guessing his previous owner was responsible. That's how you were able to buy him cheaply, nurse him back to health, and bring him here to make a big profit. I give you great credit for doing well by a mistreated animal, but thirty-five guilders is a fair price, given that you probably paid less than twenty."

"Thirty-five? You wound me, madam. That scar is from him running into a branch when he was young and foolish. He's prime stock from the cortaderia, the best horse country I know. I could perhaps be convinced to drop the price to sixty-five, because of your sweet smile."

Agatha's sweet smile was a shark's grin now. I wondered how many times she had watched her father engage in similar discussions or taken part in them herself. For my part, I would just relax and watch.

"Let's walk him again," she suggested.

The man untied the horse from the rail and paraded the horse in a circle. Agatha watched carefully, then turned to me. Guessing what she wanted, I curled my lip disapprovingly. She winked so the man didn't see it.

"He's favoring his left hind."

"He is not!" the man protested.

"Sure he is," Agatha said. "Give me the reins and see for yourself. What happened? A fall? Probably nothing that a bit of rest won't cure, but it knocks his value down. Forty guilders is all he's worth."

"Sixty, and that's as low as I go," the man said.

Agatha snorted derisively. She looked back at me, and I rolled my eyes. Agatha slowly shook her head, frowning.

"I suppose we should go back and take another look at that chestnut mare down the way," she told me.

The horse trader's mustache twitched with amusement. He glanced at Agatha as she started to turn away. I'll give him credit. He must have thought Agatha was inexperienced, but he now knew better.

"Hold on there, madam," he said. "That chestnut's a fine animal, no doubt, but you weren't here this earlier this morning. She's got a temper and a stubborn streak you don't want to deal with. Fifty-five, and I'll throw in the bridle that's on him right now."

"That bridle isn't worth the spit I'd use to try to polish it," Agatha said. "Forty-five."

"I can't do forty-five, madam. Honest, I can't."

The man looked around as though someone might come and help him. There were a few people who had gathered to watch the negotiations from a slight distance, but they were there for entertainment. He sighed dramatically.

"Split the difference? Fifty?" Agatha offered, in a conciliatory tone.

"Aye," he said, his tone admitting defeat.

"Pay the man, Mr. Falk," she said.

I counted out fifty guilders. The horse merchant noticed that doing so pretty well emptied my purse. He smiled upon realizing that and laughed softly to himself.

"Well done, fair lady," he said. "Well done."

"What's his name?" Agatha asked.

"Rufus," he said.

"I like the name. We had a dog named Rufus. He was a good boy," Agatha said.

We left with the horse in tow and headed to a tack shop. Agatha took charge there as well, obtaining a saddle that fit properly (after trying several that she deemed unsatisfactory) and all the other accoutrements at a sharp price. She paid for these items herself.

When she finished, we took Rufus to a farrier for new shoes. Agatha handled the negotiation, convincing the man to do the work immediately. We then stopped by the livery and asked them to stable Rufus with Sara for the night. The owner agreed without charging us. That let me know he had probably gouged me slightly on the cost of using Sara for the next month. I didn't care. She'd proven herself a good mount, and that meant peace of mind for me.

We then stopped and bought food for our journey, using the saddlebags Agatha had just purchased to carry things. Dried fruit, jerky, and oats for porridge, and for the animals. I was sure the priests-militant would have a kettle of some sort and might be able to feed us, but I did not want to take the chance that they overlooked us in their planning.

Our shopping expedition had taken most of the day. On the way back to my flat, we stopped by a street vendor, and I bought us an early dinner—spiced goat meat and vegetables cooked on skewers. I then bought us a decent bottle of wine to share when we returned to my quarters.

"I noticed you have a tub tucked away," Agatha said as I uncorked the wine and poured us each a glass. "Will you fix us a bath so we can begin our journey clean?"

"As long as you don't mind cold water," I said. "It's a bit too warm to be kindling the stove."

"We can warm it up together," she said with a sly smile.

I retrieved the tin tub from where I had it tucked away, along with a cake of soap and a couple of soft wash rags from an old shirt. After laying them out, I began fetching water from the fountain in the square. With a kitchen rag and some water from the first bucket, I washed out the cobwebs that had accumulated since I last used it. That finished, I went back to bucket duty.

Although Agatha teased that we would share the bath, my tub was really too small to consider it. I would, of course, offer my assistance in helping her scrub all the hard-to-reach places, along with some that were readily available. When she finished, I would take my turn.

After filling the tub just over halfway, I set the buckets down. I had worked up a sweat on the warm summer evening. I sat and took a sip of my wine as Agatha stripped off her clothes, let down her hair, and stepped into the water. My eyes were locked on her form. She had an exquisite figure, if you like women who were slim with broad shoulders. I certainly did.

"Not too bad," she commented as she eased herself down. "Refreshing, actually."

There was no room for her to stretch out. Her knees were nearly under her chin. It was clear that only one person at a time would fit. She wetted the soap and lathered up one of the wash rags.

"Hmm," she said, taking a sniff. "Lavender. From a previous guest?"

I shrugged in reply. It was, but that was not a topic I wished to discuss at the moment. Agatha was only teasing me anyway.

Lifting her feet up and placing them over the end of the tub, she slid down to submerge her head. She scrubbed her scalp with her fingers vigorously before reemerging. Her wet hair was drawn back, only slightly darker than when it was dry, as she scooched back to her previous position.

"Do my back?" she asked, holding out the wash rag with a grin.

"It will be my pleasure, Lady Agatha."

"Of course it will. You deserve a small reward for bringing the water."

I knelt behind her and took the soapy rag. Starting with her shoulders, I worked my way down, giving her a massage as I went. Agatha let out a sigh of pleasure as I stroked the muscles in her back. When I finished, she leaned back and rested her head on the edge of the tub, looking up at me.

"Now the front," she murmured.

Before I started, I bent forward and kissed her gently. When I broke the kiss, her eyes were closed, and a sweet smile adorned her face. She found my hands and guided them where she wanted them. As it so happened, she placed them exactly where I was hoping they would land.

All too soon, she opened her eyes again and pulled my hands away. She struggled to her feet and stepped out. I stood and offered her a linen cloth to dry herself. She indicated that I should do it, which was also my pleasure.

"Your turn," she said.

Her treatment of me was more perfunctory, and my bath took much less time as a result. She did not offer to assist me in drying myself either. It bothered me not at all.

When we were both clean, I emptied the tub, bucket by bucket, tossing the water out the kitchen window. The last step was to tip the tub itself out. When I finished, Agatha handed me a clean tunic and my glass of wine.

She was wearing one of my linen tunics, which looked like a shift on her. We settled onto the sofa, and she tucked herself up next to me, with my arm around her shoulders. Before I knew it, she was asleep, her head on my chest.

13

Once again, waking with Agatha in my arms was a tremendous way to start a day. She sensed I was no longer sleeping and lifted her head to look in my eyes. I gave her a peck on the nose, then went to relieve myself, noticing that the sun had just risen.

"You carried me to bed," she commented as she sat up and stretched her arms above her head.

"You were asleep."

"Sometimes I think you're too good to be true, and I'll wake up and find this was all some complicated dream," Agatha said as she rose from the bed and came to me, wrapping her arms around my middle.

"Then it has been an exceptionally pleasant one," I answered, returning her embrace.

She murmured that she agreed, then we separated reluctantly. We dressed, both of us in sturdy breeches, with linen tunics and worn-in boots. I grabbed a money pouch and checked to see that it contained at least twenty guilders. Agatha tied her hair back with a leather thong and tucked it under a felt hat of mine that she'd found. I buckled my sword on, then slung our saddle bags over my shoulders.

"That's a fine rapier," she commented when we reached the street below. "It's the only thing of yours that I found that provides evidence that you do indeed have money. Is your skill equal to the quality of the blade?"

"Better," I replied with a wink, though I was not boasting. "I did not purchase it myself. It was a gift."

"I'm no expert in arms," she said, "but we did still have a few family heirlooms left. None of them match the quality I discern in that weapon."

"The Duke of Endor gave it to me after I extracted his son from a bad situation," I said. "He told me the swordsmith was blessed by Korath, and I have every reason to believe him. The balance is perfect, and it holds an edge incredibly well. A different swordsmith told me that there are eight different types of steel used in its construction, with varying properties of strength and flexibility. It has never let me down, and I have needed it more than I care to admit."

"I noticed the sigil of Sylvaris near the hilt," she said as we walked toward the livery, "the crossed keys. Are you affiliated with the temples? Is that why they are so willing to accommodate you?"

"I'm affiliated with Sylvaris," I said, trying to dodge her question, "but not any specific temple."

I learned in my younger days to avoid mentioning my link with Sylvaris. It attracted interest of the wrong type. Many men considered it a challenge. Some women wanted to bed me in hopes that they would bear a god-touched child. Of course, if I were asked to prove my connection, Sylvaris would usually, as a matter of course, leave me empty-handed, no doubt laughing at my predicament.

"You're god-touched," she said with quiet realization. "It makes sense now."

"What makes sense?"

"Just little things," she said. "Like how you have hundreds of guilders stashed under your floorboards and yet live so simply, or your independence and somewhat solitary nature, or your anger over the situation in Lenoa."

I stopped in my tracks. The morning traffic flowed around us. We could smell fresh-baked bread and the peculiar odor of the waterfront. Agatha faced me. Her eyes were not accusatory. The look was more one of dawning understanding—of curiosity and not of greed. That was a relief.

"You're the only person I've ever met who was god-touched," she said, then took my hand and resumed walking toward the livery. "I've met a couple of others who claimed it, but they were impostors. It makes sense that someone who really was, would keep it quiet."

"Well, you're right," I said. "Sylvaris touched me when I was still a boy on the farm. Talk about being confused! The nearest temple was two days away on foot. It was over a year before I was able to go and talk with the priests about the strange things I was feeling."

"I can almost picture it," she said with a grin. "You didn't have much book learning, did you?"

"I knew my letters and numbers," I said. "Simple arithmetic—as much as a farmer would need to know. After that visit to the temple, though, my days on the farm were numbered. My father accepted what the priests told him and let me go. It was harder on my mother. My younger brother was the only one truly happy about it. It meant he would get the farm without complication."

"Did you renounce your claim?"

"That was part of the agreement my father made with the priests. He would allow them to have me, but in return, I forfeited any claim to the land."

"Did that seem fair?"

"I was a restless spirit, even then," I said with a smile. "I didn't hate farming, but I didn't enjoy it. The idea of spending the rest of my life in one place held no appeal."

"So, you stayed at the temple?"

"Not long. The priests sent me to Meropan, the main temple of Sylvaris for the entire globe. They trained me—not as an acolyte, but as something other. I learned from books, certainly, but they also made sure I was taught other things."

"Like?"

"How to handle a sword or a knife, how to box and wrestle, different languages, the art of disguise, how to change my voice, how to mimic someone's handwriting, all sorts of things. I soaked it up like a sponge."

"What are his gifts to you?"

"The most reliable one is my ability to learn languages quickly and speak them like a native. When it suits the god, I can also persuade anyone of anything, but Sylvaris is capricious. That ability has failed me in some crucial moments. I think it amuses him to pull the rug out from under me."

"Your skill with a blade?"

"I don't know if I owe that to Sylvaris," I said. "The priests didn't think so. Nor is my quickness of mind a gift from him. According to the priests, those qualities are what influenced him to choose me, not the result. I have needed to rely on both when Sylvaris has decided to have his fun."

"Does it bother you that you're not just a normal person?"

"What an interesting question, Lady Agatha! No one has ever asked me that before. No, it doesn't bother me. I am what I am. When I was young and stupid enough to boast about my connection, it caused me some difficulty, but I was clever enough to realize that I was the one who created the problem."

"Does it make you … different? From other men? In certain ways?"

"That's a very vague question. What do you mean?"

"After Voss, I wanted nothing to do with men," she said, looking down at the road and blushing. "But after I met you, I started to think … and…"

"I have no connection with Lysmera," I said, anticipating her line of inquiry.

"Then … why? It has been beyond anything I ever dreamed it could be."

"You were ready for a man who would treat you with the respect you deserve."

"You make it sound so simple, when it's not."

"So much of life can be explained in simple terms," I said with a chuckle. "It's the living of it that gets complicated."

We reached the livery, and the stableman greeted us. He went to bring Sara and Rufus out. Perhaps motivated by my generosity, both of them were freshly groomed. I gave the man a quadrans in thanks. We saddled our mounts with practiced ease and were ready to depart in short order.

The city was coming to life around us. We'd walked through mostly empty streets on the way to the livery. They were filling now. We headed to the temple of Sylvaris.

Agatha and I were walking our mounts, leading them by the reins. Her hand found mine as soon as we left the stable behind. I looked over at her, and our eyes met. She gave me a smile and swung our arms slightly.

"You're in a good mood," I remarked.

"I am. I've decided I'm glad I met you, Dexter Falk. My life has certainly changed since Zoryn sent that rainstorm."

We reached the temple a few minutes later. Rafe and Ned were there, with more than two dozen priests-militant, already mounted, with their black armor stowed behind their saddles. Seeing us, the two head priests climbed into their saddles. I let go of Agatha's hand so we could do the same.

She lifted herself onto Rufus with the grace of someone born to a life on horseback. Although her garb was that of a wagoneer, her bearing and posture betrayed the fact that she was a horsewoman. It made me smile to see it.

The group set off with a murmured word from Ned, and we followed. Rafe allowed others to pass him by. He drifted back so we could talk.

"Blessings of the day upon you, Miss Mountjoy, Dex. We have thirty-one priests-militant—the most we could muster on short notice. I've also sent messengers to Meropan to inform the head of our order of what is happening. It will be up to him to install a new head priest in Lenoa and restaff the temple. I expressed the urgency of the problem. It should not take long for new people to arrive."

"Good," I grunted. "The sooner order is restored in Lenoa, the better. It's a black mark against Sylvaris to have such a major port under the control of an evil man."

"Speaking of which," Rafe continued, "in questioning the man, Grint, he confessed that Oderic had eleven children he was holding in the cellar of the temple outbuilding. I hope we reach them before he sends them away to Molutia."

"It takes a special sort of monster to enslave children," Agatha commented, a sour look on her face.

"Any sane person would agree," Rafe said. "There could be no worse desecration of the temple than this."

We continued in silence for a time after this, as the sun climbed higher and the heat grew. The fields we passed were filled with ripening wheat. To my eye, it looked like a good year for crops.

Near midday, we encountered the first caravan coming from the east at a watering hole not far from the road. Rafe and Ned met with the leader of the group. Agatha slid from her saddle with easy grace and led Rufus to get some water. I joined her and handed her my waterskin.

"How does it feel to be on horseback again?" I asked.

"Oh, parts of me will be sore tonight," she said with a smile, "but it will be a good hurt. Rufus is a good horse, even though he is favoring his left hind leg just a bit. It seems like no more than a slight strain. With some rest once we reach Lenoa, he'll be fine."

I heard a loud whistle and looked. Ned was the one who issued it and beckoned me over. I handed Sara's reins to Agatha and went to talk.

"Harlan here," he said, gesturing to the caravan master, "just was shaken down for a 'toll' by some men wearing the armor of priests-militant. The donatives were all paid properly in Lenoa, and the crates have the seals to prove it. The leader of the gang that stopped him claimed it was a 'special assessment' due to the increased danger on the road."

"Which those phony priests have caused," Rafe snarled.

"Anyway, we're sending a group ahead to track them down," Ned continued. "You want to join them?"

"Would you like me to go with them?"

"Yes."

"Then just say so," I replied with a smile. "How many?"

"Six."

"Let me get my mount, and I'll be ready."

14

"What was that about?" Agatha asked.

I told her. For a moment, I thought she would protest that she wanted to come with me. Then she realized that her only weapon was a knife, and the bandits were wearing armor, and she changed her mind.

"Don't get hurt," was what she ended up saying, although that was not what she initially intended.

"I won't. These people are thugs, more used to bullying people than actually fighting. Besides, I'm being invited along as a courtesy. The priests-militant will take care of any combat."

As I turned to mount Sara again, Agatha clutched my hand quickly. I stopped. Looking in her eyes, I realized what she wanted. I gave her a quick but heartfelt kiss.

Climbing back in the saddle, I realized that small moment meant a lot. Agatha was, as she had said, no delicate flower. She'd faced a future not of her choosing, knowing it meant her family's survival. She'd persevered even though it turned out to be more horrible than anyone could have guessed. When her husband died, she'd set out on a new and brighter path, only to have Oderic thwart her.

Agatha was independent, with a strength of character I'd never encountered. She had decided to allow me to get close to her, physically and emotionally. I now understood better how significant that was for her.

The six priests-militant were waiting, clad in their black armor. With their visors raised, you could see in their eyes that these men were hardened warriors. The leader, named Baker, nodded at me.

"Take the lead, Mr. Falk," he said. "You track them down. We'll take care of the rest."

The priests-militant were mounted on sturdy destriers, magnificent horses. Their armor was clean but showed signs of regular use. They each carried two short lances tucked under the fender of their saddles. On their left hips were their sabers, and they wore their shields slung across their backs.

We set off at a brisk trot and reached the spot where they had waylaid the caravan less than an hour before. Tracking them was simple. The hoofprints coming and going went in the same direction.

We were in the foothills of the mountain range that bisected the isthmus, and the path curled back and forth as it headed generally upward. We came around a curve, and I stopped.

The wind was blowing from directly ahead, and I smelled the foul tang of saddle sores. About a half mile ahead was a copse of trees in an area with only a shallow slope. Twisting my head around, I looked back toward the main road. It was plain to see.

"They're in the trees ahead," I said quietly to the leader.

"How do you know?" he asked.

"I can smell them—well, not them, the saddle sores on their mounts. Bastards."

"I wouldn't have noticed it, but now that you pointed it out, I can detect it," he said.

"They can see the road from there and stay in the shade. There is probably a stream as well."

"We'll take it from here, Mr. Falk. I'll be obliged if you stay right here in case any of them get past us."

"Happy to watch the back door," I said.

I slid off Sara and tied her to a scrubby tree not far from the path. Baker and the other men unslung their shields and short lances. When he raised his fist in the air, they set off in unison, their well-trained mounts needing no kicks to get moving.

They headed to the copse at the canter, their lances grasped in their fists. These were made for stabbing down from horseback, not jousting, with sharp, bladed tips. As they drew nearer to the trees, they fanned out slightly.

I couldn't see what took place once they entered the trees. Less than two minutes later, I heard a whistle. Baker rode into view and beckoned me forward.

I untied Sara and climbed on, trotting toward the trees. The smell of saddle sores was even more apparent as I grew closer. That annoyed me greatly and was a clear sign that these men were thugs. There was no excuse for mistreating an animal. If you didn't know how to take care of them, you shouldn't have them.

There were four bodies on the ground, and one of the priests-militant was taking the armor from the corpses. Another three were stripped naked, already bound tight with leather thongs. I recognized one of them from my visit to the temple in Lenoa. The sneer was absent from his face now.

"Mr. Falk, would you please ride back and get us some shovels?" Baker asked. "We're going to have this lot bury their former comrades. We could also use some assistance bringing their mounts back."

I nodded and turned Sara around, heading back to the group. They were waiting on the road where we had turned off. Rafe and Ned rode forward to meet me away from the rest. After I told them what happened and of Baker's request, Ned assigned some of his men to provide assistance.

"What happened?" Agatha asked.

"I didn't see it, but it did not take long. Four of the bandits are dead, and three captured. I imagine Baker will have the captives dig graves for their comrades, then bring them along. It's only fair to warn you, you'll hate them more in a little while."

"Why?"

"They mistreated their horses—saddle sores that I could smell, and who knows what other problems they ignored."

"Inexcusable!" Agatha hissed.

"I agree. If the horses are the ones they stole from the priests-militant they killed in Lenoa, you'll be even more upset."

The frown on her face was like the sudden appearance of dark clouds on a summer day. We watched as six more of the priests-militant rode toward the copse. They carried shovels.

"I hate to waste daylight waiting for them to clean up this mess," Rafe said as he nudged his mount toward me, "but we don't have a choice. These men were impersonating priests-militant. We cannot allow that to pass without public punishment. I will not let them slow us down, but we'll need to have three men guard them and bring them along behind us."

A few minutes later, Baker appeared, with all but three of the priests-militant. They were leading the seven horses taken from the bandits. As I suspected, they were all destriers, showing signs of neglect. Agatha hissed when she saw them and nudged Rufus forward to meet them. The rest of us waited for Baker to approach. After a brief word with Ned, we set off for Lenoa again.

"They set the three remaining to digging a grave for the dead," Ned told me a few minutes later. "The seepage from the sores ruined the saddles. They will bury them as well. Damned idiots!"

"What will happen to the three?"

"We'll drive them to Lenoa, naked and bound. Once they arrive, they'll face punishment. What form that will take will be up to the folks from Meropan. They are the primary temple of Sylvaris, and we defer to them in anything more serious than routine punishments. It will probably be severe, given that they killed priests-militant and then impersonated them."

"Do you have salve for the horses?" Agatha demanded when she returned to us after she had inspected their backs.

"Some, but not enough to last the journey to Lenoa," Rafe replied.

"Then I must insist that someone take them back to Tallesin immediately for proper treatment. Those magnificent animals have suffered enough."

"Pardon me, Miss Mountjoy, but who made you an expert in—"

"I am the daughter of the Thane of Hessel," Agatha snapped. "Only a well-trained mareschal would know more about the care of these animals."

Her bearing and posture were suddenly different. Despite her shoddy wagoneer garb, she held herself proud, erect, and angry. Her blue eyes blazed with icy fire.

Rafe blinked, taken aback by the sudden shift in her demeanor. I'd seen glimpses of this Agatha before, the noblewoman she used to be, but it had been hidden, humbled by the fate she had accepted willingly for her family's sake.

This was like a scene in a play, when the hero suddenly strips away the rags that were his disguise and reveals himself in all his power and glory.

"I apologize," Rafe said sincerely. "I meant no offense. It's just that we are already short on numbers, and I was reluctant to send more men back. Your eye for these things is better than mine. If you say they need to return to Tallesin immediately, I bow to your better judgment. The temple in Tallesin has a fine mareschal who will see to it that these horses get proper care."

"Good," she replied curtly, her tone imperious. "If you did not listen to me, I would have taken them from you, as you clearly would not deserve to have them."

Rafe blinked again and swallowed, then tilted his head in acknowledgement of her words. He turned to Ned, who had watched the exchange and was barely suppressing his amusement at how Agatha had taken command of the situation. They murmured to one another, and Ned then had two of the priests-militant take the recaptured destriers. They headed back toward Tallesin.

Agatha watched them, erect in the saddle, then turned Rufus around and resumed progress up the road. At that moment, I could not see the rough-spun tunic and tired breeches of the wagoneer. I could only see the proud lady she displayed.

"Is she really the Thane of Hessel's daughter?" Rafe asked me a few minutes later.

"Aye."

"How, by all that's holy, did she end up like this?"

"It's an interesting story, but it's hers to tell," I said. "What she has been through would break even the most resilient. I can say that Oderic plays a part in it. After we deal with him, I hope to help her return to the cortaderia where she belongs."

"And you'll go with her?"

"I hope."

"She is right about the horses," Rafe admitted. "I hate to reduce our numbers, but it would not have been fair to those abused animals to prolong their torment by dragging them with us to Lenoa. They'll be at the temple by this time tomorrow, under the care of our people."

Rafe rode ahead to meet up with Ned. Agatha slowed Rufus and allowed me to rejoin her. She looked at me sheepishly.

"I think I overstepped—"

"Not at all," I replied with a soft chuckle. "You spoke the truth and said what needed to be said. There is no fault in that."

"Were you and the priest talking about me?"

"Yes, but only in a positive way. He acknowledges that you are correct about getting those poor animals to care as quickly as possible."

We rode in silence after that. The sun beat down on us through a clear blue sky as we climbed toward the pass. Agatha stayed next to me.

We passed two more caravans heading toward Tallesin and overtook one heading to Lenoa. Rafe and Ned conferred with the leaders of the groups we met coming from Lenoa, asking whether they had encountered the bandits earlier. They had not. They did complain about how they were treated at the temple. The amount of the donative was double the previous rate, and they demanded it in coin.

Our progress was good. We reached a point near the top of the pass as the sun set behind us. The priests-militant set up camp efficiently and quickly. By the time Agatha and I finished watering and grooming our mounts, they already had the cookfire going.

Dinner was ready in short order. Rafe drew Agatha away discreetly. They conversed quietly through the meal. It seemed to be a pleasant talk.

15

Agatha rejoined me later and drew me away from the group by quite a distance. She then spread her blanket on the ground and stretched out, beckoning me to her with a finger. I lay down next to her and pulled my blankets over us. My first thought was that she wanted to be intimate. She did, but for quiet conversation, although she did snuggle up close to me.

"I believe now," she said after a few minutes.

"Believe in what?"

"That I can return to my family. Rafe says you are not someone who makes idle promises."

"Well, we still have some hurdles to clear," I said. "Oderic being the biggest."

"Rafe seems confident that they will be able to capture him and bring him to justice. Dex, I really want to be there to see it happen, but my life will not suffer if I miss the opportunity. Rafe echoed your request for me to try to get the children to safety. Did you discuss it with him?"

"I did not."

"I can see that it's the right thing for me to do. Both of you made the same point—the children would be more likely to come with a woman than a man in the same armor that the thugs have been wearing since they stole it."

"I don't want you to miss out on seeing Oderic captured because you're a woman, Agatha. By Thalorix, you're tougher than many men I know. But you also don't have to prove anything."

"I am starting to realize that," she said.

She pulled my arm over her more tightly. Intertwining our fingers, she clasped my hand to her breast, then turned slightly and sought my lips with hers. It was soothing and tender. This was not fueled by lust; it was a desire for connection. We coupled gently, and when we separated, she backed up against me, with her head on my outstretched arm. I listened as her breathing evened out into a somnolent rhythm.

Dawn broke crisp, a slight chill in the air due to our elevation. The priests-militant were already making breakfast and watering their mounts. Agatha and I rose and tended to Rufus and Sara. We then headed to where the men had prepared oat porridge with raisins.

"Less than two days if we press the pace," Rafe said, sidling over to us. "And that is my intention. We may ride into the night this evening, in order to reach Lenoa with some of the day remaining tomorrow. I don't want that slaving bastard to have any advance notice of our arrival."

"It's possible he'll have scouts watching for us," I warned. "Men like him survive by being careful."

"I'm aware. It will be far easier if he remains in the temple. We'll have him caught like a rat in a trap. If he runs for it, things will get complicated. As a matter of fact—"

"You would like me to ride ahead."

"Yes. One man on a mule is nothing worth noting. Two dozen priests-militant is something quite different."

"I agree. Let me just inform Miss Mountjoy."

That was a difficult conversation, as I knew it would be. Agatha wanted to accompany me. All my arguments fell flat until I mentioned that Rufus might not be able to maintain the same pace as Sara. He was still favoring his left hind leg slightly. In addition, I reminded her that Sara would need to stop for water fewer times than Rufus. In the end, she acquiesced—grumpily.

Sara and I set off. She was a hardy beast, able to maintain a trot for over half an hour at a time, then resume after an equal time walking. We lost sight of the rest of the group as the road twisted and turned on the way down toward Lenoa.

As darkness settled, I came across a caravan heading to Tallesin. I rode up, making sure they were not surprised by my arrival. A single person on a mule was not much of a threat, but given how unsettled things were in Lenoa, I didn't want to take the chance that someone with a crossbow might be nervous. A man strolled out away from the campfire that was already burning.

"Mind if I share your camp this evening?" I asked, sliding from the saddle and offering my hand. "Dexter Falk."

"Anton Chamma," he said, taking my hand, giving me a thorough once-over with his eyes.

"It's just me, sir," I said. "No accomplices hiding in the shadows, although a few hours behind me are a couple of dozen true priests-militant, coming to clean up the mess in Lenoa."

"And are you on the run from them?" he asked.

"By all that's holy, no," I said with a smile. "I'm scouting ahead to make sure the desecrators are still in the temple when the rest of the group arrives."

"They were this morning," Chamma said. "I'm glad to hear that someone is on the way to sort things out. The man who calls himself the head priest is a criminal, and the acolytes are all dockside brutes. I recognized some of them. Weeks ago, someone told the Midonese Archon in Lenoa, but he washed his hands of it, claiming it was temple business and the government could do nothing."

"Technically, that's correct, but he should have sent a message to Meropan, informing them that things were awry."

"The Archon is not known for being the most upstanding man," Chamma replied. "I'd lay even odds he's benefiting from what's been going on."

"That will be a problem for the Midonese," I said. "At least the Sylvarans are coming to deal with the temple issues."

"Well, come, share our fire and our food. The good news you bring is enough to grant you a bowl."

"I need to water and groom my animal first," I said. "But I will gladly partake when I'm finished with her."

I could tell that prioritizing Sara's needs over my own convinced Chamma that he was correct to trust me. Any decent caravan master took care of his animals first. Without them, they had no way of making a living.

I took Sara to the edge of a small stream. After taking off her saddle, I allowed her to drink her fill. As she did, I groomed her quickly. When she finished drinking, I filled a feedbag and tied it on, looping her reins around the limb of a tree nearby. Two other animals were also tied to it.

After washing my hands in the stream quickly, I headed toward the fire. I could smell salt pork stew—common caravan fare. Chamma gave me a full bowl, a spoon, and a large chunk of dark bread.

"Much obliged," I said, as I sat down on the ground, not far from the others.

They were looking at me curiously, and the previous chatter died away when I walked up. As I ate, they began talking among themselves once more. When I finished, I took the bowl and spoon to the stream and washed them out. After checking to make sure Sara was finished, I removed her feed bag and returned to the fire.

"You said the real priests-militant are coming," Chamma said. "How many?"

"Just over two dozen. We're down five men since we started. We ran into a group of bandits wearing temple garb. Three men are accompanying the prisoners who survived, and two are taking their horses back to Tallesin for care," I said, then brought him up to date on all that I knew had happened.

Before turning in, I prepared everything for tomorrow's journey. The last thing I did was drink as much water as I could hold. My bladder would wake me early, and Sara and I would leave before sunrise.

Sure enough, the call of nature roused me from sleep. The gray light of false dawn was above. I woke Sara and saddled her, then set off down the road toward Lenoa.

The mule could see better in the dim light than I could, so I let her guide us. By the time the sun rose in our faces, we were nearly through the foothills and about to enter the coastal plain. It was another beautiful summer day. We continued on, alternating trotting and walking, until we saw the spires of Lenoa loom on the horizon, past ripening fields of wheat.

If Oderic had people watching the western gate of the city, it was unlikely that the appearance of a solitary traveler would arouse their interest. I entered the city without anyone taking notice, as far as I could tell. The bored city guards asked for the toll—a Midonese quadrans—which I fished out of my money pouch.

We passed by the temple. It was still as slovenly kept as when I was last there, and the same sort of thugs guarded the entrance. I kept Sara moving, not wanting to express too much interest, then headed for Ugarte's warehouse.

I left Sara at the watering trough and went to find Ferrare. He was in his office and jumped up when he saw me. His expression was one of fear mixed with hope. I raised my hands in a calming gesture.

"I'm not here to cut your balls off, Mr. Ferrare. Ugarte is satisfied you had nothing to do with the loss of the first shipment."

"Thank all the heavenly beings!" Ferrare sighed. "And the second?"

"We ran into some difficulty, but all's well that ends well. I made the head priests in Eudus and Tallesin aware of the problem here in Lenoa. They will be reimbursing Ugarte for the first shipment at Tallesin prices, which made him very happy. The priests are on the way, only a few hours behind me, with more than two dozen priests-militant."

"Even better," Ferrare said.

"Tell me what you have heard of the temple. When I rode by just now, it looked the same as it did. Have you heard anything?"

"I have," Ferrare said eagerly. "The apostate who seized control of it has grown nervous lately. According to the other merchants, he has doubled the rate for the donatives, claiming the roads are more dangerous."

"Of course they are," I said with a sour laugh. "Because his people are preying on them."

"There is also word that he has booked passage on a ship that is due in from Molutia on the tide just before sundown tonight—the *Witch of Lydia.*"

"It seems like we are arriving just in time, then," I said.

"Indeed, Mr. Falk."

"Does this ship make regular trips to Molutia?"

"That is its regular route," Ferrare said. "There have long been rumors that she carries slaves on some of her runs."

"And the Midonese government?"

"Won't lift a finger. The local archon is more fond of the money he gets from the apostate for looking the other way than he is of justice."

"If Oderic tries to run—"

"Oderic? Is that the name of the man who—?"

"Yes. I shared the description of the person we met with someone who knows Oderic. The white streak in the hair is what identifies him."

"Oderic is a name we've all heard and feared," Ferrare said, making a quick warding sign, a common superstitious response to the presence of evil, "but almost nothing was known about him. He has always remained in the background."

"Until he usurped the temple," I said. "When the priests-militant arrive, do you have an idea of where he will go? If the tide does not turn until later, he will be stuck ashore for a few hours."

"There is a warehouse that has long been rumored to be owned by Oderic. I'll have one of my men take you there."

"That would be helpful. If he has anyone watching the gates, he'll—"

"He does."

"Then he will probably bolt from the temple as soon as he gets word that the priests-militant are seen approaching. We suspect they have some children they are holding, plus the man will want to take the money he's fleeced from the merchants. If I know where he will hide, that will make our job easier."

16

Ferrare's man, Akil, showed me the building. It was not particularly large or well-located. I scouted around the building to see what sort of access it offered. There was a large door facing the street, big enough for them to pull a wagon inside. Around the back was a smaller door for foot traffic only.

Looking up, I was delighted to see a hay hood, and underneath it, a pulley attached to a beam extending out from the wall. Even better, there were no windows or other openings on that side of the building. The rope was still attached and tied to a cleat on the wall. I looked around to make sure no one was watching, then went and tested the rope. It was old and probably hadn't been used in many years. There was no way I would trust it to support my weight.

Akil showed me to a nearby chandler, where I bought a new length of rope. I spliced the new to the end of the old and fed it up and over the pulley. After testing to make sure the beam was still sound and would hold my weight, I tied the rope back onto the cleat.

Akil and I took the old rope back to the chandler. He would use it to make oakum—unraveling the fibers and soaking them in pine tar—which was useful in caulking seams between planks in a ship's hull. He gave us a few quadrans. I didn't care about the money, so I gave the coins to Akil. I just thought it was the best way to dispose of the old rope. Leaving it around for someone to find might have tipped them off to my plan. Akil and I then returned to the Ugarte warehouse. I asked Ferrare if I could borrow Akil for the rest of the day.

"Why?"

"When the priests-militant ride up, word will reach Oderic quickly. I would like Akil to wait for them and guide them to the temple first, and then to the building he just showed me. I will be watching to see what happens with Oderic and his people. Chances are the priests will find me near the harbor."

Ferrare agreed without argument. His relief at my sharing that Ugarte did not blame him for the loss of the first shipment made him pliable as wet clay. Akil was happy, since I offered him a Midonese argent—the equivalent of the Tallesin florin—for his assistance.

Hanging around the western gate, waiting for men to arrive, was probably a nice break from whatever fetch-and-carry work Ferrare would have given Akil. He set off at a jog. I left Sara tied up at the warehouse and returned to the vicinity of the temple.

There was a coffeehouse across the temple square. I took an unobtrusive seat in the shade of the awning overhanging the street. After obtaining a tiny cup of extremely potent brew, I settled in. From my location, I could see the side street where I expected to see the rats scurrying once they learned of the real priests-militant's approach.

It was not a long wait—less than an hour, by my guess. A man came running up to the front steps. He was known to the guards, who let him pass without delay. A few minutes later, the guards were summoned inside.

After some time, down the side street, I saw the gates to the rear of the temple lot open. A wagon appeared, with Oderic holding the reins. From where I was, I could not see what it was carrying, as a tarp was drawn over the contents, but I suspected the children were in the back, trussed and gagged.

The thugs wearing the armor of priests-militant surrounded the wagon on foot. There were seventeen of them. They headed toward the building Akil had shown me earlier. I waited for them to pass, then left the coffeehouse to follow, melting into the regular traffic on the streets.

My pursuit was somewhat leisurely. I knew where they were headed, after all. My only aim was to make sure they did not head for another bolt hole.

Bullies that his men were, they shouldered people out of the way. The armor they'd stolen, now showing signs of a lack of upkeep, gave them authority they did not deserve. It was easy to keep them in sight all the way to the warehouse.

I remained down the block, leaning against a stack of barrels. It wasn't long before I saw Akil leading Rafe toward me. Behind them were Ned, Agatha, and the priests-militant. Without drawing too much attention, I made eye contact with the priest and stopped them before they came into view of the warehouse. Rafe dismounted and approached.

"The temple is empty," he said. "They left it a shambles."

"Oderic and what's left of his men are in that warehouse," I said, pointing. "Unless he already has men inside, he's down to a dozen and a half, including himself."

"That tracks what we learned from Grint," Ned said, now within earshot. "Between the men we captured near Eudus and the group we just encountered at the pass, that matches the number he told us."

"I could not see what was in the wagon he brought from the temple. He covered the back of it with a tarp. If he has captives, he hid them under it."

By now, Agatha had dismounted and joined us. She grimaced when I mentioned the children. I shared with them what I knew about the entrances and how I had prepared to enter the loft area.

"It would have been far easier if he were still in the temple," Rafe said.

I could hardly argue with that. Temples were built for ease of access, with open layouts and multiple rooms. This warehouse was a large box-like building with only two street-level entrances. It would be easy to get in, but just as easy for Oderic to be waiting with knives at the throats of his captives.

"Let me climb the rope to the loft and take a look," I suggested, "and see if I can scout the premises."

"I'm coming with you," Agatha stated firmly.

"Absolutely not," I said firmly.

"Miss Mountjoy, stop!" Ned interjected quickly, seeing her get her dudgeon up, "Dexter has experience in entering and exiting places without notice. Allow him to do this by himself."

She bit back her response. I smiled at her to let her know that I appreciated her willingness to take part but also needed to act alone in this case. She frowned in reply.

"I'll be quick and quiet," I promised her, touching her hand briefly. "You can stand below and relay what I see to the others."

"Fine," she muttered grudgingly.

"Rafe, send a handful of men to watch the rear entrance. Akil can show you the way to get there without being seen."

"Good idea," he said. "I don't imagine all of them will want to stay and fight."

"Exactly. Come," I said to Agatha, taking her hand in mine so we would appear to be a couple in love, merely walking down the street.

We passed by the warehouse. Agatha, to her credit, paid it little heed, though I was sure she examined it as best she could from the corner of her eye. When we reached the corner, we turned.

The rope was still tied to the cleat. I unfastened it, then retied one end, letting the other dangle from the pulley overhead. Crossing to it, I gave it a tug to take up the slack. Before starting, I offered a silent prayer to Sylvaris for assistance on behalf of the children.

"Wish me luck," I said with a grin when I finished my plea, then started to climb hand over hand.

The rope, being new, was rough and bristly. It made it easy to grip, but I also knew it would leave tiny splinters in the palms of my hands—an annoyance, to be sure, but nothing debilitating. Besides, it wouldn't be the first time I'd needed to deal with them. If all went well, Agatha could help me remove them later.

I made it to the beam quickly, then leaned over to open the entrance to the loft. It was latched shut from the inside. Clinging to the rope with one hand and my crossed ankles, I drew my sword with the other hand and inserted it into the gap between the door and the wall, lifting up.

I heard a snick as my blade reached the latch. Using my sword, I pried the door open slowly, then slid my sword back into the scabbard. There was no shout of alarm, so I hoisted myself up a bit and reached up to the beam. I walked myself forward with my hands, hanging from the beam.

Nearing the opening, I could see, in the dim light, a floor a few feet below. I swung my feet up to the bottom edge, then grasped the upper with my hands, one at a time. Not wanting to remain silhouetted, I quickly and gently lowered myself to stand on the rough planks of the loft's deck. After giving a quick wave to Agatha, I moved to the side.

Pressing my back against the wall, I could see dust motes in the light filtering through the gaps in the boards. The loft smelled of old hay, but there was none to be seen. I doubted the owner of the building had used this part of the space for years.

The loft extended only a third of the length of the building. Lowering myself to all fours, I crept forward. As I neared the edge, I heard a young voice whimper, followed by a snarled reprimand and what could only have been a cuff to the head that silenced the child.

Looking down, I could see a group of eleven children. The oldest was no more than nine or ten years of age. All of them looked miserable, with tear tracks on the cheeks of their dirty faces. The bandits were arranged here and there, sitting on the floor or on the few crates inside. The wagon which had carried the children was in front of the main door, with the mules still in harness. In the bed of the wagon were four strongboxes of substantial size. These likely held the donatives Oderic had extorted from the merchants since taking control of the temple.

Oderic himself was pacing back and forth, the white streak in his hair a magnet for my eyes. He had the look of a man who knew that time was his enemy. According to Ferrare, the tide would not turn for hours yet. The *Witch of Lydia* would not enter the harbor until then.

The men were clad in the armor of priests-militant, with various weapons close at hand. I saw swords and three crossbows. The crossbows were a complication. They had not brought them from the temple, or I would have seen them earlier. There was a man sitting by each of the windows to the street. From the loft, there was an old ladder to the ground floor. It looked untrustworthy, plus it would be seen by all of Oderic's men.

I started to creep back to where I'd entered. In the corner of the wall where I'd entered was a hole in the floor of the loft. As had been the case outside, there was a rope over a pulley attached to a roof beam. That would be the way I reached the ground.

I returned to the door through which I entered. Agatha was still there, waiting. I beckoned her closer so I could keep my voice down.

"Eighteen men, including Oderic. Eleven children, all young. The wagon is right in front of the main door, with the mules still harnessed. He has the children behind the wagon, in the center of the space. Men are posted at both windows. They have three crossbows. Go tell the priests to bring the men as close to the main entrance as they can without being seen. When they hear a ruckus, they will need to move fast. Come back when they're in place."

"What are you going to do?" she asked.

"Cause a ruckus," I said with a grin. "Don't worry. It's one of the things I do well. I'm going to get my hands on the crossbows first."

Agatha nodded and jogged off. Remembering that she did not want to alert the men inside that anything was happening, she slowed to a leisurely walk before she reached the corner of the building. I remained near the door, waiting for her return.

While the minutes ticked by, I was formulating a plan of action in my head. The crossbows were critical. If I could disable them, we stood a better chance of avoiding casualties.

Agatha returned. Rather than speaking, she nodded to let me know she had delivered my information. I returned the gesture, along with a confident grin, and blew her a kiss. She scowled, clearly frustrated at not being able to play a more active role.

Back on all fours, I crept to the opening I spotted earlier. The rope was old and smooth, and I worried whether it would bear my weight. Looking down, I saw a couple of large crates underneath. That made things easier. I would ignore the rope and lower myself to the top of one of the crates.

Before making my move, I accessed my link to Sylvaris as the priests taught me back when I was still a boy. It was a metaphysical thing. It is difficult to describe to someone who has never experienced it. There is a spot within my body that I can find with my senses, but if you cut me open, you would find no trace of it. Nevertheless, it exists, and I know how to find it.

I "opened" the connection and prayed to Sylvaris for his aid—not for myself, but for the children. As I did, I could feel the tingle on the back of my neck, alerting me to the presence of numinous power. It was the strongest connection to the god I had ever experienced up to that point in my life.

It gave me confidence that Sylvaris would not play one of his jokes and abandon me in the midst of turmoil. Whether that was because of the children, or avenging the wrong done to his temple, I did not know or much care. I just accepted it and started to lower myself down to the crate.

17

None of them noticed me as I slipped silently down to the top of the crate. A quick hop, and my feet were on the floor as I crouched down to hide. I withdrew my blade carefully and considered my next move.

The crossbows were a priority. I could render them useless with a few flicks. The bigger problem was the children. From where they were huddled, I could probably hold Oderic's men at bay for a few seconds if no one was behind me.

Staying low, I started to move carefully along the back wall of the warehouse, staying in the shadows. Sylvaris was still with me, judging by the tingle I felt. He would make me difficult to spot.

Four of Oderic's thugs were playing dice near the rear entrance to the building. On the ground in front of them, I could see the gleam of the gold they were wagering. Oderic must have given them a taste of the spoils, and like the blockheads they were, they were already gambling their newfound wealth away.

They would be behind me if I stood forth to guard the children. I hoped Rafe and Ned had their men at either entrance ready to move. As I watched, one of them started to celebrate his roll, but suddenly fell silent.

"Whazzat?" he muttered. "Djou hear that?"

"Boss," one of the others called, "someone is out back."

"Probably the Archon's man, coming to shake me down. Open the damned door and tell him to bugger off," Oderic snarled. "He doesn't see another coin from me until we're safely aboard the *Witch*."

The dice players grumbled, one of them saying, "You're the one what heard summat. You look."

"Any a youse touches my money and I'll slit yer throat," he said as he heaved himself to his feet.

He threw open the door. I was expecting three or four priests-militant to come barging through, but nothing happened. The man stuck his head out in the alley and looked both ways.

"Nuthin' here, boss," he called back. "I must not a heard what I reckoned I heard."

"All four of you, get off your asses and check both ends of the alley," Oderic snapped. "Do it now."

Reluctantly, the other three rose and headed through the door, bitching to the one about being spooked by the wind. I was delighted to see them go. While I didn't know what they'd heard, I guessed there was probably something, and at least two of them would encounter a priest-militant.

That also gave me the cue to move. As quickly as I dared, I dodged between crates to get close to where the three crossbows were resting. With one more silent plea to Sylvaris, I stepped out and reached the devices in two strides.

With quick flicks of my wrist, the sharp edge of my blade sliced the hempen bowstrings without difficulty. By the time Oderic's dull-minded thugs realized I was in their midst, the crossbows were neutralized. The brutes were slow to react, startled by my sudden appearance.

"Behind me, children!" I called. Then shouted as loud as I could, "Now!"

The second yell was for Ned and Rafe. An instant later, the front door burst open, with true priests-militant charging through. Oderic spun from glaring at me to the entrance of the soldiers.

"Get the brats!" he screeched at his men.

Two of them tried to rush past me to reach the children, now screaming in fright, but my blade was too quick for them. One fell to the floor, clutching his throat where blood spurted out. The other, I impaled in the center of his chest, the sharp tip of my rapier slowed hardly at all by the stolen armor he wore. I raised my foot and kicked his body away, freeing my sword.

The other thugs did not know whether to follow Oderic's orders, face the incoming priests-militant, or try to escape. Two more tried to reach the children, and I dispatched them as quickly as their predecessors. Three had turned to face the priests and were already falling to the ground. The others tried to make it through the front entrance, only to run into the next group of priests.

In the confusion, Oderic had jumped onto the wagon and flicked the reins. The mules, already frightened by the sudden commotion, jerked forward, trying to escape. Oderic careened out into the street, hauling hard to the left. The mules were only too eager to get away.

As the wagon lurched to the left, an angry shout greeted it from someone Oderic had nearly run over. The only things remaining in the bed of it were the strongboxes. He was able to take none of the children.

The fighting inside the warehouse took only a few seconds. Only two of Oderic's men survived to surrender. A moment later, they were joined by the four who had been playing dice. The priests dragged their unconscious forms in from the back door.

Agatha came running in after a wave from Ned. She found me with her eyes, and I could see that she was relieved. She then looked past me and saw the children, rushing over.

"It's safe now, dear ones," she said, dropping to one knee to address them on their level and spreading her arms. "We've come to get you home."

The five youngest immediately ran to her. All eleven of them were crying, scared, relieved, shaken. Agatha embraced the little ones as best she could. I saw tears on her cheeks as well.

Sensing the worst part was over, I jogged out to the street, looking for Oderic and the wagon. He had already disappeared from sight, having turned a corner. I could tell he had turned to the right from the direction people were looking.

"Rafe," I called out. "I'm going to follow him on foot for as long as I can. Have a couple of your men mount up and follow as best they can. Try to find out where Oderic is heading. He still has time to wait before his ship will arrive."

When Rafe nodded, I set off at a jog. Reaching the corner, I turned to the right. I continued running to the next intersection.

"The wagon that was speeding along?" I shouted to the bystanders. "Which way?"

Several people pointed for me to continue. At each intersection, I asked the same question. It was three blocks further along when they told me to go left.

Before I reached the end of that block, I heard the rhythmic clink-clop of the iron shoes of the mounts of the priests-militant. Three of them approached at a canter, with a fourth horse for me. They slowed, and I mounted quickly.

With a strong destrier underneath me, I was confident I would be able to catch up with Oderic. At every intersection, we asked people where the wagon had gone. Having been nearly run over by Oderic, or having witnessed this, they were most helpful.

The mules pulling the wagon were not accustomed to maintaining speed, but their fear gave them wings at the beginning. We were approaching the harbor, the peculiar odor of it growing stronger with each block we traversed. Oderic was hoping to reach the docks and hide somewhere until the *Witch of Lydia* arrived.

The priests-militant riding with me said nothing. We were traveling quickly, but not at a reckless, out-of-control pace. Rounding another corner, we could see Oderic and the wagon several blocks ahead.

Without having said a thing, the three priests-militant nudged their mounts to a gallop. The road ahead was clear, everyone having jumped out of Oderic's way. It only took a press of my knees for my horse to match the pace of the other three.

The harbor was in sight now, and the masts of the ships at anchor were like a winter forest with the leaves having fallen away. I wondered where Oderic was heading, then answered my own question. The owner of the *Witch* had to have a warehouse near the docks. Daylight was fading, and the tide was starting to come in. The *Witch of Lydia* would be tying up soon.

We were closing the gap. Oderic was lashing the mules, trying to drive them faster. It wasn't doing much good. He drove right to the front entrance of one of the buildings and yanked savagely on the reins with his left hand to stop the mules, while hauling on the brake lever with his right.

"Open up, damn your eyes! Open up!" I heard Oderic yell.

The wagon clattered to a stop. Oderic climbed into the bed of the wagon, grabbed one of the strongboxes, and jumped to the street. He scurried into the smaller door set into the middle of the larger one. It slammed shut behind him.

The priests-militant slid from the backs of the horses only seconds behind. One of them raised his booted foot and smashed the door open. A crossbow bolt hit him in the left shoulder for his trouble. One of his comrades yanked him to the side.

"Are more of you coming?" I asked the third priest—the first words we'd spoken since they rode up to me.

"Should be," he said with a slight shrug. "If they can follow our trail."

"Between the wagon and us, we caused enough commotion that folks will remember which way we went. Since they have crossbows in there, trying to barge through the front door would be stupid. I'll need to think of something else."

The one with the crossbow quarrel in his shoulder grunted deeply as he tugged it out. He threw it on the ground and spat on it. He moved his left arm experimentally.

"Let's start by getting the wagon out of the way," I suggested. "The strongboxes in the back are probably full of the donatives this scumbag collected. That money belongs to the temple."

The injured priest decided this was a job for him. He took the reins and led the mules, still panting, around in a half-circle and toward the temple. The other two priests waited, looking to me for further instructions.

I turned my attention back to the building. The front door was wood, but the walls were brick. There were no windows at street level, but there were on the second story. I went around to the side.

The only thing I saw that held any promise was a downspout, a tube of thin lead that channeled rainwater from the roof, but it ended eight or nine feet above the cobbled pavement of the street. It was not in the best repair, but it did come within arm's length of a grimy window. It was the only way I could see of getting into the building without facing the crossbows inside. I retrieved the reins of the horse they'd lent me and led him over to that corner.

"What are you doing?" one of the priests asked.

"You can help," I said. "Hold him steady. I'm going to climb up and stand on the saddle and see if I can reach that downspout."

"Perhaps we should wait for the others," he suggested, clearly dismissing my idea as too risky.

"I would certainly wait for your comrades before trying to go through the front door again," I replied.

As I climbed up to stand on the saddle, I once again noticed that I was almost tingling with asomatous energy. I'd felt connected to Sylvaris many times in my life to this point, but never with the power I was experiencing now. If I were a more trusting soul, it would have given me great confidence. Unfortunately, Sylvaris had made it a regular habit to abandon me in times of need. He did seem to enjoy his little jokes.

The priest held the horse steady, and I was able to grasp the downspout with both hands. Pressing the balls of my feet against the wall, I started to climb. The lead tube shook and swayed as I moved. A few of the bolts anchoring it to the brick wall gave way above me, falling on my head. The tube itself was thin enough that my grip was bending it.

I made it to the level of the windowsill and was able to reach it with my left hand. At least it was brick, but it was covered with bird crap. I brushed it off as best I could to get a better grip. As soon as my fingers had a firm purchase, the downspout separated from the roof, leaving me dangling.

Fortunately, the priests below were alert and caught the pipe before it crashed to the ground, preventing it from making too much noise. I was swaying, hanging by my fingers until I managed to get my right hand on the sill. Falling from this height wouldn't kill me, but it would probably hurt.

"Gentlemen, I need to break the window to get in. Would you kindly go back toward the front entrance and cause a commotion?"

"What do you want us to do?"

"Stay out of crossbow fire, but start hollering, demanding that Oderic come out and face justice. I imagine that will provoke a response."

18

The two of them took the horse away. While I was clinging to the windowsill, I heard the click-clop of other shod horses arriving. I twisted my neck and saw Rafe with a few more of the priests-militant.

One of the men who had been with me quickly conferred with Rafe, who looked over and gave me a cheeky wave. Even though I tried to take some of my weight on my toes pressed against the wall, my fingers were getting tired, and I hoped they would do something soon. We were also losing daylight.

I did not need to wait much longer. Rafe and the priests-militant began shouting to those inside the building. Their message was that cooperation would mean a lesser punishment, but Oderic would face the full force of the god Sylvaris's wrath no matter what. If they continued to resist, the rest of them might share the same consequences.

I could hear the shouted responses from inside the building. Most of them were curses, so I will spare your eyes, dear reader. It was just the sort of uproar I needed. I reached up with my left hand and smacked the windowpane hard.

The glazing around the glass was weakened by time and probably shoddily installed to begin with. The entire pane fell inside. I did not hear it break. That emboldened me, and I pressed hard on the pane next to the first. It gave way with only slight pressure. Again, when it fell, it must have landed on something soft, as I did not hear the tinkle of broken glass.

When I cleared the lower section of the window, I hoisted myself up, grasping the inner edge of the sill. Scrabbling with my toes, I managed to get halfway through. I could see the four panes I'd knocked out lying on coils of old rope. They were broken, but into large pieces, not shattered.

Heaving myself further, I got my left knee up and over the sill. The people downstairs were still engaged in a shouting match with the priests outside. I twisted myself through, careful that I didn't break any more of the glass. Once I had my feet underneath me, I withdrew my sword and crept toward an opening I could see in the floor. Above the opening was a block and tackle, obviously used to hoist things up to this level for storage. The ropes appeared to be in good condition. It was a mechanism that still saw regular use, I figured.

I looked down to the floor below. There were a half-dozen men armed with crossbows, and Oderic standing behind them. Unlike the other criminals we encountered earlier, these were not wearing the stolen armor of priests-militant. That helped confirm my earlier guess that this warehouse belonged to the owner of the *Witch of Lydia*, not Oderic.

As I peered down, I had the strangest feeling. It wasn't anything communicated in words, but I understood clearly that I was to capture Oderic alive. As I considered it, the feeling was reinforced. When I realized that Sylvaris wanted Oderic to face the grisly punishment stipulated for people like him, I felt confirmation.

I must admit I offered a slight resistance mentally. The sentence of being dragged, racked, and gutted was horrible. I did not want to think that the god that I served was so cruel.

The feeling that I must take Oderic alive grew stronger in response to my reluctance—not in a hostile way, but more in a calm, confident manner. I realized that I was not the judge. That was the province of Thalorix. For Sylvaris to press me in this implied that the judge of souls approved the penalty. As Oderic was a trader in human flesh, there could be no punishment too harsh.

Fine, I thought. *Alive it will be.*

The ladder to the ground level was too exposed, too slow, and I would turn my back on my foes. The block and tackle was clearly the right means of getting down. I approached it, grabbed the hook on the lower pulley, and swung into space.

With a strange whirring sound, the rope fed through the pulleys as I dropped to the floor. The two men nearest me heard the sound and turned. My blade flicked out, quick as thought, forcing his crossbow down. On the return stroke, I slashed his throat.

The second man was lifting his weapon to fire it at me. I danced toward him, batting the crossbow aside with my left arm and burying the tip of my rapier deep in his chest with my right. Neither man made a sound beyond the gurgle of the dying, but our movement drew attention.

I leaped behind a crate and heard two crossbow quarrels thud into the wood. Rather than continue around the crate, I reversed my steps. The two men whose bows were still loaded were looking the wrong way. When they saw me, they turned and fired but missed.

The other two men were trying desperately to reload their weapons, pointing them toward the floor with a foot in the stirrup as they hauled the bowstring back into position. They took too long. I was on them in two strides, dispatching the nearer with a thrust into his chest, then kicking the weapon of the other from his grasp.

The two who fired most recently did not even attempt to reload their weapons. They grasped cudgels and approached me. The one whose weapon I kicked away scrambled to find an implement with which to attack me.

I say this with all due humility, but dockyard brutes with cudgels stood no chance against me. One gift that never failed me was my skill at swordplay. I was far too quick and capable, and I disarmed all three in a matter of moments, while yelling for Rafe to come in.

A priest-militant charged through the door, wary of a crossbow bolt. When he saw the three bruisers backing away from me, he hurried over. Other priests followed him when they saw they need not fear being skewered by a crossbow. In less than a minute, the three remaining thugs were on their knees with their hands in the air.

It was then that I turned to look for Oderic. He was nowhere to be seen. I spotted an open door on the rear wall. I raced toward it, skittering into the alley at a run with my blade drawn.

As soon as I cleared the door, Oderic, the bastard, fired a crossbow at me. The quarrel hit me square in the front, and lodged in my right side, just below my ribcage. As soon as he fired, he dropped the weapon and started running away.

The pain took a moment to register, but when it hit, it blossomed with full force. I staggered to a stop and switched my rapier to my left hand. With my right, I grasped the butt end of the bolt and yanked it out. The pain took my breath away.

"Dexter!" I heard Rafe call behind me.

"He's getting away, Rafe!" I said, gesturing in the direction Oderic went as I turned to face the priest.

"You're wounded. Do you think you can ride?"

"Only if the horse gets here quickly. I'm going to need to run if it can't."

"Bring my horse around and a mount for Falk!" Rafe hollered into the warehouse. "Quick as lightning!"

I stood, gasping from the pain in my side, holding my left hand over the wound. Blood was oozing out from between my fingers. Rafe looked at it as he approached.

"We should bandage that."

"No time," I blurted. "His ship might already be nearing the pier. If he gets aboard, he'll get away. We can patch me up later."

Two of the priests-militant rode round the corner, leading two other mounts by the reins. Rafe took the one; I, the other. Hoisting myself into the saddle caused a new spasm of pain, but I gritted my teeth and swallowed the moan I wanted to voice.

"This way?" Rafe asked as he set off in the direction I initially indicated.

"Aye," I gasped, as the jolt from the horse's first step on the cobbles generated a new wash of pain.

"He's on foot?"

"Aye," I gasped again.

I clamped my jaw shut as Rafe started off at a trot. My horse matched the pace, and we headed down the alley and into the street. We turned left, heading to the waterfront. The other two priests-militant followed us.

The feeling of Sylvaris's presence made itself known again. As it did, the pain in my side faded. I was still aware that I was wounded, but it was no longer an issue of immediate concern.

"There he is," Rafe called, pointing ahead.

Three blocks away, I saw the white streak in Oderic's hair as he ran around a corner. Rafe nudged his mount to a canter. Mine followed his lead, and we moved quickly down the center of the street.

People were gawking. They'd seen Oderic running for his life, and now there were three priests-militant chasing him along with me, whatever I was. We reached the intersection where we'd seen Oderic turn. As we rounded the corner, we ran straight into a squad of the Archon's constables, eight men standing in our way with pikes lowered menacingly.

Oderic was nowhere to be seen, but I knew this was his doing. Rafe pulled his horse up short, and I did the same. The wound in my side protested the sudden movement, but the pain was not as sharp as a few minutes earlier.

"Halt in the name of the Archon!" the man in charge of the squad barked.

"This is temple business," Rafe snapped.

"How can it be?" the man demanded. "The head priest just told us to stop you."

"That man is no more a head priest than you are Zoryn," Rafe said. "He is an apostate and a desecrator of our order. Sylvaris demands that we bring him to justice."

"Sounds like a matter for the Archon to sort out," the leader said smugly.

"If you don't let us pass, he'll board a ship and escape any sort of justice," Rafe said, nudging his horse closer to the men blocking our way.

"If you don't back off, priest, you'll face your own justice here and now," the man snarled, brandishing his pike in a threatening way.

A crowd was gathering, attracted by the confrontation. I could almost feel the tension between Rafe and the squad leader. It was suddenly clear what I should do.

"Gentlemen," I said calmly, feeling all the gifts of Sylvaris's persuasion at my command, my voice coming out smooth and silky with no hint of the pain I was feeling, "there's no need for this. You know the man who asked you to stop us—Oderic. He's a slaver—you probably know that as well. It likely disgusts you, but you've been paid to ignore it. This man is the legitimate head priest of the temple of Sylvaris in Eudus. The head priest from the temple in Tallesin is on his way, following us. They have come to bring Oderic to justice, and the god's will shall be done. That is not for the likes of mere mortals like us to debate.

"If you stand in his way, the god will demand that Thalorix judge you in league with Oderic. If your assistance allows Oderic to escape today, you will pay the same penalty he will—dragged, racked, and gutted. Your wives and children will be forced to watch. Or you can stand aside, confident that you have done the proper thing in this instance. If you are expecting some sort of financial reward from Oderic, I am sorry to tell you that he has no money other than what he carries on his person. He has been forced to leave all his strongboxes behind."

Seven of the men, including the leader, were lowering their pikes. I don't know whether the threat of punishment swayed them, or if it was the disappearance of whatever reward Oderic promised. One man, however, was unswayed.

"Don't listen!" he screeched. "The Archon will pay us!"

"Oh, shut up, you fool," the leader snapped, as quicker than I could react, the tip of his pike flew up under the man's chin. "If what the man says is true, there ain't no money in it for the Archon no more. That means no coin for the likes of us. And I didn't see Oderic lugging no strongbox with him. Stand aside, you idiot, or I'll cut you down myself."

With that, the men of the squad stepped aside and allowed us to pass. The one only did so because the tip of the leader's pike forced him back. Rafe urged his horse forward toward the docks.

19

We neared the harbor. It took us a minute to scan the different piers before we found Oderic from his shock of white hair. There was a ship slowly approaching where he was with furled sails. It was no more than fifty yards from the pier.

"That's the ship, Rafe," I said. "Hurry."

With a squeeze of his knees, his destrier surged forward. I followed, a fresh stab of dulled pain accompanying the horse's first steps. The other two priests-militant were right behind me.

Oderic was at the end of the pier, shouting at the sailors. I couldn't make out the words, but it sounded like Molutian. The ship eased up to the end of the pier as Rafe and I rode onto the shoreward end. As I watched, the sailors lowered a gangway, and Oderic scrambled aboard.

"Back to sea!" he screeched.

As Rafe and I thundered down the planking of the pier, people scattered to get out of our way. Two destriers riding abreast down the pier left no room for anyone else. Rafe crashed into a fishmonger's cart, knocking it over and spilling its silvery contents, as the owner jumped into the water to avoid being trampled.

I saw the sailors frantically adjusting the sails to do as Oderic demanded. In the confusion, the gangway was still lowered. We reached the end of the pier.

The gangway was only five feet away. I slid from my horse's back, the wound in my side issuing a dulled complaint. Taking as deep a breath as I was able, I sprinted forward, leaping through the air to wrap my arms around one of the stanchions on the edge of the gangway.

Oderic darted forward and started to saw at the ropes supporting the gangway with his dagger. I quickly pulled myself onto the main plank and reached the side of the ship before he succeeded. He turned his attention to me, swiping at me with his weapon. I blocked his blow with my left forearm, feeling the blade slice into me.

Then I was on the deck and withdrew my sword. Oderic was screaming at the sailors to help him fight me off as he backed out of my reach. In the midst of this charged atmosphere, a thought reminded me that I needed Oderic alive.

Three of the crew came to Oderic's side, armed with sturdy cutlasses. I could sense the ship was pulling away from the pier more quickly now. The other members of the crew would be able to help Oderic soon. Standing in the stern of the ship, I saw a man better dressed than the others. I figured him for the owner.

Before I could think of how to persuade him to surrender Oderic, he urged the sailors with him to attack me. The deck was an organized jumble of ropes and tackle. No doubt everything was in its proper place for a seaman, but to me it represented dangerous footing.

The first sailor lunged forward, swinging his cutlass with great strength but no finesse. I ducked underneath and gashed his arm as it swept over my head, causing him to drop his weapon and howl in pain. The second man lunged forward, his blade held in front like a spear. I danced out of his way and stomped the bottom of my foot against the side of his knee as he went past. He crumpled to the deck.

Oderic continued to retreat aft. The one sailor by his side no longer held any confidence that he would succeed in attacking me. Then, with perfect clarity, I knew how I would get Oderic off the ship alive and uninjured—well, mostly uninjured.

"You the owner of the *Witch*?" I called to the man in the stern.

"Aye."

"Did you happen to notice what Oderic brought on board? Or failed to bring, as the case might be?"

"Don't listen to him, Lucius!" Oderic shouted.

The owner narrowed his eyes, weighing my words. His crew stood still, waiting to see if he would signal them to join Oderic. They could see one of their mates clutching his arm with blood trickling through his fingers, and the other rolled into a ball, moaning about his ruined knee.

"No strongboxes," I said. "No children to sell in Molutia. He left everything behind, chased out of Lenoa by the true priests-militant, come to set things right. He has no hope of regaining any of his loot—not in Lenoa, at any rate, and probably nowhere on the continent after word gets out about him and his desecration of the temple of Sylvaris here. Return to the pier, hand him over to the priests-militant, and you're guilty of nothing other than putting a non-paying passenger ashore. As far as I know, there's no crime in that. Give him safe passage, and you'll suffer the same torment he will."

"Lucius, you know I'm good for it," Oderic pleaded. "Think of all the money you've made because of me."

"Dirty money," I commented. "Slaver money. And he doesn't have any of it except what he has in his money pouch."

The owner stood silent for a moment. Finally, he nodded, having reached a conclusion.

"The man's got a point, Oderic," he said, and jerked his head at one of the members of his crew. "I've never liked you or your business."

That man stepped toward Oderic. Realizing he was about to be betrayed, Oderic seized the crewman who was standing by his side. He twisted the man's arm up the middle of his back. Oderic put his dagger to the man's throat.

The other members of the crew froze. I did not. Oderic now had his back to me. I strode forward and clouted him on the side of his head with the hilt of my rapier. He dropped like a jute sack of sprouts.

"Much obliged, stranger," the owner said with a tight smile. "Get us back to the pier, men. And truss that piece of meat up nice and proper for the priests of Sylvaris."

In less than a minute, two men had Oderic's hands and feet secured. The others worked the sails, and the ship began reversing course, returning to the end of the pier. Waiting there were Rafe and Ned, and a handful of priests-militant. I did not see Agatha.

"You did me a favor, stranger," the owner said, suddenly appearing at the ship's rail next to me. "It has been dirty money. Oderic caught me at a time of weakness. The *Witch* got hit by a bad storm on the way back from the Kryyder

Islands. It would have been the last load of the season and would have made me a pile. Unfortunately, a couple of the hatches gave in. Seawater ruined the entire shipment. We were lucky to keep the *Witch* afloat. It cost everything I had, and everything I could borrow on my good name to make her seaworthy again. But when I went back to my customers, they wouldn't touch me. The man whose shipment was ruined blamed me, when it was him who begged me to make the run so late in the season. Somehow, Oderic found out the trouble I was in, and offered a way out."

"Did you know it involved slaves?"

"Only when he dragged 'em aboard. And because of that, whatever was left of my reputation was shot. No one likes a slaver."

"Then why help me now?"

"Because someday I will stand before Thalorix and have to answer for what I've done. Maybe by helping you and the Sylvarans, I can even things out. If Sylvaris is real happy with me, maybe I can restore my good name. But it had to start sometime, and I decided that today was maybe the best chance I'd ever get."

"I'll make sure the priests know."

He returned to the stern of the ship, guiding the *Witch of Lydia* back to the pier. Rafe and Ned were waiting when the gangway was lowered. Two members of the crew carried Oderic across.

"You'll regret this, Lucius," Oderic screeched. "I'll make sure of it!"

Lucius snorted and turned away.

"The Archon will free me," Oderic hollered. "I demand that you send word to him!"

"Faced with sanction from the order of Sylvaris, the Archon will be fortunate if he keeps his head attached to his shoulders," Ned said with a laugh. "The Midonese don't much care for slavers and those who help them."

I crossed to Ned and Rafe and quickly shared with them that the owner was responsible for Oderic's capture. I explained briefly that unfortunate circumstances had forced him into business with the man. Ned nodded and crossed to the gangway.

"Permission to come aboard?"

Lucius grunted his approval.

"Mr. Falk just told me we owe you thanks. Will you be in port long? I would like to speak with you to see how we might reward you for your assistance."

"The only reward I need is good, clean business, Your Grace."

"Then let's talk about how we can help make that happen, if you will be here tomorrow."

"Ain't got nowhere else to be."

While Ned spoke with the owner, I talked with Rafe.

"He's alive, as the god demanded," I said.

"Sylvaris spoke to you?"

"In his way. He made it clear to me that he wants Oderic alive."

Rafe's eyes narrowed. He tracked Oderic's progress along the pier. The bound man was still spitting curses and threats as the priests-militant carried him to a horse and threw him over the saddle.

"The Meropans will see that he receives the full measure of justice. But that's in the future. Your wound needs tending. You've bled more than you might realize."

Truth be told, I was beginning to feel the onset of exhaustion. I touched my hand to my side, and it was covered in blood when I pulled it away. My shirt was soaked, and the upper part of my breeches as well.

"Aye, I think I'd best get off my feet soon," I said.

"Ordinarily, I would take you back to the temple, but it's a pigsty right now. Let's get you to an inn and summon a healer."

"Where is Lady Agatha?"

"Ned tells me that she is helping with the children. She might be upset to have missed this, but she is performing an invaluable service. The little ones were clinging to her."

"I saw that briefly."

"Let's get you to a reputable inn."

"The mule I rented," I said. "It's at Ugarte's warehouse. Someone needs to tend to her. She's been a good girl."

"We'll see to it," Rafe said.

He needed to help me into the saddle. Halfway up, I ran out of strength. Now that I'd accomplished Sylvaris's bidding, his presence had disappeared. I felt the full pain of my wound and was growing light-headed.

By the time we reached an inn near the temple, I was close to falling from the saddle. One of the priests-militant helped me down then into the building. I didn't remember much after that.

The sharp pain in my side woke me with a start. A woman I didn't know was poking at the wound, holding a candle for light. Slightly disoriented, I figured out quickly that I was in a bed, and it was dark outside.

"Shh," she said. "Lay still. I'm a healer from Vionelle's temple."

"Hurts," I mumbled.

"I'm sure. It missed your guts, thank all the heavenly beings, or there wouldn't be much I could do for you."

"Mhm."

"The biggest problem is the blood you lost. Red meat, fish, and leafy greens for you to rebuild your strength. I'm going to stitch you up and give you a poultice. I'll instruct your lady friend on how to check your dressings."

"Where is Agatha?"

"Here," came her voice from the dark corner of the room.

"Please hold the light, miss," the healer requested. "I need both hands now."

Agatha approached and took the candle. I could see her scowling face in the light. I mustered a weak smile in return. It did not soften her expression.

"Over here," the healer directed a minute later, and then I felt the needle pierce my skin.

Compared to the pain of the wound, her stitches were a trifle. I did my best to keep from wincing. Fortunately, she finished quickly. She then bandaged the wound, explaining more to Agatha than to me that we need to keep it clean and dry. She also explained how to treat the rope splinters in my hands by soaking them in tepid saltwater and using clean tweezers to pull them out. The healer would check on me three days hence and provide further instructions.

20

"You're upset with me," I said once the healer left.

"You got hurt."

"It happens sometimes. You've seen my scars. This isn't as bad as some."

"It's the first one I've been around for."

"How are the children?" I asked, trying to deflect her.

I shifted my posture on the bed to sit up more, so I could look her in the eye on the same level. It pulled at my stitches and sent a twinge through me. Fortunately, whatever herbs the healer put in the ointment she spread over the wound before covering it served to dull the pain slightly.

"We've already returned four to their parents," Agatha said proudly. "The rest are being cared for at Vionelle's temple until we locate their parents. The Vionellans have sent messengers to the places where the children said they came from. By morning, even more will be claimed."

"That's good. Thank you for helping."

"I was upset with you, you know. For treating me like, well, like a woman. And I'm upset that you got hurt. But the way those children reacted to me, it reminded me of how lost and alone I felt when Voss took me away from my family and my life. No one should have to experience that. When I realized what the children and I had in common, I wasn't so mad at you any longer."

"But you're still a little bit angry," I pointed out.

"I would have liked to see Oderic trussed up like a bird ready for the oven."

Her comment made me laugh, which proved to be unpleasant. Agatha noticed me wince. I saw on her face a feeling of sympathy for me at war with her dissipating dander. Sympathy seemed to win out after a few moments.

With a small sigh, I eased myself back into the pillows behind my back. The events of the day were catching up to me all at once. I thought to rest my eyes for just a moment, but the next thing I knew, light was streaming in through the window.

Agatha was draped over my left side, her head on my chest. She must have been awake, as she sensed I returned to consciousness. As she lifted her head to look at me, I started to stroke her blonde hair with my left hand but quickly stopped. The rope splinters were making their presence felt.

"I do enjoy waking up with you," she said quietly. "How are you feeling?"

"Like someone who took a crossbow quarrel in his side yesterday, so not too wonderful," I said. "My hands hurt, and I am really thirsty. I'm not complaining, mind you, just giving you an honest report."

"Good. Cry if you must, but don't whine. I can't stand whiners."

"Noted. I could also use the chamber pot. Just to warn you, I'm feeling a bit wobbly."

Agatha uncurled herself from my chest and slid off that side of the bed. She came around and offered me her hands. I took them, and she helped me up to where I could swing my legs off the bed.

With my left hand on her right shoulder, I stood carefully. My wound yipped at the movement, but my bigger concern was my legs. I was more than a bit wobbly. Agatha helped me shuffle slowly to the chamber pot in the corner.

"Do you want me to hold it for you? Your aim might be off, and I don't want a mess."

It took me a moment to realize she was joking with me. "No, thank you. I think I can manage."

"Pity," she said. "I've always wondered what it would be like."

Agatha's eyes sparkled with the mischievous glint I'd learned to recognize and appreciate. From the very first time we crossed paths, in the rainstorm near the pass, she'd teased me. However much life had tried to beat her down, that sense of humor must have helped carry her through.

"Another time, Lady Agatha. As long as you can keep me from falling, I'll make sure my aim is true."

When I finished, she guided me back to bed. I saw my clothes, or what was left of them, in a blood-soaked heap on the floor. After she helped me plant my butt on the bed, she attended to her own needs. I turned my head to give her privacy.

"The healer cut them off you," she said, noticing my glance at the clothes. "She didn't want to waste time. Then she used them to prevent the bed linens from getting too bloody. I'm afraid you're stuck here at my mercy until I fetch your other clothes."

"Sara," I said, remembering I'd left the mule tied up at the warehouse.

"Rafe sent one of his men to deal with her. I told him where you kept the receipt from the livery, and they will return her to his counterpart here in Lenoa."

"Thank you. She is a dependable beast and deserves good treatment."

"Like me?"

"The only trait you share with a mule is stubbornness, Lady Agatha. In you, it is one of your more admirable qualities. You would not have survived thus far without it. Besides, you're much more fun to ride."

Agatha's eyes opened wide at my rude and inappropriate remark. As soon as it passed my lips, I realized I should not have said it, even though it was exactly what I was thinking. The amount of blood I'd lost was making me goofy in the head.

"I'm sorry," I said quickly. "That was … I feel like I'm drunk, but not pleasantly so."

"I think you need food," she said, with a smile of forgiveness. "Red meat and leafy greens, the healer said. I'll go to the kitchen. I'll also ask for a basin of warm saltwater so we can work on your hands."

Agatha left, and I relaxed against the pillows, still ruing my vulgarity. The wound was starting to throb. Whatever ointment the healer daubed onto it was no longer as effective at dulling the pain. Yesterday, Sylvaris gave me the strength to carry on despite the injury. Today, I did not feel his presence, and I was left to fend for myself like every other mortal.

She returned more quickly than I expected. Either that, or I dozed off. She brought a tray loaded with different items: a steaming bowl of stew, a large chunk of bread, a smaller bowl with what looked like spinach, a pitcher of water, and a small basin. After she set the tray down on the end of the bed, she poured me a cup of water.

"Drink first. The healer told me that you need water as much as you need the right sort of food."

"Where is your food?" I asked before I drained the cup.

"I ate in the kitchen," she said.

I realized then that I must have fallen back asleep while she was away. She set the bowls of stew and spinach on my lap and handed me a spoon. She then brought the basin over to my left side, took my hand, and dunked it in.

I focused on eating. While I was normally indifferent to spinach, there was something about it right now that was making me almost crave it. I attacked it first. When I finished, I started on the stew.

This was no watery slop. The broth was more akin to a sauce in its thickness. Most of it consisted of meat. There was just enough seasoning to blend everything together wonderfully. When I finished, Agatha took the bowls and spoon from my lap and handed me the bread.

"You'll need to gnaw on this one-handed," she said. "I'm going to start pulling splinters."

While she'd been away, she found a pair of tweezers. The soaking had loosened the skin of my hand enough that she was able to pull the rope splinters out easily. She finished with that hand just after I finished the bread.

"Let's soak your right hand now," she said as she came around the bed.

"Are you going to play nursemaid for me all day?" I asked.

"Goodness, no," she said with a laugh. "After I finish this, I'm going to go check on the children, and then visit my solicitor. Now that Oderic is in the custody of the priests, I can finally come out of hiding."

"It won't compensate you for the years you've lost, or the pain you've suffered," I said.

"No, but what I've endured has taught me a great deal about myself and others. I will certainly appreciate the good things in life much more. The gods work their wonders in mysterious ways."

"They certainly do."

When she judged my hand was ready, she set the basin aside and started plucking the splinters. When she finished, she loaded everything back on the tray and left the room. She appeared a few minutes later with a bowl of hot water and a clean rag.

"Time to change your dressing," she said.

With deft fingers, she removed the bandage the healer had applied. Using the rag and hot water, she gently cleansed the area. When she finished, she put a clean dressing on.

"There. As good as I can do. The healer will be by to check on you later. Do you need anything before I go?"

"Just a kiss, to let me know that you forgive me for my foul mouth earlier."

She grinned, then gently pressed her lips to mine. When the kiss ended, she whispered in my ear, "It goes both ways, you know. You're lots of fun to ride, too."

Agatha gave me a naughty wink when she pulled away. She stood, took the basin and rag, and headed for the door. There was a little extra swivel in her hips as she walked away. She looked back to make sure I noticed, and grinned when she saw that I had.

The door closed behind her with a soft click. I drifted off to a dreamless sleep almost immediately. When I next woke, it was to feel the healer poking at my wound.

"Drink," she said, handing me a cup of water. "The wound is clean. No signs of infection, but there's no guarantee one won't develop. You are to stay just as you are—flat on your back—for two more days. After that, limited exercise, but no riding until I say so. Understand?"

"Yes, miss."

"You have quite a collection of scars. This is by no means the first time you've been wounded seriously. Have you learned to listen to the healers?"

"Yes, miss."

"By disobeying our instructions, no doubt. I'm sure Vionelle taught you not to do that."

"Yes, miss."

"I brought you something to eat. Is there anything else you need?"

"No, miss."

"Very well," she said as she stood. "I'll return in two days. In the meantime, if the wound becomes inflamed, send someone to the temple immediately."

She handed me a plate. On it were two slices of bread with meat and lettuce in between. I waited for her to depart before tearing into it. My appetite, at least, was healthy. I knew from experience that this was a good sign.

The next thing I knew, someone was in the bed with me. The plate that held my lunch was still on my lap. I blinked several times as I regained my wits. Agatha sensed I was conscious again.

"Well, hello there," she said with a smile. "You looked so peaceful and content, I thought I'd join you."

"How long have you—?"

"I just got here. If you are asking for the time, it's just past mid-afternoon."

"How are the children? Did you see your solicitor?"

"Only two of the children are still at the temple, but their parents are on the way. I happened to be there to witness one reunion. It was awfully touching."

"I imagine so. Tears and hugs?"

"Plenty of both."

"And the solicitor?"

"Things are … complicated."

<h1 style="text-align:center">21</h1>

“Complicated? In what way?” I asked.

“Remember I told you that I maintained the fiction that Voss was still alive, before Oderic came after me?”

I nodded.

“As far as the courts are concerned, Voss has never been declared dead.”

“But he is.”

“Most definitely. I helped bury the body. My solicitor knows this and knows where the corpse is interred. He also has the sworn statements from the household servants that Voss fell down the stairs while drunk and broke his neck. Voss left no will, so I, as his wife, inherit everything. The only hitch is that my solicitor needs to inform the courts that Voss is deceased.”

“Even though he has been dead for years.”

“Exactly. Without a body or a formal declaration, the courts treat him as missing. There shouldn’t be any problem, other than needing to grease a few palms in order to get the matter expedited.”

“You still have access to the money, though.”

“Not any longer. After he died, I acted as my husband’s ‘agent’ and moved the money from his accounts to where my solicitor could control it. My solicitor has managed it conservatively but well, growing it by a healthy sum. The problem is that now, until my husband is ‘officially’ dead, I have no access to the money.”

“Agatha, do not let that worry you. I have an account with a banking house here in Lenoa, and—”

"Oh, my solicitor has advanced me some funds. He knows, more than anyone, that I'm good for it."

"Oh. That's good, I suppose."

"It is good. I could have returned hours ago, but I have been clothes shopping."

"Really?"

"If I'm going to return home, I don't want to show up in these rags. We will need to spruce up your appearance as well."

I couldn't argue with that. She had only seen me in functional clothing. In a wardrobe back in my flat, I had a few nice things, but I wore them only rarely.

With my goal of returning Agatha to her father and allowing her to resume her existence as the daughter of the Thane of Hessel, it would not do for me to arrive looking like a dusty tradesman. The right appearance would prevent too many questions that were best ignored. If I looked like a man who not only knew how to use a sword, but also which fork to use at the Thane's table, I would gain ready acceptance.

"Fair enough," I agreed. "Once I'm allowed out of bed, I'll visit the tailor and the cobbler."

"No need. I've already done so on your behalf."

"What? How?"

"The clothes from your saddlebags that you left at Ugarte's warehouse, and your boots. I'm having several outfits made, and more refined footwear," she explained, looking particularly pleased with herself.

"Excuse me?"

"Don't get your breeches in a twist, Dex. The tailor is good, and so is the cobbler. I have much better taste in clothes than you do. So it's only logical for me to pick them out. When we arrive in Hessel, you will look as though it is not unreasonable for us to have met."

"Do you intend to hide what your life has been like since your father gave you away?"

"I don't intend to smack him in the face with it when we first arrive. He and my brother know it was unpleasant. Over time, I'll educate them as to the degree."

"That's perhaps the kindest approach you could take."

"I love my father. I don't blame him. If I told him the truth all at once, it might kill him."

"You know better than I."

"Yes, I do."

"No lace. No ruffles," I said.

"Of course not," she said with a laugh. "I want to dress you up, not emasculate you. You will also need a better mount. Showing up on a rented mule will not be acceptable."

"I understand, but I thought I explained to you why I don't already own a horse."

"There is no animal at any livery stable that would be presentable when we arrive home. A horse like Rufus will barely meet expectations. And that is, of course, the answer."

"What is?"

"You shall take Rufus, and I am buying a new horse. The market day for livestock is tomorrow, so expect me to be gone for a good portion of the day."

"Agatha—" I tried to object.

"Of course, you'll need better tack, and the saddle on Rufus will be too small for you," she continued, ignoring my protest. "I went to a saddler while I was out, with a pair of your breeches to get the right measurement for your … seat. The healer will not allow you to travel for at least a week, and that will be plenty of time for him—"

"Agatha," I interrupted. "Thank you, but you're spending money like it's water from a well."

"It's my money to spend."

"Not yet."

"It will be. And I suffered for it—this you know. You are helping me reclaim my life. Let me dress you for the part you will need to play."

"And what part is that?"

"Well, I can't introduce you as a vagabond solver of people's problems, can I? Our story needs to be more … plausible."

"And have you given this some thought? What sort of tale we will tell?"

"I have. To spare my father's sensibilities for the time being, we will tell him that I took over Voss's business. That much is true, to a point. I will have accompanied one of the shipments because I needed to negotiate with a new customer in Tallesin. We cannot let him know I was just a simple driver. That would distress him no end. You happened along and helped me and my people fight off some bandits who ignored the seals on our crates. Over the balance of the rest of the journey, you fell in love with me. I resisted your charms as long as possible, but your persistence and good manners eventually won me over. It's romantic enough that folks will want to believe it. I'll share the gritty truth with them once they are used to having me back."

"We will need to work on the details," I said with a smile.

"We will have time," she said, as she leaned over and planted a solid kiss on my lips.

"Where are you headed now?" I asked when she stood after the kiss ended.

"The healer left a note for me downstairs, so the temple of Vionelle. I should also check in with Rafe or Ned and make sure they returned Sara properly. I'm also curious as to where things stand with Oderic."

"You want to see him in chains and gloat."

"That would be unbecoming," she sniffed, then broke character, laughing, and admitted, "You're darned right I do."

She was out the door again, leaving me to my thoughts. Her excitement about returning home with me in tow was palpable. I allowed myself to wonder what life on the cortaderia would be like.

The door opening woke me again. It seemed all I was capable of doing was eating and sleeping. And Agatha was carrying a tray that smelled of dinner. When the aroma registered, my stomach rumbled audibly, causing her to laugh.

"The healer said not to expect you to do much more than you have been," she said. "Food, sleep, and time will be the best medicine."

The tray held a thick slab of roast beef and a hearty portion of green beans. It smelled as though the beans had been cooked in bacon grease—perhaps my favorite way to prepare them. Without minding my manners, I dug into the food.

"The children have all been returned to their parents," Agatha informed me as I gobbled my dinner. "Sara was returned to the livery. Oderic is being held in the root cellar of the temple of Sylvaris. The irony is that it is where he was keeping the children, and it has not been cleaned since."

"Does that mean—?"

"His thugs weren't too concerned about the cleanliness of the children, so, yes, it's disgusting. The rest of the temple is being purified, and a mareschal has come to tend the destriers. All of them have saddle sores as bad as the ones we saw on the way here."

"What else?"

"Rafe says they are waiting for the priests from Meropan before they do anything with Oderic. In the meantime, the Archon has attempted to stick his nose into things, claiming that Oderic should be turned over to a Midonese court."

"As soon as the Archon got his hands on Oderic, Oderic would be killed. The Archon does not want information about his involvement to reach the capital."

"That's exactly what Rafe and my solicitor said. My solicitor claims that there is no possible way that the Archon did not know about Oderic's slaving activity."

"Well, by the time the priests from Meropan are finished, Oderic will tell them everything," I said. "It will be a matter of public record. At which point the Archon better have a berth on a ship before the Midonese get their hands on him. The rumors are that their punishments are even worse than what Oderic will face."

"Rafe said the same. You're finished. Here—drink this. The healer gave it to me."

She handed me a small vial. It smelled sickly sweet when I pulled the stopper. I drank it in one swallow, finding that it tasted as sweet as it smelled.

"What was that?"

"No idea," she said with a shrug.

"You've been a busy bee today, haven't you?" I remarked.

"Yes, I have," she admitted with a pleased sigh. "You cannot imagine what a relief it is to be able to move through the city without hiding my face. And to be taking concrete steps regarding my return home—I didn't believe you, you know. Yet, it's going to happen. It's getting difficult to contain my excitement."

"You're a remarkable woman, Lady Agatha. No one would have found any fault with you if you had broken long ago. But you didn't merely endure, you grew stronger."

"There's no need to sweet-talk me, Mr. Falk."

"Not my intention. You are simply an admirable person, and I applaud you."

"I would reward you for your generous thoughts, but the healer says we must not indulge ourselves in that way until after she sees you the day after tomorrow."

"I'll look forward to it," I said, "as I always do. In the meantime, your company is enough."

Agatha smirked, but there was a softness in her eyes that was very different from her guarded expressions when we first met. She was allowing me to see inside the tough shell she had developed. I realized it was a gift more valuable than any clothing or saddlery she might buy for me with Voss's money.

She tucked herself against my sound left side, her head on my shoulder. We talked about her day. It was only a couple of minutes later that I realized the healer had given me a sleeping draught. Despite having spent most of the day unconscious, I could not keep my eyes open.

22

The next day brought much of the same. I spent the day in bed but did not sleep around the clock as I did the day before. Agatha spent most of the day at the livestock market. When she returned at dinner time, she was able to tell me all about her new horse, a gray gelding named Chester.

The healer had given her another bottle for me to drink. It was the same stuff as the night before, but I swallowed it down like a good soldier. Within minutes, I was sound asleep.

When the rosy light of dawn woke me on the third day, I felt better than I believed I had any right to. Agatha was still snoozing, with a cute catch to her breathing. I eased myself from under her arm and made my way to the chamber pot. Though I felt weak, I was steady on my feet. When I finished, I saw Agatha peering over at me.

"You should have woken me," she grumbled. "I would have helped you."

"But you looked so peaceful," I said as I slid back under the sheet.

"What if you'd fallen on your face?" she demanded, crossing her arms over the thin shift she was wearing.

"Then I would have felt pretty foolish, lying on the floor without a stitch on. When will you give me back my clothes, by the way?"

"When the healer tells me. She advised me to keep them away from you in case you tried to do more than you should. You know that the ones you were wearing when you were wounded are ruined anyway. The inn took them. They will wash them and then use them for cleaning rags."

As she was speaking, she rose from bed and went to the window. She stretched in the morning light. From my angle, I could see every curve of her body under the gauzy garment she wore.

With her golden hair loose about her shoulders and the light filtering through her shift, she seemed like a painting I'd once seen of the goddess Calithra, the patroness of arts and literature, and the inspiration of poets and troubadors. But Agatha was real—very real—and I could see the strength of her frame in addition to the sensuous curves. She turned and caught me gawping. Her lips curved into a naughty smile.

"Like what you see?" she said as she sashayed toward me.

"Oh, yes," I said as I reached for her.

"Ah, ah, ah," she said as she batted my hand away. "The healer will be here soon, and I don't want her to think I've been allowing you liberties that go against her instructions."

"A kiss, then?" I asked.

"I'll permit it," she said as she presented her cheek to me. "No more than that until we scrape the whiskers from your face and she approves you for further activity. A bath wouldn't hurt you either. When I get dressed, I'll arrange that."

"You don't need to get dressed on my account," I suggested.

"You'd like it if I took even this little thing off, wouldn't you?" she said, lifting the hem of the garment teasingly.

"Indeed, I would."

"I'll tell the healer that you've made progress. You're starting to think with your little head again."

She turned her back to me and did take the shift off, only to put her breeches and tunic on. When she turned back to face me, she noted my look of mock disappointment. She wagged her finger.

"I'll go see about getting you something to eat, and arrange a bath for later," she said, then left the room.

When the door shut, I conducted a quick assessment of my condition. I was weak, but no longer wobbly. The stitches in my side tugged, but that was only an annoyance. Where the quarrel hit me no longer produced the stabbing pain it did at first. It now felt like a deep bruise, as though someone had punched me there with all his might, using a pole. I would need to be mindful of it, but I was hoping the healer would let me get out of bed.

Agatha returned not long after, bearing breakfast and a basin with steaming water. Along with the basin of water, I noticed shaving equipment. She allowed me to eat, then had me sit on the edge of the bed.

My beard had grown since I last shaved in my flat in Tallesin. Though I had not looked in the mirror, I'm sure I looked fairly scruffy. With deft strokes, Agatha removed my whiskers.

"You've done this before," I commented halfway through.

"I have. It's been many years. As a little girl, I once saw my father shaving, and I was fascinated. After I peeped on him one too many times, he lifted me up and taught me how to do it. I did it until the novelty wore off, and I realized it was just a chore, but I still remember what he taught me."

She finished and wiped the remaining soap from my face with a rag. With her hand on my chin, she tilted my head first one way, then the other, examining my face like a sculptor evaluating his work. Satisfied, she straightened up with a smile.

"That will do," she said. "You're almost handsome without the beard. A bath, however, is most definitely in your future. You still have dried blood all over, and you smell like a wet goat."

A knock on the door interrupted her critique. The healer did not wait for a response but strode into the room. Agatha stepped away from me to allow the woman to approach.

She removed the bandage first, bent over, and examined it from close up. She even sniffed, checking for the smell of infection. When she was satisfied, she took my face in her hands and tilted my head back, looking at my eyes.

"Good," she grunted a moment later. "The wound is not seeping. You have avoided infection. The bolt missed your liver, from what I can tell. There is no yellowing of your eyes."

"Can he bathe?" Agatha asked.

"You can wash him, but I would not immerse the wound yet. How do you feel?" she asked, addressing me.

"Not strong, but reasonably steady."

"You'll be a bit feeble for another week to ten days," she said. "That's from the blood loss. Stay with meat, fish, and leafy greens, but you can get out of bed now. Don't try to do too much, but fresh air and sunshine will also help speed your recovery. You can snip the stitches in another three days. I won't need to see you again unless there's a problem."

"Thank you, miss. May we compensate you for your assistance?"

"The help your lady gave us with the children would be enough to balance the scales," she said with a smile. "Besides, we are all grateful to you for bringing that pig Oderic to justice."

Agatha saw her to the door of the room and followed her out. I could hear them exchange a few quiet words. It was a bit later before Agatha returned, but when she entered, one of the inn's maids followed her with a tub. I scrambled to pull the sheet over my nakedness.

It was not a tub for bathing. This was a circular washtub, roughly three feet in diameter. Behind the maid came a boy with two buckets of hot water. Over the next few minutes, more buckets followed until the tub was half full.

"Come on, now," Agatha said. "Get over here and dunk your head. I want to wash your hair first. Then you'll stand in the middle, and I'll clean the rest of you."

I crossed over and knelt down, needing to do so gingerly. Agatha gently pushed my head forward, indicating that she was serious about me putting it in the water. I did so carefully, working my fingers through my hair to make sure every strand got wet.

When I straightened up, Agatha had some sort of paste in her hands and began working it into my hair. It smelled faintly of lilac and produced a thick lather. She worked it all through my hair, and I must admit her hands massaging my scalp felt wonderfully decadent. When she was satisfied, she tapped me on the shoulder.

"Soak your head again and get the soap out."

I bent over and did my best to rinse the suds from my hair. Before I was able to finish, I needed to come up for air twice. Finally, I could no longer feel any of the soap still lingering.

"Looks like you got it all. Now stand in the middle of the tub, and I'll get the rest of you."

Carefully, I rose from my knees. Agatha offered me her hand, and I was not too proud to take it. When I stepped into the middle of the tub, I turned to face her, only to find that while I had been bent over, Agatha had removed her clothes and tied her hair back.

"I need to wash you, and I don't want to get my things wet," she explained, but her mischievous grin told me she was enjoying teasing me.

The teasing continued as she used a rag to wash me, turning me back around and starting with my shoulders, then working her way down. Once she had my back cleaned, she pressed herself against me closely, reaching around to wash my chest. I couldn't help but react to what she was doing.

"Are you enjoying torturing me?" I complained.

"Yes," she said. "Yes, I am. Too bad we can't do anything about that just yet. The healer suggested we wait for another day or two."

"Arrgh!" I groaned, exaggerating my frustration for comic effect.

Agatha giggled in response but then started to wash my lower torso and legs. She was very careful and gentle around my wound. It took her only a couple of minutes to finish after that.

"Step out of the tub," she said.

She dried herself and then handed me the slightly damp towel. While I was getting the water off, she quickly dressed. She then crossed to her bag and withdrew a tunic, a pair of breeches, stockings, and my boots.

"You're allowed to dress and get out of the room. I'm to take you to the square outside where you are to sit," she said, emphasizing the word sit, "and watch Lenoa pass by."

"Will you be with me?"

"No. Things to do, people to see," she said. "When you're hungry, return to the inn, and they will feed you."

"Who is paying for this?" I asked. "Not you, I hope."

"Ned made the arrangements," she said. "So, the temple is."

When I finished dressing, we headed out of the room. I needed to hold the handrail on the stairs going down—not because I was in danger of collapsing, but because I wasn't entirely trusting that I wouldn't. When we reached the ground floor, we crossed through the common room and went outside.

The inn was on a market square, and the business day had already begun. Agatha guided me through the hustle and bustle to the fountain in the center. When we reached it, I sat on the broad stone edge.

"Behave," she said. "Watch the people. When you get hungry or thirsty, go see the innkeeper. He'll take care of you. I'll be back in time for dinner."

"I'd like to go with you."

"The healer said that would be too much activity. According to her, you've already shown that you're a fast healer. She also says your wound cost you a great deal of blood, and that you should be grateful that you're alive. You need to be patient while your body renews itself. Your strength will return. Enjoy the fresh air and sunshine. Watch the people."

She shut off further protests by giving me a serious kiss. When she broke away, she immediately strode off. All I could do was watch her, slightly out of breath. Agatha certainly knew how to shut me up.

It wasn't as though I had been sentenced to misery. Observing the comings and goings in a market square can be very entertaining. Listening to buyers and sellers haggling over prices was almost like sport to me.

When my stomach rumbled, I returned to the inn. The innkeeper, warned by Agatha (I learned later), had been maintaining a loose vigil over me. He quickly bustled me into the dining room, where I devoured a larger-than-usual lunch. When I finished, I returned to my spot next to the fountain and awaited Agatha's return.

23

My peaceful afternoon was interrupted when I heard a high-pitched voice breathlessly calling my name. I stood to see where it came from. A boy of eight or nine years old was looking around, calling, "Dexter Falk?"

"Over here, boy," I replied.

He came jogging over. His face was flushed red as though he had been running. He was still out of breath.

"I'm Dexter Falk."

"I'm to tell you that the lady was arrested. She said you'd give me an argent (the Midonese equivalent of the Thetlarian florin) if I told you,"

he said, sticking his hand out.

"I'll need more information, son, but if you answer some questions, the argent is yours. The lady had blonde hair?"

"Yes, sir."

"Who arrested her?"

"The Archon's constables."

"Where?"

"In Eldryne Square. I can take you there," he offered quickly.

"I know where it is," I said. "What else can you tell me?"

"That's pretty much it, sir. The lady caught my eye as they were putting her into a coach and told me to find you and tell you what happened. She said you'd give me an argent if I did."

"Did you see the constables when they took her?"

"Yes."

"Where was she?"

"She'd just come out of a door. It wasn't a shop, though."

"For another argent, can you show me?"

"Yes, sir," he replied enthusiastically.

"You'll need to move slow," I said. "I was hit by a crossbow bolt a couple of days ago, and I'm not my usual self."

"Don't worry, sir. I'll stay with you."

"Here's the argent she promised you, and there will be another when we get to where you saw this happen."

I handed him the coin, and he clutched it tightly in his left hand. He took my hand with his right, and we started off. He kept the pace reasonable, looking up to check on me every so often. My wound didn't hurt, but I found myself getting short of breath, even as slow as we were walking.

"You need to stop, mister?"

"For a minute, yes," I said.

"How did you get hit by a crossbow?"

"I was chasing a bad man. He shot at me."

"The one who was keeping the children in the temple of Sylvaris?" he asked eagerly.

"That's the guy."

"Sir, you're famous. Everybody is talking about it, except no one knows your name."

"That doesn't bother me. In fact, it's probably better that way. I was just doing the right thing."

"The lady who got arrested—is she your wife? Why would they arrest her if you're the one who—"

"She's not my wife. She's a … friend," I said, not knowing how to respond properly to the lad.

In truth, I considered Agatha to be far more than a friend. For the first time since my teens, I was in love, though I had a difficult time admitting that to myself. And right now, I was worried sick about her.

We resumed walking and reached Eldryne Square before I needed to stop to catch my breath again. The boy led me to the right. This square was not a market like the one where I'd been sitting. This was a quiet piazza. The only retail establishments were a coffeehouse and a bookseller.

"Here, sir," the boy said. "She came out of this door, and the constables grabbed her."

There was a small brass plaque next to the door. "Julius Bellows" was engraved on it. I did not know the name of Agatha's solicitor, but guessed this was him.

"Good job, lad," I said. "I'm going to give you another argent now, but how would you like to earn a third?"

"Another?" he said, his eyes opening wide.

For a boy of his age, three argents was *wealth*. The youngster was decently dressed, so not a poverty case. His father probably worked in one of these buildings, which is why the boy had been here when they took Agatha. With this amount of money, he could buy sweets enough to keep himself and his friends sick to their stomachs for more than a week.

"Yes."

"What do I have to do?"

"Go to the temple of Sylvaris. Ask for Ned or Rafe. They're head priests from temples in other cities, but they are nice men, so don't be frightened. Tell them what happened to the lady and bring them here as quick as you can. When you return, I'll have another argent for you."

I handed the boy the coin I'd promised for delivering me here. He clutched it in the same fist as the other, then took off at a run, weaving around the other pedestrians like a minnow in a stream. It made me smile, despite the circumstances. Oh, to be that young again and have that kind of energy.

I turned to the door and raised the knocker. After banging it three times, I listened to see if anyone would acknowledge my presence. There was no sound, but through the window next to me, I saw someone standing in the shadows, peering out at me.

"Mr. Bellows?" I called out. "I'm a friend of Lady Agatha's. I need to know what happened so I can help her."

The shadowy figure moved out of my sight. The door opened a crack, revealing an older gentleman. Through his spectacles, he eyed me suspiciously.

"What's your name?" he demanded in a querulous voice.

"Dexter Falk."

"Oh," he said with a look of recognition. "You got here fast. How did you know?"

"A boy came and found me. I just sent him to the temple of Sylvaris for additional help. What happened?"

"The Archon's men must have been waiting outside my office," he said. "I didn't see what took place. After I walked Lady Agatha to the door, I shut it and was returning to my desk when I heard the hullabaloo outside. I hurried back to the door in time to see the wagon drive away. One of the constables came to me and presented a writ claiming that, because she murdered him, Voss's entire estate is forfeit to the Archon. I have until the end of the day to file an appeal of his judgment."

"Can he get away with that?"

"Yes and no. It depends on the judge. And the one who will hear this case … well, the Archon owns him. He will deny my appeal. I will need to turn over ownership of all the assets to the Archon."

"But she didn't kill him."

"And I have the affidavits from the household staff—eyewitness accounts— that prove it. The judge will deem them as inadmissible, claiming that Lady Agatha bribed them."

"This is preposterous!"

"Oh, it won't stand," Bellows said. "We'll need to appeal to the capital, and they will overturn the ruling. The Archon will be forced to return the assets, and—"

"The Archon won't be here," I stated firmly, just short of a shout.

"What do you mean?"

"A couple of days ago, we apprehended a man named Oderic."

"A notorious gangster," Bellows commented. "When you say, 'apprehended,' by whom?"

"The temple of Sylvaris has him in custody. Sometime last winter, Oderic seized control of the local temple and has been pretending to be the head priest. In addition to extorting larger-than-customary donatives, he has also preyed on the spice merchant, Ugarte. That is how I became involved. And, he had children imprisoned in the temple. He was planning to sell them in Molutia."

"What does this have to do with the Archon?" Bellows asked naively.

"Oderic could not have gotten away with anything unless the Archon was part of it."

"And you have proof of this?"

"Mr. Bellows, it's common sense. It is inconceivable that Oderic could usurp the temple without the Archon knowing about it."

"Oh, I agree, laddie, but you need proof. Physical, tangible evidence for a judge to examine."

"What about a confession from Oderic?"

"It depends on who obtained the confession."

"Priests from Meropan, the center of the Sylvaran order, are on the way to Lenoa to try Oderic on religious grounds."

"That would be an acceptable confession," Bellows admitted. "But his confession would need to go to the capital. They would then rule on the Archon, and subject him to civil punishment."

"Except the Archon won't wait for that to happen. He will grab Voss's estate, sell the assets as quickly as possible for whatever price he can get, then sail away before the Midonese come after him."

"Ah. I understand the urgency."

"Besides the money, Lady Agatha should not be in jail," I said.

"Oh, I agree. But there is very little we can do about it. I will go to the judge and file the appeal and request bail for Lady Agatha. He will deny both, and demand that I surrender ownership of the assets in the Voss estate tomorrow."

"How much is the estate worth?"

"Almost half a million dinars," Bellows said. "Voss was quite rich. There are rumors that the money was earned through illegal means. The Midonese government would have a stronger case to confiscate the money by pursuing that angle, but it would take time. And, at this late date, they would have great difficulty compiling the evidence."

"The Archon won't be able to get anywhere near full value for the properties," I said. "He needs the money too quickly. If he reaps a hundred thousand dinars from it, he'll be satisfied. Then he'll hop on a ship, and we'll never see him again."

"A hundred thousand dinars seems hardly worth it," Bellows commented.

"That will be on top of all the other bribes he's taken since he was installed as Archon," I pointed out. "He's been in place for more than ten years—"

"Thirteen, to be precise," Bellows corrected.

"With what he can realize from the Voss estate, he'll probably have half a million himself. Where and when is this hearing to take place?"

"Here. I'll show you the writ," Bellows said, handing me a piece of parchment. "I am to appear in the Hall of Magistrates, before Judge Tarchis, before the close of court business today. That's in less than two hours."

I scanned the document quickly. Unlike most official writs I had seen (not that there have been many), this was not in the usual ornate clerical calligraphy. Instead, it looked somewhat hastily scrawled. The language was the usual legalese obfuscation: Agatha Voss (née Mountjoy) was hereby accused of the murder of her husband by means of poison, according to "witness testimony" and "physical proofs." The deadline for appeal was clearly stated, and the confiscation of assets pending decision was demanded.

"Is it unusual to have such a proceeding with such tight time constraints?"

"It's unheard of," Bellows said.

"And you see no hope of winning the case, as things stand now?"

"None."

"Then I'm afraid I must ask you for a favor, Mr. Bellows, on behalf of Lady Agatha."

"What is that?"

"I need you to gather all the documents pertaining to this—ownership of the Voss assets, the affidavits from the servants, anything and everything at all—and disappear for a few days."

"Where would I go, Mr. Falk, where the Archon's men cannot track me down?"

"The temple of Sylvaris. The same boy who brought me here is collecting one or both of the head priests who came with me to capture Oderic. They will give you sanctuary in the temple. Even the Archon dare not violate it."

"But that will still leave Lady Agatha a prisoner."

"That will be my problem to solve."

24

Almost on cue, there was a knock on the door. "Dexter Falk? Julius Bellows?" I heard Ned call from outside.

I nodded to Bellows to open the door. Ned and Rafe were both there, along with the boy who brought them. I quickly retrieved an argent from my money pouch and gave it to the youngster.

"Well done, young man. Thank you for your help."

"Thank you, sir," he replied with a grin, clutching the three silver coins in his fist and skipping off.

Bellows ushered them in, and we went back to his office. By now, my energy was nearly exhausted. I collapsed into a chair while I brought Ned and Rafe up to speed.

"Mr. Falk was correct to offer you sanctuary," Rafe said. "Lady Agatha shared her story with me personally, and I am as convinced of her innocence as you. We agree with Mr. Falk's assessment of the Archon's intent. In fact, the Archon has sent representatives to the temple, demanding that we release Oderic into their custody. We have refused, citing the established precedence of religious law over temporal concerns. That has not stopped them from other attempts, using different arguments. It is clear to us that the Archon wants Oderic silenced before he is implicated."

"But I'm no particular devotee of Sylvaris," Bellows protested.

"That does not matter. Pack the documents you need, and we will take you to the temple where you will be safe."

"But what about my other files? They are all important, and if I fail to appear at the court, the Archon's men might—"

"We will station some priests-militant to protect your belongings," Ned said.

"But what about Lady Agatha?" Bellows asked. "She is in the Archon's cells. I can't imagine they are treating her gently."

"As I stated earlier, that's my problem to solve," I said.

Rafe looked at me with a cocked eyebrow. I was pretty sure he could tell that my words were just bravado. The walk from the inn to Bellows's office had nearly exhausted me, and I'm sure it showed.

"Dex, you're in no condition to do anything," Ned said after looking me up and down. "You look like you're on the verge of collapse. You'll need to let us handle this."

"I agree that I'm in no condition to fight my way through the guards, but there might be another way to free her. You have to let me come along. You know what I can do when the god is with me."

"We saw it just a few days ago, Dex, but you've also told me that Sylvaris has a habit of abandoning you in times of need."

"That's when I'm capable of extracting myself. I think it amuses him. But the shape I'm in right now—I think he'll see me through."

"Dex, if you get in the way or can't keep up, we'll leave you behind."

"Fine."

While we were arguing, Bellows finished gathering the documents he wanted. He'd stuffed them into a stout leather satchel. We left his office. Bellows locked the door behind us. Rafe held out his hand for the key so some of the priests-militant could stand guard while Bellows was away.

Ned helped me up behind him on his horse. The healer had told me not to ride, and I felt it pull my wound open as I climbed up. I held onto Ned as we returned to the temple.

The change in the appearance of the temple was dramatic. It had been only three days since Oderic left, but already the temple looked clean and well-kept. I could feel the presence of the god's numen, which had been absent on my earlier visits. We rode through the gate at the side to the outbuildings behind the temple building itself.

I slid down, again feeling a twinge from my wound. Looking down, I could see a spot of blood on my tunic. Ned noticed it as well.

"You're in no shape to—" he began again.

"Ned, I'm coming along. Give me a jacket so I can cover this up. If I'm right in my guess, we won't be able to fight our way through to her. I'll need to talk her out of jail. If it comes to swinging blades, I'll run or crawl away, I promise."

Ned stalked away, clearly unhappy with my obstinacy. He returned a moment later and tossed a short, quilted jacket at me. I thanked him and started to put it on. He came over and assisted me, as it was a bit snug in the shoulders, making it difficult to put on.

"Can you ride?"

"I'll have to, won't I?" I retorted.

He walked away again, presumably to arrange a mount for me. I took advantage of his brief absence to draw upon my connection to Sylvaris as I described before. With the connection opened, I begged Sylvaris to help me. I admitted to the god that I loved Agatha and could not bear to have anything bad happen to her. Before I finished my plea, the hair on the back of my neck stood up. The pain from my wound disappeared, and I felt strength returning to my limbs. I thanked the god as profoundly as I ever had, then finished my prayer.

Ned returned, leading his destrier. He was followed by a priest-militant leading a bay gelding, already saddled. Rafe and a group of eight more priests-militant followed.

"Are you sure you're capable of this, Dex?" Ned asked.

"I am. You will need me—you'll see."

"If you fall out of the saddle before we get there, I'm leaving you in the street," he stated grimly.

"You've given me fair warning. I'm still coming."

I gripped the saddle horn and pulled myself up. It did not hurt as much as when I climbed behind Ned outside Bellows's office, but I could tell I was doing some damage to the wound. The healer would be upset with me.

"The Hall of Magistrates is in the western portion of the city center—not too far. We'll approach from side streets. I'll let you attempt to talk the guards into letting her go free, but if you feel like you will fail, get out of the way and let us convince them with cold steel."

We set off at a trot, the priests-militant forming up around me. I shook my head. Rafe or Ned had issued instructions to them to treat me as though I were fragile. It amused rather than annoyed me. The streets were busy with afternoon traffic. Seeing true priests-militant riding along in a formation, their black armor well-kept and gleaming, caused people to stop, step aside, and follow us with their eyes. It was clear that we were moving with purpose. We reached the Hall of Magistrates by a side street and halted before coming within the view of the main entrance.

"Well, it's your show now, for a few minutes at any rate," Rafe said. "If it turns sour, holler and we'll come get you."

"I'll be fine," I replied with a confidence that seemed strange, given how weak I'd been feeling not long before.

I slid from the back of the horse with more grace than I should have been able to muster, and, leading him by the reins, I strode toward the corner, around which was the main entrance. Checking the spread of the bloodstain on my tunic, I adjusted my jacket to hide it. The four guards noticed me when I rounded the corner.

They were typical Lenoan constables. Burly men clad in quilted vests under chainmail, with smooth helmets and pikes. They moved to block the entrance as I approached.

"State your business," said the one with a sergeant's chevron on his sleeve.

"Urgent temple business, gentlemen. I'm sure you can help me."

The words flowed out of my mouth like honey. I could feel Sylvaris was with me. With his backing, it wasn't necessarily the power of my arguments, but how my voice could hypnotize my audience.

"The woman you arrested earlier, Agatha Voss, is completely innocent. She is here because the Archon wants to steal her money before he must escape himself. You see, the Archon was taking bribes from a slaver. His masters in the capital will have his head for this, as we can all agree that slavery is detestable."

"The Archon said she's to be held until the trial," the sergeant replied, but his voice was uncertain already.

"A trial? The Archon doesn't have time to wait for a trial. Oderic, the slaver, has already admitted everything. Messengers are already on the way to the capital with his signed confession. The Archon will be lucky if he's only dragged, racked, and gutted, as will be Oderic's punishment. I need to share with you, gentlemen, that the chief priests of the Sylvaran order are on their way from Meropan, and they are *not* happy. Anyone who has helped Oderic or the Archon will be found guilty under ecclesiastical law. The Midonese government will not protect you. They don't dare oppose any of the religious orders. If you refuse to release the woman, so be it, but think of your wives and children, and how horrible it will be for them to witness your execution. Give her to me, and you will be found blameless. Sylvaris himself demands this."

"Aye," the sergeant replied dully, his eyes having taken on a somewhat glazed expression. "Get the woman. Bring her out."

It took a few minutes, during which time I waited anxiously. In the past, it was times like this when Sylvaris would pull the rug from under my feet, leaving me to fend for myself. From the tingle on the back of my neck, however, I felt he was still very much aiding me.

Agatha emerged, her eyes blinking at the sudden brightness of the late afternoon. She was slightly disheveled but seemed unharmed. Her eyes widened when she saw me. Before she said anything, I put my finger to my lips. I feared that her words might break the enthrallment that currently held the guards.

I put my foot in the stirrup and lifted myself into the saddle, feeling my wound again. I offered my hand to Agatha, and she climbed up behind me. With my knees, I nudged the bay forward and toward the corner where the priests-militant were waiting. Before we reached it, the sergeant's reverie faded.

"Halt!" he bellowed. "Halt, I say! In the name of the Archon!"

I squeezed the bay's flanks more tightly, and he broke into a canter, getting us around the corner and out of sight. We could still hear the sergeant shouting, then whistling as he sounded the alarm.

"Time to go, men," Ned called out, seeing us approaching rapidly. "Form up as before. The constables will be coming after us in just a moment."

"Dexter," Agatha said into my ear, "how did you get me out?"

"That was all Sylvaris's doing," I said. "I was just the instrument he used."

"You're bleeding again—quite badly."

"Oh, well," I said, feeling rather noble and brave at the moment.

Behind us, I heard shouts. I guessed it was the mounted constables giving chase. I thought about turning my head to look but then remembered my wound and realized it was a bad idea. There was nothing I could do about our pursuers anyway.

I sensed a crossbow bolt whizz past my head. It would have required an exceptionally lucky shot to hit me. Firing a crossbow from the back of a moving horse was an acquired skill that I doubted any of the constabulary had mastered.

I heard Rafe issue a command. Later, I learned from Agatha that he and four of the priests-militant had turned, with their lances lowered, to face the constables. The constables wisely reined in and followed us at a more sedate pace.

We continued at a canter through the city streets, with Ned shouting, "Make way! Make way!"

Folks jumped out of the street to let us pass. We did not stop until we reached the rear of the temple. I heard orders being shouted to close the gate as I brought the bay to a stop.

I felt Agatha slide off from behind me. When I tried to dismount, I nearly fell on top of her. Somehow, she managed to keep me on my feet.

"Help!" she cried out.

25

When I woke, I had no idea where I was. It was not the room at the inn. My head felt as though it held only pocket lint and not brains. The ache in my side was back.

Wherever I was, it was daytime, but I sensed it was raining. I moved my head carefully to assess my surroundings. Agatha was seated to the side of the bed, her chin on her chest. She was holding my hand in hers.

Slowly, I remembered what happened. I guessed I was in a room in one of the temple outbuildings. The room was cool and comfortable, and I could now hear the rain falling outside.

Shifting slightly, I felt the pull of new, tighter stitches—much tighter, painfully tight, in fact. The ache underneath still felt like a bad bruise, as though I'd been rammed with a sharp stick. It was worse than it had been, but manageable. Agatha sensed my stirring.

"You're awake," she murmured, squeezing my hand.

"How much time has passed?"

"Just the night. You collapsed in the courtyard. The priests carried you up here like a sack of grain, then summoned the healer. She was quite displeased with you. When she stitched you back up, she muttered something about making sure you'd feel it. She did seem to yank on the thread quite hard."

"That explains what I feel down there," I said.

"She also said that you somehow managed to avoid doing too much damage, except to the stitches. Unfortunately, the scar will now be slightly bigger. Then she roused you and made you drink a different kind of sweet-smelling stuff, and you went back to sleep."

I lifted my head and pulled up the sheet to check the wound. There was a fresh bandage on it, but no trace of blood seeping through. I dropped my head back onto the pillow.

Agatha was looking at me strangely. Her expression was one of both concern and frustration. She was wearing the same clothes as when we retrieved her from the Archon's cell. Her cheek was smudged with dirt, and I could see where she'd been crying. Whether that was while she'd been in jail or after, I could not tell.

"You're an idiot, you know," she muttered, more as though she was talking to herself than addressing me. "Mr. Bellows would have arranged my freedom today, and you wouldn't have needed to nearly kill yourself."

"Have you spoken to Mr. Bellows?"

"No, and it may be some time before I can. The priests told me I can't leave the temple until they say."

"Mr. Bellows is here as well," I said, "claiming sanctuary, just like you. It is because he did not feel he could gain your freedom that we acted. Accusing you of murder was just a pretext for the Archon to seize the Voss estate."

I explained to Agatha what we discussed with Mr. Bellows. As I did, I saw the gleam of understanding soften her gaze. The furrow in her brow disappeared, and she no longer seemed upset with me.

"Mr. Bellows would not have been able to resolve this?" she asked.

"No, but don't take my word for it. Speak to him, and he can explain. I don't think you would ever have been released from that jail."

"So, you're saying you're not an idiot?"

"I make no claim either way. Talk to Mr. Bellows and make your own decision."

"I will," she said.

Her expression was much more kindly now. She stood and headed for the door of the room. Before she reached it, she turned around, darted back, and gave me a quick peck on the lips.

I must have dozed off again. The sound of the door opening woke me. Agatha appeared, with Bellows right behind her. I struggled to sit up.

"I've informed Lady Agatha that she would probably never have left that cell alive without your intervention, Mr. Falk," he said.

"Thank you. And the estate?"

"I have all the documents. The Archon can't touch any of it. He would be wise to give up and focus on preparing to leave Lenoa. Once word reaches Ogier, his masters will come for him. Until then, however, we must stay here. The Archon's men surround the temple grounds. They will not risk Thalorix's judgment by committing a sacrilegious act—assaulting a temple of the gods—but they will apprehend us if we attempt to leave."

"Without the documents, can the Archon gain control of the assets?" I asked.

"His pet judge can make any ruling he wants," Bellows said with a smile, "but as long as I have the papers, the Archon can't do a thing."

"Couldn't he simply seize the properties?"

"He would need to know what the estate owns, which would be difficult but not impossible to learn," Bellows explained. "That will take time to figure out. Once he does know what the assets are, the Archon wants to turn them into cash, meaning he needs to find a buyer. No one will want to risk paying even a small fraction of the worth of the assets, knowing that the courts will return ownership to Lady Agatha once I present the documents. The buyer would lose whatever he paid the Archon. With the Archon gone, he would have no relief. No, as long as we stay here, we've stymied the Archon."

"So?"

"We wait," Bellows said.

"You heal," Agatha added.

"Will there be anything else, Lady Agatha?" Bellows asked.

"No. Thank you. I felt it would save time for you to speak directly with Mr. Falk."

"By your leave, then," Bellows said, nodding, then turning to the door.

Although we could not leave the temple, the Archon's soldiers did not restrict access to it. Other than Mr. Bellows, Agatha, and me, folks could come and go as they pleased, including the priests-militant. Agatha prevailed upon them to retrieve Rufus and the horse she had just purchased. When she received word that they were ready, she also had the tack she had bought delivered, and the new clothing she had commissioned.

She delighted in displaying her new outfits. None of them was what I would call fancy. Instead, they were what she had been accustomed to wearing at home on the cortaderia.

A typical ensemble was a linen blouse over what seemed at first glance to be a skirt that reached to mid-calf. It was not a skirt, however, but a cleverly designed pair of trousers, allowing her to ride without sacrificing modesty. Coupled with those pieces were new riding boots, and either a vest or a short jacket. She had also purchased a hat with a flat, broad brim.

I was not allowed to don the clothing she bought for me until the healer visited three days after we rescued Agatha. The healer told Agatha that, as long as I did not do anything stupid, I would not open the wound. I was permitted out of bed and allowed light exercise that would not strain the stitches.

The clothing she purchased for me was simple, but clearly a substantial upgrade over my usual attire. In it, I no longer looked like a tradesman, yet the clothes were nothing like the idle rich would wear. There were no ruffles and no lace. The pieces were suitable for a working member of the upper class, in particular, someone who might be found on the cortaderia.

The best were the boots. These were riding boots, made from supple leather, that reached just below the knee. They fit perfectly. I shuddered to think what they cost.

Since I was allowed light exercise, Agatha and I strolled around the temple grounds. She showed me her new horse, and I became better acquainted with Rufus. The best part was that, after dinner, Agatha decided my light exercise would include honoring the goddess Lysmera, with the stipulation that Agatha would be in charge.

The next day saw the arrival of the contingent from Meropan, led by the Archpriest himself. I had met Azar years before when I went to Meropan as a boy for training, after my link to the god was discovered. His presence was an indication of how seriously the temple viewed what Oderic had done.

Azar was the only person I'd met who possessed a stronger connection to the god than I did. When I first arrived in Meropan, I thought I was there to become a priest. Azar explained that I was not meant for the priesthood. The god had other plans for me. He never explained what those plans were, but I was utterly convinced that he was sharing the god's will.

"What am I supposed to do?" I had asked when the man who was the archpriest at the time judged that my training was as complete as they could make it and sent me from the temple in Meropan.

"Sylvaris will let you know," the old man had said.

It was a cryptic and completely unsatisfying answer. Nevertheless, I had managed to thrive and prosper in my own way. I had learned when the old man died that Azar was named the new archpriest and had been pleased for him.

"Dexter Falk!" he exclaimed upon seeing me. "The dispatch Rafe sent mentioned your name prominently in this mess."

I crossed to him slowly, the pain in my side only a reminder to take things slowly, but not much of a hindrance. Azar came to me, arms outstretched and embraced me. He pulled back and examined me with a critical eye.

"You're wounded," he remarked, and then in a much quieter voice whispered, "and you're in love."

"Yes, to the first, and perhaps, to the other."

"Dex," he said with soft remonstrance, "you might be hiding it from yourself, but you cannot hide what's in your heart from the god we serve—and what he knows, I know."

Azar had demonstrated this ability to me years ago. He had already been marked as the one who would assume the archpriest's position. It was unsettling to hear it from him, nonetheless. I had not yet admitted it to myself.

"Archpriest, may I present Lady Agatha Mountjoy, the daughter of the Thane of Hessel," I said, remembering my manners, having left Agatha's side to greet him.

Agatha stepped forward. She dropped a graceful curtsy, as though she did such a thing every day. The formality of her greeting caused Azar to laugh. The sound of his pleasure was warm and genuine. When she straightened, he stepped forward and folded her in an embrace no less close than the one he gave me.

"My dear Lady Mountjoy, there is no need for such ceremony. Let me look at you."

Agatha straightened, and a blush came to her tanned cheeks. She did not expect such familiarity from an archpriest. Azar held her at arm's length and examined her with a twinkle in his eye and a broad smile.

"Rafe mentioned you only briefly in his dispatch," he said. "To do your story justice would have required another full message, and even then, he would have omitted much of your suffering."

"Are you a seer?" she asked wonderingly.

"I see what Sylvaris deems it is important for me to see," he said. "He has always allowed me to read Dexter like a book printed with large type, for instance. In your case, enough to know of the hardships you have faced. I'm glad Dexter has been able to aid you in returning to your true path. You are not there yet, but the day is not far off."

"You've been right in the thick of things," he said, turning back to me. "I'm completely unsurprised to find that someone stabbed you."

"It was a crossbow bolt, actually," I replied.

"Probably when you came charging around a corner, in pursuit of your quarry."

I laughed, shaking my head at the accuracy of Azar's guess.

"That's how it happened, isn't it?" he said, clapping his hands with delight. "How marvelous! The god played a bigger part than usual this time, didn't he, Dex?"

"Aye."

"Because that man was an abomination and desecrated this temple. I understand he is waiting in the root cellar for my arrival. Well, he will need to wait a little longer. We have been on the road since receiving Rafe's message, and I deserve a good meal and a few glasses of wine. Tomorrow will be time enough for the unpleasantness. Lady Agatha, will you do me the honor of sitting with me at dinner? I find your strength fascinating, and I want to hear your story from your own lips."

Azar had the strongest charisma of anyone I'd ever encountered. He was directing it all at Agatha now, and she was in his thrall. Azar knew what he was doing. He winked at me to show that it was all just in fun for him.

26

"What happened tonight? Agatha asked later, when we were in bed.

"What do you mean?"

"Tonight, with Azar," she said. "It feels as though he cast some sort of magic spell over me. The spell has worn off, and that's the only reason I know there was one."

"You know I am god-touched," I said. "Yet the strength of my connection to Sylvaris is like the moon behind a wispy cloud, compared to Azar's sun at noon on a clear summer day. What happened to you wasn't a spell. It's just that he can channel the god's charm more than any other person in the world."

"But he could see—"

"He can read people with incredible insight. He said in the courtyard that he sensed your strength, much as I did when we first met, but he still wanted to hear your story from your own mouth. I'm sure he is as impressed as I am."

"It was strange. I felt as though I was basking in his attention. He made me feel as though the difficulties I have faced were not random instances of misfortune, but part of some greater fabric."

"That is probably true for all of us."

"It was intoxicating. I felt half-drunk."

"It can feel that way."

"What will happen tomorrow? With Oderic?"

"Azar and the others from Meropan will question him. They will find the truth, then issue the sentence. It is likely that they will send a messenger to Ogier to inform the king that the Archon was involved with what happened. As much as they will pass judgment on Oderic, that message to the king will also seal the Archon's fate."

"Will he face the same punishment?"

"I don't know. There are rumors that the king tailors punishments according to a person's worst fears. If anything, it might be more horrible than what Oderic will undergo."

"Will you need to witness it?"

"No, thank all that's holy. I hope we are far away when that takes place."

"Good. I've seen enough ugliness. Help me think happier thoughts."

I came up with an idea, and Agatha embraced it enthusiastically. When we finished, she fell asleep on top of me. I held her in my arms until I thought she was asleep.

"I love you," I whispered into her hair.

"I love you, too," she murmured back, surprising me.

Agatha woke first. I felt her slip from bed. I cracked my eyelids to watch her dress. Somehow, she sensed I was peeking and managed to put an extra wiggle in her hips.

"Did you enjoy spying on me?" she asked as she tied her hair up.

"I certainly did."

"Well, get up, slug-a-bed. Your light exercise means no more meals in bed."

I groaned theatrically but sat up and swung my legs out of bed. The pain from the wound was fading fast. Agatha handed me some of the new clothing she'd had made for me—shirt, stockings, breeches, and the boots.

"You clean up nicely," she said. "One little thing, though."

She moved behind me. I felt her gathering my hair. She pulled it to the back of my head.

"There. Much better. Your hair has grown long enough that it looks better in a queue."

"Did you tie it with a fancy ribbon?" I asked worriedly.

"A black ribbon. It's not even shiny. Don't worry," she laughed. "No one will make fun of you."

Her voice was a teasing lilt, making me uncertain. Perhaps she used a brightly colored or embroidered ribbon. She fiddled with it, then drew her fingers lightly over the nape of my neck, giving me a pleasant shiver.

"You almost look like a proper gentleman."

"Where do I fall short? It can't be the clothes."

"It's because I know you, Dexter Falk, and you're a scoundrel at heart—my scoundrel, at least."

"I am. I meant what I said last night, Agatha."

"As I did," she said as she came in front of me and raised her head to kiss me quite thoroughly.

"Time to eat," she announced when she drew back. "No more lounging around like a privileged lordling."

"With my hair pulled back, I probably look more like a pirate," I muttered with a pretend growl.

We headed to the refectory, where the priests-militant and the officials from Meropan were breaking their fast. The room hummed with conversation that paused only momentarily when we entered. Rafe spotted us and waved us over.

"Porridge, bread, and fresh fruit over there," he said. "Help yourselves, then join us."

Rafe and Azar were at the table with him. They were engaged in a quiet discussion that seemed serious. Agatha and I went to the sideboard where the food was waiting and filled bowls and plates.

"Good morrow, Dex, Lady Agatha," Azar said when we returned. "Join us. We have much to discuss before the unpleasantness begins—at least for me."

Agatha paused and curtsied to Azar. He smiled and shook his head. Even though he mentioned he did not care for the formalities, Agatha was all too aware that he was an archpriest.

"Dexter Falk," he said to me. "Look at you. You appear to be almost respectable."

"Agatha said the same thing—almost. Apparently, I fall short because she's aware that I'm a scoundrel."

"In my case, it's because I remember the scrawny farm boy who showed up in Meropan with a hole in the knee of his breeches," Azar said. "Are you a scoundrel, Dex?"

"Only when I need to be," I said.

Azar chuckled. That the highest-ranking member of the order would have a sense of humor seemed to surprise Agatha. Azar was not one to put on airs. His robes were the simple gray worn by even acolytes. The only finery on them was the silver of the small, crossed keys of Sylvaris embroidered over his breast.

"Speaking of scoundrels, we have one with whom we need to converse. Dexter, I would like you to join us. Lady Agatha, you may observe if you wish. It will be interesting, but he may say some things you would find highly unpleasant."

"Will you … will you torture him?" she asked.

"There will be no need," Azar said. "I will persuade him to tell me everything without anyone touching him."

"The same way you managed to convince me to share all my trials and tribulations last night over dinner?" she asked.

"Fundamentally, yes. I imagine Oderic will be even more reluctant to talk, but he will regardless. Let's put this chore behind us."

He stood, brushing the breadcrumbs from his robe. I think Agatha was slightly surprised that crumbs would dare to land in the lap of the archpriest. It took her a moment to process that, then she stood.

With Rafe, Ned, and a pair of priests-militant and a scribe, we followed Azar. The temple had no facilities for holding prisoners. Oderic had kept the captive children in the root cellar, and that was where he was being held, along with the six of his accomplices who surrendered or were captured.

"Are his men still with him?" I asked.

"Aye," Ned confirmed. "They face the same sentence. Killing true priests and acolytes, desecrating the temple with slavery—they must pay the full price for their transgressions.

The priests-militant unbarred the door. When it opened, a wave of stink issued forth. Rafe and Ned had not cleaned the room after they regained control of the temple, and with seven men jammed inside, on top of the filth already present from the children's captivity, the smell was enough to make me gag.

"Oderic," Azar called.

The criminal shuffled out, his hands and feet manacled. His hair was matted, and his expression was sullen. He only looked up when he stopped, and then his close-set eyes fixed on me.

"You," he hissed. "I should have killed you."

"You missed," I said.

"And who is that with you? Voss's whore of a wife? Is she special to you? You should know how Voss used to share her with his friends after he finished with her."

"You're pathetic," I said calmly. "Only someone sick of mind and heart would take pleasure in beating a woman senseless and then raping her. But then, a man who snatches children from the streets to sell as slaves has no conscience and is beyond redemption."

I glanced at Agatha to see if his words hurt her. From her posture and expression, they only served to anger her. She had drawn herself up straight, and her blue eyes glared at Oderic with cold fury.

"Oderic," Azar said, his voice serene, "tell us of your crimes against my god, my order, and against your fellow man."

"You'll get nothing from me. I deny everything. The Archon will see me free."

"The Archon will soon be running for his life, Oderic," Azar said. "We've sent word to Ogier, to the king, with evidence of the Archon's involvement in your sordid business. The Archon will wish his punishment were as light as yours. I understand the king goes to great lengths to devise unique punishments that match the darkest fears of those who betray him. Confess your crimes now, in the hope that Thalorix will take your acknowledgement of guilt into account when he weighs your deeds."

As Azar spoke, I sensed asomatous energy flowing from him. It was stronger than I'd ever experienced before. Oderic could feel it, too. His expression softened from the callous sneer into one of resigned acceptance.

"It was the middle of Zorynth, and the port was shut down. I knew the temple would be idle. My men and I entered in the middle of the night and started killing. The priests, the acolytes ... we slit their throats as they slept. We dumped the bodies in the harbor before dawn. We needed to hold some until the next night, there were so many.

"I took the robes and pretended to be the head priest. We drank the cellar dry for two months, until trade resumed in Teryssan. Then, we collected the donatives. I demanded them in coin. No bank would have allowed me to convert a draft. The Archon learned what we had done. He agreed to keep quiet for a quarter-share of what we took."

"What about the children?"

"The Archon knew we took them. He agreed to look the other way if I paid him half what we expected to gain. I cheated him and only gave him a quarter."

"Were there other children that you sent to Molutia earlier, after taking over the temple?"

"No, but I've sold dozens of 'em in the past. Voss was part of it, but his bitch found out and snitched on us. Made things more difficult."

"Have you been looking for her all this time?"

"Sure. Would have killed her if I ever saw her."

"Did you know that the Archon would try to seize Voss's estate?"

"No, but it doesn't surprise me. Archon's a greedy bastard."

"Why did you take the spice shipments?" Azar asked. "The donative was paid. Didn't you think that would arouse suspicion and draw attention?"

"Made a hundred times more from the first shipment of spice as all the donatives added together, and didn't need to share with the Archon," Oderic said with a shrug. "With the money from the second shipment, plus the slaves, I could have gone anywhere in the world and set myself up in style."

"Thank you for your honesty, Oderic," Azar said. "We'll have a confession ready for you to sign in a little while. I'll be back to see you when it's ready."

The priests-militant took Oderic under his arms and half-dragged him back into the root cellar. The thrall that Azar held him in seemed to break, and Oderic started screaming curses. Only the door slamming shut silenced them.

27

"You captured everything?" Azar asked the scribe.

"Every word, Your Eminence," he said. "I should have two copies for him to sign finished in a bit more than an hour."

"Very well. Once I get him to sign, we need to send one to Ogier and let the king know."

"Won't the Archon's men try to stop any messenger we send?" Agatha asked.

"I have a feeling the Archon won't stay around to issue the order," Azar said, his eyes twinkling with mischief. "You see, the punishment for Oderic and his men will be to be dragged from here at the temple to the Archon's palace, then racked, and gutted. We don't have a rack, but the Archon does. It is customary to 'borrow' his. I will be calling upon the Archon shortly to inform him that we have need of his equipment. While I'm there, I will let him know that Oderic has signed a confession, attesting to the Archon's knowledge of and involvement with the whole mess."

"At the same time, Rafe and I will be calling upon every ship in the harbor to let them know that providing the Archon with passage from Lenoa will be a serious offense," Ned said. "Someone may choose to defy our edict, but we can deal with him later."

"If the Archon somehow manages to obtain passage," Rafe continued, "he will leave as soon as the tide turns. Should he be prevented from sailing away, chances are better than even that he will realize that there is nowhere he can go and decide he has lived long enough. His only hope will be that his wife and children can escape with some portion of the loot he has extorted during his time in office."

"Once the scribes draw them up, we will send some of the priests-militant out to post notices announcing the punishment," Ned shared. "This kind of savage cruelty never fails to draw a huge crowd. The rack only holds one person at a time. With seven men to work through, it will be an all-day event."

"You sound almost gleeful," Agatha admonished.

"I apologize, Lady Agatha. I was being sarcastic. These punishments turn my stomach. I wish I did not have to be there."

"Truth be told, Sylvaris weeps for the necessity," Azar added. "But Oderic and his men killed priests and acolytes, stole in the god's name, and desecrated his temple with slaves. Though Thalorix will judge them in the afterlife, mortal flesh needs the occasional reminder that fiendish crimes have the most dire consequences. Word of what takes place tomorrow will spread across the entire globe, reminding people that none of the gods are to be taken lightly."

We walked outside into the courtyard. The bright sunshine helped to dispel the miasma that lingered from the visit to the root cellar. Agatha held my hand as we walked in a circuit around the grounds.

"Will you need to witness the punishment?"

"No, thank all that's holy," I said. "I know that no one here wants to watch, let alone administer it, but the priests must do their duty. The life of a priest of Sylvaris is, in some ways, more difficult and challenging than what priests and priestesses of the other gods endure. Yet all of them were called to service in some way."

"But you are god-touched. Why are you not a priest?"

"A question I myself asked long ago. Azar, before he became the archpriest, informed me that it was not the path Sylvaris chose for me."

"And what is your path, then?"

"Right now? Walking around the courtyard, holding the hand of my lady love. I do not know what the god intends, but I know what I want."

"Which is?"

"You in my life."

I pulled her close, my arms around her waist. We fit together like pieces of a puzzle, her head on my shoulder, my nose buried in her blonde hair. She squeezed me gently.

"Well, you have that."

Over Agatha's shoulder I saw Rafe approach just as he cleared his throat to announce his presence.

"Azar wants you to come with him to meet the Archon," he said.

"Is that wise? I was the one who talked the guards into releasing Agatha. They will surely recognize me."

"Have you forgotten all the things we taught you in Meropan, Dexter Falk?" I heard Azar say with a laugh as he came out into the sunlight. "Can you no longer alter your appearance?"

"Of course I haven't forgotten, but all my things are—"

"This is still a temple of Sylvaris, Dex," Rafe chided. "Oderic didn't touch the … supplies. He probably never thought to make use of them. Come. I'll help you."

"I won't need your help, Rafe, but thank you."

"What are you talking about?" Agatha asked.

"Give me a few minutes, and I'll show you," I said. "It will be quicker than explaining."

Azar beckoned me inside and led me to a room with racks of clothing, along with wigs, mustaches, and beards displayed on formless heads, secured with pins. I scanned the clothes and picked out an ensemble similar to what Bellows might wear—the drab clothing of a solicitor. The breeches and jacket were a dull brown. I searched for shoes that would match the look and fit my feet without too much of a problem.

After I donned the clothing, I perused the other accoutrements. Rather than a wig, I found a neatly trimmed beard and mustache that matched my hair color. Finding the jar of spirit gum, I affixed it to my face, patting it down to make it secure. I reached behind my head to the ribbon Agatha tied my hair with. Pulling my hair much more tightly to my head, I then tied it quickly, giving me a more severe appearance.

I checked my appearance in the mirror. Not quite as prosperous as a solicitor, but I would pass for a minor bureaucratic functionary. Azar would garner most of the attention. People would look at me and immediately dismiss me as unimportant. I headed back outside.

Agatha saw me, and her expression was … interesting. She knew it was me but would have walked by me on the street if she had not been forewarned. Azar chuckled at her reaction.

"That only took minutes," she said.

"It's something I've been taught, and I will admit I'm rather good at it. What do you think of when you see me?"

"Like a clerk of some sort—someone more comfortable with parchment than people."

"Good. That was my intent. All eyes will be on Azar. They will see me and make a quick judgment that I am unworthy of their interest."

"Do you do this sort of thing often?" she asked.

"When I need to. I have different clothes and other things in my flat in Tallesin."

"I didn't see any beards or things like that."

"You didn't look in the right boxes. I have beards and wigs stored there, too."

"Huh," she grunted skeptically, her hands on her hips.

"Come along now, Dex. Let's go see the Archon," Azar said, already mounted.

A priest was holding the reins of Rufus, already saddled. Mindful of my wound, I got up carefully. Nothing seemed to pull or tear.

"Are any of the priests-militant accompanying us?" I asked.

"No need," Azar replied. "In fact, a quiet approach serves us better."

I understood immediately. Arriving in the midst of a phalanx of priests-militant in their gleaming black armor would raise the Archon's hackles and draw the attention of passers-by. A lone priest (who certainly looked like nothing special) accompanied by a mousy clerk, would alarm no one. Besides, I was confident that Azar could prevent anyone from accosting us.

The Archon's palace was atop a hill in the center of the city. Its appearance betrayed its origins as a fortress, later converted into a sumptuous residence. Well-appointed guards stood in front of the heavy iron gates.

"State your business!" one barked when we arrived.

"We are here on behalf of the temple of Sylvaris," Azar said, as I felt asomatous energy emanate from him. "The Archon will want to see us immediately. You will allow us to pass and announce to the Archon that the archpriest of Sylvaris is here."

"Aye. The archpriest. Open the gate," he said, instructing one of his companions.

One of the other guards unlocked the gate and swung it open. The leader jogged ahead of Azar toward the front entrance of the building. When we reached the steps, Azar dismounted. I followed his lead. A groom appeared from the shadows and took the reins of our horses.

"We won't be long," Azar said. "Keep them here."

The groom nodded and stood still. The guard who had run in front of us had been speaking with someone I reckoned was the seneschal. He beckoned us forward.

"This is highly irregular," the seneschal stammered. "No one sees the Archon without having an appointment."

The seneschal was a fussy man, with a doughy complexion and sweaty jowls. He was almost as fat as Ugarte, and he wore gaudy rings on every finger. His beady eyes darted toward me but quickly dismissed me as being of no consequence.

"I'm sorry," Azar said unctuously, "this is not a request. The Archon will thank you for taking me to him."

"And who should I say is here?" the seneschal asked, his attitude having changed in the blink of an eye.

"The archpriest of the order of Sylvaris, and his assistant."

"Of … of course, Your Eminence. The Archon is in his chambers. Let me take you to him straight away. Please follow me."

The seneschal did not proceed through the main corridor in front of us. Instead, he took us to the side and then into a much narrower passage. I sensed we were indeed heading into the residential area of the palace instead of any formal audience chamber.

The corridor was ornately decorated, with tapestries worth small fortunes. The few pieces of furniture were intricately carved, with gold and mother-ofpearl inlays. We walked on a checkerboard of gleaming black-and-white marble. When we reached a door with gold facings, the seneschal knocked.

"I apologize for disturbing you, Your Excellency," the fat man said, "but the archpriest of the order of Sylvaris is here."

"The what?" I heard the Archon shriek. "Send him away immediately!"

"I'm afraid it's too late for that," Azar said as he walked past the seneschal. "Besides, I have an urgent request, and you will want to hear what else I have to share."

I followed Azar into the room. The Archon was barely half-dressed. It was not a good look for him. He once was a skinny man, with narrow shoulders and a hollow chest, but now sported a round belly that poked out above the pajama trousers he was clutching to his waist.

Beyond the Archon, I saw his bed. In it was a woman, kneeling. She was much younger than the Archon and in the prime of her beauty, now trying to cover herself with the sheet. Her eyes were wide with a mixture of fright, shock, and curiosity.

"What … what are you doing here?" the Archon stammered.

"I've just finished a conversation with a man named Oderic. He confessed to murdering our priests, usurping our temple, and engaging in slavery. He, along with six of his associates, will be dragged, racked, and gutted tomorrow. I have come to request the use of your rack, as we do not maintain such a device in our temple. It is the long-established custom that local leaders lend us such equipment when we have need of it."

"You did not need to bother me with that," the Archon complained. "The seneschal could have seen to it."

"Ah," Azar said, stroking his chin thoughtfully. "I suppose that's true. In that case, I apologize for disturbing you."

Azar turned to the door and took two steps. A look of relief washed over the Archon's face. It vanished when Azar stopped and turned back.

"Of course, there is the matter of why you did nothing about his sacrilegious actions."

28

"You say this man usurped the temple of Sylvaris?" the Archon asked. "I knew nothing about it."

"You are foolish to attempt to lie," Azar commented. "Oderic has shared everything with us. A written copy of his full confession, signed by his own hand, is on the way to Ogier even as we speak."

The Archon's face paled as his hand twisted the waist of his pajamas nervously. Behind him, the girl was watching, her eyes wide like a startled doe as she realized that the Archon had just lost all of his power and authority. The Archon's eyes flicked back and forth, as though he sought a way out.

"Yes, he named you as an accomplice, Archon. You knew about his taking control of the temple, and about his slaving. He bought your silence."

"What can I do to convince you to recall the messenger? Surely, there must be something? A significant donative to the temple?"

"A donative?" Azar replied with a harsh laugh. "Oderic murdered priests and acolytes in their sleep. He desecrated the temple with the chains of slavery. He preyed upon the very people who sought divine protection from Sylvaris. And, you, Archon, the king's chosen ruler of Lenoa, who besmirched his royal name, you think a donative will balance the scales of justice?"

"Please," the Archon said. "Oderic threatened me. He forced me to—"

"Again, you try to lie. Oderic told us quite a different story. When you learned what he was doing, you compelled him to pay for your silence. No, there is no way you can buy your way out of this mess."

"I'll—I'll abdicate—leave. Just let me take my family away. I'll leave all my money for the temple."

"Your wife and children may yet live, Archon, but you will find there is no ship in the harbor that will take *you* anywhere."

The realization of his predicament swept over the Archon, and I saw the shameful stain of wetness bloom in the crotch of his pajamas. He looked as if he was about to cry. Azar continued to stand dispassionately.

"There are two things you can do, Archon," Azar said. "First, you must absolve Lady Agatha Mountjoy from any accusation that she murdered her husband. Her solicitor has sworn affidavits from eyewitnesses who saw Voss fall down the stairs while drunk and break his neck. You must relinquish any designs on the Voss estate and declare that it is the sole property of Lady Agatha. Then, when you have done that, I will allow you to make arrangements for your wife and children to travel to Ogier in order to throw themselves upon the king's mercy."

"But what about me?" the Archon whined.

"You're welcome to appeal to the king's mercy," Azar said and shrugged.

The Archon's face crumpled. He released his grip on his pajamas, which slid to the floor, revealing his unflattering nakedness. He might have seemed pitiful to some, but my heart held no sympathy for him.

"You should leave now, child," I said to the girl.

She started, surprised to be addressed. With the sheet wrapped around her, she got out of bed and scurried to a side door in the chamber. I wondered where her clothing was, since she did not stop to retrieve any.

"Be a man, Archon," Azar said harshly. "Accept the consequences of your actions. Compose yourself. Summon a scribe and draft the declaration absolving Lady Agatha. Instruct your wife to take the children to Ogier and have them leave this very day."

"Fetch the scribe," the Archon said to the seneschal, whom I saw was still standing in the doorway. "Then tell my wife to take the children to Ogier immediately. I will come see her when I finish with the archpriest."

"Yes, Your Excellency," the seneschal replied as he turned away.

The Archon bent and pulled his pajamas back up and tied the drawstring around his waist. It was, perhaps, more dignified than standing naked, but the stain of his urine still betrayed him. We stood, motionless and silent. I could tell the Archon was thinking, trying to develop some argument that would save his skin. Yet every scheme crashed upon Azar's calm resolve like waves breaking on a rocky crag. A scribe knocking at the door broke the tableau.

"Your Excellency, I am here as requested."

"Draft a declaration. Lady Agatha Voss, née Mountjoy, is hereby absolved of any and all culpability in the death of her late husband. As he died intestate, she is the sole inheritor of his entire estate, effective immediately."

The mousy clerk went to a small writing desk against the wall and began scratching furiously with his quill. His writing produced the only sound in the room. When he finished, he dusted the parchment with pounce to dry the ink. Satisfied, he stood and took it to the Archon.

"Let me look," Azar said, extending his hand.

The Archon handed it over. Azar scanned the document and nodded in satisfaction when he finished reading. He gave it back to the Archon and gestured for him to sign it. The Archon returned to the desk and added his signature, his hand shaking.

"Your seal as well," Azar instructed.

This produced a slightly comic flurry. The scribe needed to find a taper, which took some searching. He then struggled to light it. I could tell the Archon wanted to snap at him, but Azar stood there calm and patient, which convinced the Archon to restrain his temper. Once lit, the scribe dripped the sealing wax onto the bottom of the document, and the Archon pressed his ring into it.

"Go now," the Archon said to the scribe as he handed the document to Azar, who immediately passed it to me.

"I would advise you to see to the safety of your wife and children," Azar said. "We will show ourselves out."

I followed Azar out the door and back to the entrance. We encountered the seneschal again, and Azar reminded him that the rack needed to be brought out from wherever they kept it and set up in front of the palace by morning. The groom holding the reins of our horses was where we left him. It appeared as though he had not moved an inch. Our return seemed to snap him from a spell.

Carefully, I mounted the saddle, feeling the tug of the stitches the healer left in me. We rode slowly away from the palace. Azar was the one to break the silence when we were down the street.

"If he has any sense, he'll kill himself before the sun sets," he muttered.

After that, we continued in silence through the busy streets of Lenoa in the middle of a normal working day. None of the people we passed had any inkling of the momentous events that had just transpired. No one paid us any special attention.

"And that will be the end of it?" I asked eventually.

"Lady Agatha is free and clear. We will show the document to the officer in charge of the soldiers stationed around the temple and tell him to return to the barracks. It has already been an eventful day, and we will return just in time for lunch."

Azar's casual remark made me laugh. It had indeed been a busy morning. And the best part was that I carried a document freeing Agatha from Voss forever.

When we reached the temple, Azar found the officer in command of the Archon's soldiers. He asked me to produce the Archon's decree for the officer to read. The man looked it over, then grunted in satisfaction.

"Never did understand what we were doing here," he grumbled. "The men will be gone as soon as I pass the word, Your Eminence."

He turned on his heel and began barking orders to his men, instructing them to form up. Azar continued into the courtyard of the temple, and I followed him. As I slid gingerly from the saddle, I saw through the gate that the small column of soldiers was beginning to march away. When I turned back around, Agatha, Rafe, and Ned were waiting for us.

"Lady Agatha, I bear in my hand your deliverance," I said pompously, giving her a sweeping bow, but caught myself before bending too deeply, as the pain in my side counseled me against it.

I held my pose until Agatha crossed to me and took the parchment from my hand. She read it quickly but carefully. When she finished, she threw her arms around my neck but quickly recoiled.

"That beard is awful," she commented.

"I'm sorry."

"But I'm free? I'm really free?" she asked, turning to ask Azar.

"You are. Someone should tell Mr. Bellows that he can leave as well," Azar said.

"The Archon put up no fuss?" Rafe asked.

"He made a brief attempt, but when he realized his words had no effect on His Eminence, he pissed himself."

"He did what?" Agatha gasped.

"You heard me correctly the first time," I said.

Her eyes widened, and then she burst into a peal of laughter. The sound was so infectious that Rafe and Ned could not help chuckling. It was a welcome change from the tension I had felt since Oderic's interrogation.

"It will take a day or two for things to settle down, I imagine," Azar commented. "But Mr. Bellows should be able to handle the formalities when that happens."

"Thank you," she said, releasing me and crossing to Azar to kiss his cheek firmly.

He blushed. I think it's the first time anyone has ever seen him embarrassed. He reached his hand up and held it to the spot her lips had touched. She crossed back to me and planted a much more serious buss on my lips.

"I'll show you even more gratitude later, once you get rid of that ridiculous beard," she whispered in my ear with a low growl.

"Dexter, I appreciate you joining me this morning, but you are still recovering," Azar said. "Go change out of your costume. After we have lunch, I want you off your feet for the rest of the day."

"I agree, Your Eminence," Agatha said. "He pushes himself too hard sometimes. I want him healthy as quickly as possible."

I went back into the temple and to the room where the costumes were and stripped off the clothes I borrowed. It took some time and aquae vita to loosen the spirit gum that I'd used to fix the beard to my face. After I removed the beard, I needed to wash thoroughly. When I finally finished, I joined the others who had already started eating lunch.

Once there, I learned that Agatha had decided we would return to the inn. It was hard to argue with her reasoning. It was much more comfortable than the acolyte's cell I had been using in the temple outbuildings.

She took me outside, and we found Rufus and Chester already saddled and waiting for us. Agatha had packed all of her new purchases in the saddlebags while I had been fussing with removing my disguise. We made the short ride to the inn. Upon arriving, the innkeeper asked us where we had been for the last few days.

"Something came up," I said. "Have you let out our room?"

"No, sir. Everything is as you left it, but if you did not return today, I would have needed to free them for others. We will be full tonight."

"Why is that?"

"The punishment," he said. "Notices are posted all over the city. Word is spreading quickly, and by tonight, I expect people from nearby towns will come to the city to watch."

"That's horrible," Agatha said.

"Aye, miss, there's no question about that, but it's good for business."

A boy carried our bags up to the room. As the innkeeper promised, it was as we left it—tidied by the maids, though. Agatha unpacked, and I stretched out on the bed and watched.

"What next?" I asked.

"We stay here for a few days while Mr. Bellows sorts everything out and you heal. Then, we ride for Hessel."

"Are you excited about returning home?"

"Yes, but also wary. My family has not heard from me. Suddenly appearing will be a shock. I hope a pleasant one."

"I suspect your father feels great guilt over what he did to you."

"He did not know Voss was a monster. The family desperately needed the money, or they would have been forced to sell everything. I know I've painted a pretty picture of life on the cortaderia, but the business side of things can be violently competitive. Because of our indebtedness, we were at a grave disadvantage. A couple of our neighbors would always try to take advantage. Fortunately, we had other neighbors who stood up for our interests. Without them, we would never have lasted as long as we did, but even with their help, the family needed Voss's bride money."

29

The innkeeper's prediction was correct. By nightfall, the inn was packed with guests, some sleeping two to a bed. In the common room and dining room, conversation centered on tomorrow's spectacle.

"Why do people take such pleasure in this?" Agatha asked me over dinner.

"I think the answer varies depending on each person," I said. "Some people are here because it's an event, almost like one of the feast days for the gods. They don't really relish the reason for it; they just enjoy the excuse to go out and take part in the overall atmosphere. For some people, it is a sense of reassurance that there is justice in the world. The punishment of most criminals is not a public spectacle, so people don't see the perpetrators facing the consequences of their misdeeds. Even though this is one of the most extreme forms of punishment, it reminds them that other, lesser sentences are also being carried out. And finally, some take pleasure in the misery of others. If they aren't sick and twisted souls, who are—I hope—a very small number, seeing something like this tells them that their own lives are not so bad."

"But the punishment?" Agatha protested quietly, "I understand that Oderic and his men committed great sacrilege. Engaging in slavery is unpardonable. But why subject them to such torture? Why not just hang them and be done with it? This sentence feels as evil as the deeds they performed."

"I'm no religious scholar," I said. "Azar would be able to answer this better than I, but I feel that there must be more to it than vengeance."

"I'm glad we're not watching tomorrow."

"As am I."

A new buzz note entered the conversational hum in the dining room then. It began at the door and moved table by table. When it reached our neighbors, I overheard what the subject was.

"They're learning that the Archon killed himself," I whispered to Agatha.

"How?" she asked, her fork frozen in midair.

"None of them will know," I said. "But everyone will have a theory. It doesn't matter in the end."

"You're not surprised," she said.

"No. As horrible as the punishment Oderic will face tomorrow, the king is well-known for sentencing officials who betray him to fates that play upon their worst fears. When Azar told the Archon that the only thing he could do was to send his wife and children to Ogier to plead for the king's mercy. There would be no clemency for the Archon, but if he forestalled any further embarrassment to the king, his family might be spared."

"Will the king punish his family?"

"From what I have heard of him, no," I said. "The king will quickly determine whether his wife played any part in the Archon's decisions. The children certainly did not."

"And you don't think his wife influenced him?"

"Judging by what Azar and I saw today, no. When we interrupted the Archon, he was with a concubine,"

Agatha shook her head slowly in disgust. We finished eating, listening to the other diners speculating about the manner of the Archon's death. My guess was poison, but I didn't really care all that much. The Archon struck me as a coward. He would choose the least painful way of ending his life. There were several poisons that would have done what he wanted.

After we finished eating, we strolled around the market square. There was a festival atmosphere, with more people out than usual. Agatha held my hand as we window-shopped.

When darkness crept in, we headed up to our room. Agatha was quiet as she undressed. She slid under the sheet and tucked herself up to me.

"You're thinking hard about something. Can I help?" I asked.

"My life has changed so dramatically since you showered in the rain in front of me. I was resigned to my life as it was, for a few more years, at least. And suddenly, all my wishes are about to come true. Even more than I dared dream, actually."

"Is that a bad thing?"

"By all that's holy, no!" she said with a sweet peal of laughter, as she turned to face me.

Her joyous mood led to some vigorous activity, at least on her part. I was still well aware of my wound, and it limited my role. Nevertheless, we both enjoyed ourselves immensely. When sleep overcame us, Agatha was lying mostly on top of me, as I stroked her back.

We stayed well away from the proceedings the next day. The streets of Lenoa were as empty as I had ever seen them. It was not until late in the afternoon that people started returning to the inn. Neither of us cared to hear them recounting what they'd seen, so we retreated to our room until dinner.

Two days later, Mr. Bellows came to the inn with his satchel. Every bit of Voss's estate was now in Agatha's name. He asked what she wanted to do with the various properties.

"Mr. Bellows, you have done an admirable job of safeguarding my interests," she said. "If you are willing, I would like to have you continue to do so for the time being. I am returning to Hessel in a few days. All I need for the present time is a hundred dinars."

"Are you sure that will be enough, Lady Agatha?"

"To reach home comfortably, it will be much more than enough. If I find that there are problems in Hessel that require more money, I will write or return in person."

"Very well, Lady Agatha. I will continue to manage the estate as before, at the same fee. I can have the bank deliver the money to you before the end of the day. When do you plan to leave the city?"

"In two or three days, depending on how Mr. Falk feels."

After Bellows left, Agatha decided I should visit the healer at Vionelle's temple. The stitches could be removed, and Agatha wanted to know more about when it would be safe for me to engage in a long journey. Hessel would be a ride of more than two weeks.

We went to the common room to wait for the bank delivery. Just after the bank messenger arrived with a money pouch for Agatha, one of the priests-militant strode in. When he saw me, he crossed immediately.

"The archpriest would like to see you at your convenience, Mr. Falk."

"Is this an urgent summons, or a casual one?"

"It did not seem urgent, but with him being the archpriest…"

"We are heading to the temple of Vionelle. We will stop by on our return," Agatha said.

"I'm sure that will be fine, my lady," the priest said.

The healer was less aggravated with me when she inspected my wound. She snipped the stitches and pulled them. Agatha asked when I would be able to embark on a long trip.

"He could probably leave tomorrow, but you must watch him carefully to make sure he does not overtax himself," she said.

After thanking her profusely for doing her best with such a bad patient (me), and learning that the temple of Sylvaris had provided compensation for her time and effort, we left. It was a short walk to see Azar. The priest-militants on duty at the temple steps waved us right in.

"Ah, there you are, Dex," Azar said when he saw me enter the office he was using. "Right on time."

"You didn't specify a time," I said.

"Perhaps not, but you are here just when I wanted you to be. Good day to you, Lady Agatha," he said with a slight bow in response to her curtsy. "I'm afraid I need a couple of minutes with Dex alone. Temple business. If you would be so kind as to take a stroll in the courtyard, I will send him out soon."

Azar waited until after Agatha departed. He gestured for me to sit facing him. His face bore his usual kindly expression. I was trying to read him but failed as I always did.

"You are heading to Hessel with Lady Agatha tomorrow," he said, stating it as a fact and not an attempt to fish for information.

"Yes."

"Good. It is clear that you love one another. She will have more need of your assistance in the future."

"Then I will provide it."

"Of course. Dex, do you ever wonder why Sylvaris did not choose you for the priesthood?"

"It used to trouble me greatly, Azar, especially when I was told to leave the temple in Meropan. Somehow, I ended up on the path that has brought me thus far, and I haven't questioned it for years."

"The training that the archpriest put you through was different from what priests-militant experience. You know that, don't you?"

"I realized it at the time."

"I thought you did."

"Is there a point to these questions, Azar? I don't mean to be rude, but you are being rather cryptic."

"I am, aren't I?" he said with a chuckle. "I'm still ill-at-ease with the punishments we inflicted. Sylvaris let me know we were doing as he desired, but he also feels remorse—much as I do, I suppose. Anyway, to the reason I asked you to come."

He picked up a sealed envelope from the desk and handed it to me. It was addressed to me. I started to open it, but he stopped me.

"Not now, Dex. That letter is for you to read at some point in the future."

"Fine. When?"

"That, I cannot answer. All I can say is that you must remember to carry it with you, but otherwise not think about it at all. When the time comes for you to open it, you will remember this conversation and read it then. I'm sorry to be so enigmatic. It will make sense eventually."

Such were Azar's powers of persuasion that I questioned him no further. In the days and weeks to come, I always made sure I had the letter with me but otherwise would forget about it entirely. It is easy for me to understand now, but I am afraid, dear reader, that you must wait for me to disclose the letter's purpose at the appropriate time in the story.

With that, our meeting was over. Azar stood and ushered me into the courtyard. He embraced Agatha and me and wished us well on our journey to Hessel.

"What was that about?" Agatha asked as we left the temple grounds.

"He just wanted to thank me for the role I played in bringing Oderic to justice," I said, truly believing that this is what we had discussed.

I was aware, dimly, of the letter in my pocket, but it did not seem important. What was important was Agatha's hand in mine as we strolled back to the inn. The next day we would start for Hessel.

"I'm wondering what your father will think of the scoundrel you're dragging home with you. It will be like a lost puppy. 'Daddy, he followed me home. Can I keep it? Pleeeaaase?' I'll bet you even pulled that trick on him when you were a girl."

"How did you know?" she said with a peal of laughter. "He was a scruffy old thing, missing an ear, and you could count every one of his ribs. I begged Father to let me keep him. That dog followed me *everywhere* and couldn't stand to be on the other side of a closed door from me. He died just before ... just before I had to leave. Anyway, you're slightly less mangy than he was. And in the clothes I had made for you, you look almost respectable."

"Almost."

"Close enough that he won't take note of your appearance until after he gets over seeing me. When I tell him of how you helped me, you will look like a prince to him."

"What about your mother? You never talk much about her."

"I think when my mother realized that my father's intention was to, in effect, 'sell' me to the highest bidder, she started to distance herself from me emotionally. She recognized the dire necessity but did not like it. I think pushing me away before the time came was the only way she could cope. I remember them having bitter fights. It was only later that I realized it was about my father's plan for me. How will she react to my return? She will probably be even happier than my father but will temper her reaction because of him."

I pondered what Agatha's life had been like growing up. She had shared that her family had been indebted to the point of ruin, yet they still owned horses and cattle. My upbringing was admittedly quite different. Our farm was no vast estate, protected and preserved over the years. Animals were expensive to own, and we considered ourselves fortunate to have a single mule. My father's family had held it for generations, but we certainly did not consider it an "ancestral holding." Our existence was pretty thin most years.

Agatha seemed to hold no bitterness toward her father for the decision he'd made. I hoped I would never need to face a choice like that. Giving away your daughter to save the family was a move of horrid desperation.

30

Dawn came crisp and clear. After breaking our fast, Agatha and I went to the inn's stable and saddled our horses. One of the inn's boys brought down our saddlebags. I attempted to settle our bill with the innkeeper, but he informed me that one of the priests-militant had already paid the account in full the night before.

That out of the way, Agatha and I mounted and headed to the south gate of the city. We were both dressed in the clothing Agatha had purchased. I must say, she looked like an idealized painting of a lady of the cortaderia. Her blonde hair flowed down her back, underneath the wide, flat-brimmed hat that was tied loosely around her neck. She rode with an easy grace.

It was as though Chester was an extension of her body. Rufus moved easily beneath me. The slight hitch in his left hind leg was gone. It occurred to me that Rufus was the first horse I'd ever owned, and that wouldn't have happened without Agatha.

We rode in silence as the outskirts of the city gave way to cultivated fields. Wheat fields gave way to an olive grove. We reached a small hamlet, a few houses clustered at a crossroads, that had a well next to the road. While we let the horses drink, Agatha gave me an appraising glance.

"Not a mangy puppy any longer," she said. "Nor a vagabond. You could almost pass for someone important."

"If they see me in your company, they will automatically assume that I am a man of consequence," I said. "Otherwise, you would not permit me to ride with you."

We remounted after the horses drank their fill. The road south to Swardle was well traveled, a vital artery of trade. We passed caravans heading in the same direction, but little traffic heading north.

"The traffic will change in another month and some," Agatha said, "when they begin driving the cattle to Lenoa. They'll wait until the crops are harvested, then let the cattle graze on the stubble as they travel."

We did not press ourselves too hard. When we reached a sizable town in the late afternoon, Agatha declared we would spend the night at the inn. She was mindful that my stamina was not what it should be.

When we stopped, we groomed our horses. For me, it was a chance to repay Rufus for carrying me all day. It was also an opportunity for him to get to know me better. Because of my injuries, I had not spent much time with him, and I wanted to develop a level of trust. So far, I was very pleased with him. Agatha clearly had a good eye for horseflesh.

We continued on the road south for seventeen days, stopping each afternoon at an inn. Our pace picked up slowly each day. I was feeling better, and I could tell Agatha was growing excited about seeing her family again.

The fields through which we passed changed. After two weeks, we no longer saw crops under cultivation. Instead, we were now in the grasslands of the cortaderia. Midday of the eighteenth day, we passed a stone marker that I would not have noted except for Agatha pointing it out.

"We have just crossed into our holdings," she said. "We'll be home before nightfall."

We rode on, the sun now past its zenith. A herd of cattle was crossing the road, and we reined in while a group of six mounted herdsmen, vaqueros, she called them, guided them with whistles and yips. The one closest to us tipped his hat to Agatha, but I saw him study what he could see of her face under the broad brim of her hat.

"Miss Agatha?" he asked hesitantly, reining his horse in.

"Marco?"

A curious mixture of expressions passed across his features. There was joy at seeing Agatha, but I also sensed pain. The pain was not that of losing Agatha years ago, but something more recent.

"Aye, miss. It's good to see you. You here for the funeral? I'm afraid you're too late."

Agatha's face went pale. Her eyes widened with shock. Poor Marco looked dismayed, realizing that she knew nothing about any death.

"Whose funeral?"

"You din't know?" Marco asked, realizing he'd just given her an awful piece of news. "Your brother, miss."

"What happened?"

"We been losing cattle, miss, ever since old man Whitman died last year. His son—"

"Arkady? Or Dmitri?"

"You din't know, miss?"

"Marco, I haven't heard anything from home since I left."

"Mr. Dmitri died just afore the old man. Some say it broke the old man's heart. Others ain't so sure. Anyway, your brother was sure Arkady was stealing our stock and rebranding 'em. Mr. Arkady changed the Whitman brand after he took over, and you can overbrand ours with it. He and Mr. Arkady got into it a few times about it. Then, four days ago, Mr. Elias didn't come home for supper. We went out lookin' for him at first light. We found his horse, Cisco, and, not far away, your brother. His neck was broke, like he fell. But I ain't so sure. Your brother—"

"Elias rode like he was born with reins in his hand, and he and Cisco…"

"That horse wouldn't throw him for nothin'. And where we found him, there weren't no holes or rocks, no sign a snakes, just close-cropped grass. No, Miss Agatha, I don't hold with him fallin'. Someone done him in. Too many bruises for just a fall, but nobody asked me."

Agatha's knuckles were white where she clutched the reins. I reached over and touched her arm, just to let her know she wasn't alone. She didn't react. Her eyes were distant, like she was searching for a storm on the horizon.

"Marco," I asked, "tell me more about Arkady Whitman."

"Beg pardon, sir, but who're you?"

"It's fine, Marco," Agatha said, yanking her mind back to the present. "This is Dexter Falk. I owe him my life. It's a long story, and I promise to tell you everything when I can, but you can trust him. I do."

"Yes, miss. Mr. Elias was convinced that Whitman was stealing our cattle. It mighta started with picking up strays, but then he started taking dozens at a time. Mr. Elias caught him on the property with his men twice, and they had some words. Mr. Arkady, well, he's mean like a spoiled cat—sneaky. His smile don't never reach his eyes, and you don't never want to turn your back on him. The men they got working the Whitman place're all new since he took over. Don't none of them look too savory."

"Why didn't Elias take it to the Council of Thanes in Corwig?" Agatha asked. "They don't hold with cattle thieves."

"He was planning to, but..."

"What's my father doing about it, Marco?"

"Your daddy? Hain't seen him. Your mama says he's takin' it hard. She looks like she's ready to spit nails, though. Sorta like the look on your face right now."

Marco shifted in his saddle. His face, weathered by years of the unrelenting sun on the cortaderia, was creased with worry. He kept his eyes on Agatha.

"Miss Agatha, I din't mean to drop that on you all a sudden. I thought you knew, and that's why you're here."

"Marco," she said in a kindly tone, much softer than I would have expected, "you didn't do anything wrong. Thank you for sharing what has happened. Mr. Falk and I are returning at exactly the right time, it seems. We need to get to the house and see my parents. I promise I will tell you where I've been—it's not a happy story, for the most part, but the ending hasn't been written."

"Well, you couldna come at a better time, or worse, I guess," Marco said. "It's good that you're here, that I can say for certain. Nice to meet you, Mr. Falk."

Marco rode off to join the other vaqueros, of whom two had lingered just out of earshot. Agatha did not move. I nudged Rufus closer to her. The expression Marco used, about looking like she could spit nails, was on target. I decided I never wanted to give her a reason to look at me that way.

"Let's get up to the house," she said finally.

She pressed her knees, and Chester started up the road. Rufus and I stayed beside her. We rode in silence for a few minutes.

"How are you feeling?" I asked eventually.

"Sad," Agatha admitted. "Angry. Selfishly disappointed."

"Why disappointed?"

"I thought my homecoming would be a joyous event," she said quietly, "but it won't be now. It will just serve as a reminder of other unpleasantness."

"I'm sure your parents will be happy to see you."

"Yes, but the bitter will outweigh the sweet."

"Tell me about your brother," I asked.

"Elias was four years younger. He was a good boy, growing up into a good man when I left. The whole point of marrying me to Voss was to enable Elias to take over free of debt," she said. "I don't think he knew about it, or he would have argued against it."

"Were you close?"

"Not at first. There was enough of a gap between us that I realized my status changed from 'only child' to 'older child.' I resented him for that. Not long after, I started to learn that being a woman was an additional handicap here in Swardle. It wasn't until a couple of years before I left that I realized that it wasn't Elias's fault. As I said, he was a good boy. You remind me of him in certain ways—your kindness and respect."

"What about the Whitmans?"

"Father and Mr. Whitman had their disagreements, but they were mild. Cattle get lost and cross boundaries. They were usually able to sort things out without resorting to harsh words. Whitman's primary complaint was that we didn't do enough to keep our animals off his land, and he was right. We just saw Marco with five other men. Before I left, Marco would have had two men helping him, at most. Anyway, our relations with the Whitmans were not hostile, but they weren't the friendliest. Mr. Whitman offered to buy a portion of our land. Father always refused, and I think Mr. Whitman felt my father was being stupidly stubborn."

"What about his sons?"

"Dmitri was a couple of years older than me. He was my first crush."

"Why didn't—?"

"The Whitmans might have had enough money to purchase some of our land, but not enough to cover all of our debts. Mr. Whitman wouldn't have agreed to do it anyway. The Whitmans felt our family had been foolish. And, in the case of my grandfather and great-grandfather, they were correct. Dmitri was a good man. His younger brother Arkady was bad in every way that Dmitri was good."

"I realize you were dealing with the shock of learning about your brother, but Marco hinted that he suspected Dmitri and his father did not die from natural causes."

"I did not notice that," she admitted. "From what I know of Arkady, it's believable. I doubt their father would have split their lands between the two, so Dmitri would have inherited the entire holding. Arkady would have received nothing. My mother will know more."

Agatha did not volunteer any more information, and I sensed she needed to be allowed to process her emotions. I felt great sympathy for her. In addition to losing her brother, there was the realization that her sacrifice and all the horrible things she went through ended up being for naught. The whole point of marrying her to Voss was to clear the family's debts so her brother could prosper.

This meant that Hessel would be Agatha's in time. I believed that she was capable of succeeding. It might end up for the best, but at a horrible cost.

31

It was late afternoon when we saw the main house. Perched on a small rise, it projected a faded grandeur. Even from a distance, I could see that it was in need of a coat of paint.

We rode up to the front door. Agatha sat motionless on Chester for a couple of minutes. I knew she was steeling herself for what was to come. Then, she nodded, as if confirming something to herself, and dismounted.

I followed suit, the tug in my side from the wound only a faint reminder now. Agatha tied Chester to the rail in front of the house slowly and deliberately, delaying the next step. I looped Rufus's reins next to Chester's and waited while Agatha crossed to the foot of the front steps.

She climbed them as though her feet were encased in lead. I had to think that she would have run up them if not for the news of her brother's death. I followed, a pace behind. Agatha stood at the door. She raised her hand to the knocker, then thought better of it. Instead, she opened it.

"Hello?" she called.

Over Agatha's shoulder, I saw a woman enter the main hall. She looked like an older version of Agatha, with the same strong features, blonde hair, and square shoulders, but terribly drawn in the face. When she realized who was at the door, she stopped dead. A moment later, she collapsed to the floor, having fainted dead away.

I shouldered past Agatha and rushed forward, kneeling and picking up her mother's unconscious form in my arms. She was completely limp, but I could tell she was breathing. I stood and gave Agatha a questioning look.

"In here," Agatha said, pointing to the left.

I followed Agatha into the room—a parlor. The furniture in it was old and of fine quality, but it did not seem as though the room saw much use. There was a divan, and I laid Agatha's mother on it. Agatha moved quickly to sit next to her and gently laid her hand upon her face.

"Mamma?" Agatha asked. "Mamma?"

It took an anxious couple of minutes, but eventually her eyes fluttered. She opened them wide to see Agatha staring at her with concern. Her mother's look changed from confusion to recognition.

"Agatha? Is that really you?"

"Yes, Mamma."

"By Serethyn's grace!" she breathed.

Her mother reached up her hand tentatively, as though Agatha might suddenly disappear. She touched Agatha's cheek gently, and Agatha leaned into her hand. Sitting up, she wrapped her daughter in a fierce embrace.

"Oh, my child! My dear sweet child!"

The two of them were rocking back and forth on the divan, both crying. I stood silent, not wanting to disturb their moment. I felt like an intruder. Eventually, her mother pulled away.

"Let me look at you," she said, then noticed me. "And who is this?"

"This is Dexter Falk, Mamma. He's … he's the reason I'm here. He helped me escape the nightmare I was trapped in."

"Lady Mountjoy," I said, bowing, "I'm pleased to meet you, although I wish the circumstances were better."

"You've heard then?" she asked Agatha.

"Yes. We ran into Marco. He told us about Elias. He thought we had heard. It's just Serethyn's own timing that brought us back now. Where is Father?"

"He has hardly left his study except to go to the privy since hearing about your brother, except for when we buried him yesterday. He won't eat or drink. His heart is broken—and perhaps his mind has snapped—because of what he did to you, and now losing your brother. He had no idea what a monster Voss was. When he realized what he'd done to you, it shattered him. He has not been the same strong man you remember."

"But I'm here now, Mamma. I'm alive and well, thanks to Dexter."

"We only ever received the one letter from you, a couple of years back, when you told us that you were still alive but would not be able to contact us. That's all we knew, and we feared the worst."

"Mamma, it was as horrible as I'm sure you imagined, at least, until Voss died. I thought I was free then, but his business partner … well, I needed to go into hiding. I was working as a wagoneer, staying away from anyone who might recognize me."

"But you're here now. What changed?"

"Dexter," Agatha said, and she reached over and clasped my hand. "It's a long story, and we will tell it complete soon, but Dexter freed me."

Her mother had the same piercing gaze as Agatha. She looked me up and down. I met her eyes, letting her form her own opinion.

"Falk, is it? Northern name, if I'm to guess," she stated.

"Yes, my Lady."

"Let's dispense with that right now," she growled. "You may call me Julia. Your family?"

"No one of consequence, Miss Julia."

"Are you being modest or truthful?"

"Truthful. Poor farmers, with scarcely an argent to their name."

"Good. No need to flinch from that. You've clearly made something of yourself, and you brought my daughter back. That alone earns you a warm place in my heart. Please sit. The two of you must have ridden all day, and I'm sure you're parched. My little fainting spell interfered with my good manners."

"Mamma, I can get us some water," Agatha said. "Why don't you try to get Father from his study and meet us here?"

"Seeing you will either kill him or bring him back," Julia said. "Either is better than what he is now."

Julia rose from the divan, and I saw in her the same grace Agatha possessed. She smoothed her skirt unconsciously. Her eyes stayed fixed on Agatha for a moment.

"I'll fetch him but prepare yourself. He's only a shadow of the man you remember."

"I'll get us some water," Agatha said as her mother left the room.

I was thirsty, and a drink of water would be welcome, but I suspected Agatha was using this as an opportunity to compose herself. My thirst reminded me that the horses needed water as well. That might give me a convenient excuse to leave the family to their reunion.

Before Agatha returned, the door opened again. Julia was with a man who looked much older, though I reckoned he was roughly the same age as his wife. He had been tall, but now his shoulders were stooped. His hair, gone white, was unkempt, and his clothes looked like he had been sleeping in them.

"What's so all-fired important that you're bothering me, woman?" he complained. "Him? Who's he?"

"He's the man who brought your daughter home."

"You must be seeing things, woman," he snapped, clearly dismissing me. "Agatha's dead. She's never coming home. I killed her, just the same as that poisonous toad Arkady Whitman killed Elias."

His timing was perfect, as Agatha returned that very moment, bearing a pitcher of water and some glasses. For her part, Agatha quelled her reaction. She crossed to the table and set down the tray before turning to her father.

"I'm not dead, Father," she said, stepping into his line of sight.

It seemed as though his vision cleared at those words. He opened his eyes wide and blinked. Agatha crossed to him and knelt, taking his hands in hers.

"Agatha? Oh, praise Zoryn and all the other gods! Agatha?"

"Yes, Daddy."

I decided this was a good time to water the horses. None of them noticed me leave the room. I went out the front door and untied both animals. On the ride up to the house, I'd seen the stables behind, so I headed in that direction. A groom appeared shortly after I rounded the corner of the house. He was older than Marco by a good bit but looked to have a sinewy strength to him.

"Who're you?" he demanded, his hands on his hips.

"My name is Dexter Falk. I arrived with Lady Agatha a little while ago. She introduced me to Lady Julia, and she is just now seeing her father."

"Miss Agatha?"

"Yes."

"By all that's holy!" he muttered. "You here for the funeral? You're a day too late."

"The first we heard of it was from Marco on the way up to the house," I said. "We had no idea."

"What're you doing?"

"I was thirsty, and I figured the horses were, too. It gave me a reason to slip out while they—"

"Oh, I'll bet there's all kinda hugging and crying goin' on," the man said. "You're probably smart to let them work it out. If you talked with Marco and Lady Julia, you know things are a mess right now. Come with me. We'll get your mounts situated."

"And you are?" I asked.

"Gus. Gus Polever. Been the groom here for … well, for longer'n you been alive. Which one is hers?"

"The gray. Name's Chester."

"Gimme his reins. I'll take care a him. He's a good-looking fella. Glad to see Miss Agatha din't forget what I taught her."

"She chose my horse, too—Rufus."

"Aye. He'll do."

Together, we watered the horses, then unsaddled and groomed them. Gus kept a watchful eye on me, making sure I was being thorough. I must have done a good enough job—he didn't stop me to correct me.

"I'll take care a feedin' 'em," he said. "You been gone long enough that the tears'll be about ready to stop. Just head in through that door there, then follow your ears. You'll hear 'em, I'm sure."

"Thank you."

"Thank you, too, mister, if you really brought Miss Agatha back."

"I did, Gus."

"Well, it's too damn bad you din't get here a few days ago. Mister Elias might be alive if you had. But, better now than never, I s'pose."

I left Gus and crossed to the door into the kitchen. I smelled roasting fowl, but there was no one there. I heard the sound of talking from the front of the house. A plump woman was clearly eavesdropping. She jumped in fright when I appeared beside her.

"Shh," I said in a whisper, holding my finger to my lips. "Is the crying done?"

"Who're you?" she demanded in a whisper.

I was getting tired of the same question but answered her politely and quietly.

"I'm guessing you're the cook?" I asked. "No one was in the kitchen."

"Yes, I am, Mr. Falk. Martha."

"Well, as you can see, there will be two more for dinner."

"Gracious!" she hissed. "I didn't even think … there won't be enough with just one bird."

"Relax, Martha. Some additional vegetables and biscuits, and it will all come out fine."

"I'd better get busy. Will you please ask Miss Agatha to come see me when she can? We've all missed her so much."

32

None of them noticed when I reentered the room. I didn't feel the tingle of Sylvaris's presence, but figured he was the reason I was somewhat invisible to them. It was only when I poured myself a glass of water from the pitcher Agatha had brought in that she realized I was there.

The cheeks of all three of them were stained with tears. And yet, despite the emotional strain, both Agatha's mother and father looked healthier—more alive—than when I'd left the room. It was particularly noticeable in her father.

Still sitting, his posture was now erect. His eyes seemed clearer. Color had returned to his skin, although some of that was due to the tears that had been shed.

"Father, this is Dexter Falk," Agatha said. "He is the man who made it possible for me to come home."

Her father stood and offered his hand. His earlier survey of me had been dismissive. This was more evaluative. I clasped his hand.

"Mr. Falk, my daughter hasn't had the chance to tell us much yet," he said, his voice clear and strong but tinged with a slight rasp. "If you are indeed the reason she is here, then you will always be welcome in my house. Please sit and join us. I believe the deluge of tears is over now, though there may still be a few sprinkles. Julia, dear, I think we need something more than water. Will you please pour us something?"

Julia went to a sideboard. There was a decanter of sherry. She opened a door in the piece and withdrew four glasses. Agatha came and helped hand them out, giving her father the first, and me the second. She sat next to me on the divan.

"Zoryn, and all the other gods, we give thanks for Agatha's return," he said, and took a sip.

We all followed suit. The sherry was quite good—dry, crisp, with a slightly nutty hint. It cut through the dust in my throat even better than water.

"Agatha, please tell us what happened after the wedding, if it's not too painful," her father asked. "I learned later that we married you to a monster. You heard me apologize earlier, but I can never hope to forgive myself until I know the full extent of your suffering."

Agatha grasped my hand tightly. She took a strong swig of her sherry, then set the glass on the table. She cleared her throat and began. When she reached the part where we met, Martha called us to the dinner table. Agatha had originally hoped to spare her parents the worst details of her time, but the death of her brother changed everything.

Her father, Elias, Sr. (I was instructed to call him Eli), sat at the head of a table that could have held two dozen. His wife sat to his right, and Agatha to his left. I was given the seat next to Agatha.

"Let us give thanks to all the gods for Agatha's return," Eli said.

We all joined hands, and Eli said a short prayer of thanks. He then began to carve the single roasted fowl. We would not have much meat, but Martha had added some fried potatoes and green beans. While Eli was carving, Julia poured everyone a glass of wine.

The dining room reflected the former elegance of the house. Still a grand room, with polished hardwood floors, high ceilings, and ornate plaster moldings, it seemed to me to need a fresh coat of paint. None of it was peeling, but the atmosphere was dull and drab.

While we ate, Agatha resumed her tale, beginning with our meeting. She left out the telling of how we showered together—too spicy for her parents, who had just met me. Yet, as the story continued, it was clear that Agatha and I were together. I sensed no disapproval from either her mother or father.

When dinner was over, we adjourned to the parlor where we had been earlier. Julia lit some candles, as the light was fading. Eli poured everyone a small nip of port.

"Father, why does everything look so shabby?" Agatha asked. "I would have thought—"

"After clearing our debts, our first priority was restoring our stock, repairing the fences, and getting the entire operation back on solid footing, including hiring the hands that we'd been forced to do without for so long," he explained. "Your brother did a magnificent job, and last year, operations posted the best profit of my lifetime—by far. With another good year, we planned to use the money to start work on the house. But, even before losing Elias, it won't be a good year, I'm afraid."

"Why not?" I asked.

Eli set down his port glass with a heavy sigh. He ran his fingers through his graying hair. The candlelight made the lines in his face more prominent.

"It started when Dmitri died at the end of last summer, the middle of Marivelleth."

"The older Whitman boy?" I offered. "Marco told us a little."

"Dmitri died. Arkady said it was from a snakebite. The only problem is that the venom in the snakes in these parts doesn't act that fast. To die in under a day, the person bitten is usually in terrible poor health to begin with, and Dmitri was hale and sound. Anyone with any sense suspected right off that Arkady poisoned his brother. I think Mikhail, the boys' father, came to realize that. He supposedly died in his sleep but given that everyone already suspected Arkady killed his brother, it was easy to figure he killed his father, too. Probably smothered him."

"Isn't there any sort of sheriff or—?"

"The law is several days' ride away," Eli said. "I sent word to the magistrate when Dmitri died. By the time the message reached him and he came out, Mikhail was dead as well. And here's the thing—Arkady left both bodies out in the sun. It was uncommonly hot for that time of year, and by the time the sheriff arrived, there wasn't any way to tell what might have happened to either one. Both bodies had gone bad. There wasn't any way to tell what happened to them."

"The sheriff poked around for a day," Julia added. "Asked a lot of questions, but there were no witnesses. We were all pretty sure Arkady killed them both, but none of us had any proof. Without anything tangible to go on, the sheriff couldn't do anything. He shrugged his shoulders and rode back to Corwig."

"We started losing cattle that winter. Agatha, you know we always had a problem with strays. We didn't have the men to keep a better watch on them or the money to keep the fences up, even if we had the men to repair them. It was always a sore spot with the neighbors, Mikhail included. But he always returned any of our animals that wandered onto his property. He might give me a piece of his mind, but he was always fair. When we were able to get on top of things after … after…" Eli could not continue and seemed to deflate right in front of my eyes, remembering what he did to his daughter.

"When we got back on top of things, our neighbors were happy for us," Julia said, taking over the narrative. "There were still times when cattle knocked fences down, but as often as not, the neighbors needed to come calling on us to find their strays, instead of us always going hat in hand to them."

"That winter after Arkady took over, he changed the Whitman brand," Eli said, having regained his composure. "Elias took one look at it and knew the only reason Arkady did it was to overbrand any of our strays and claim them as his own. That winter, when we noticed a few head missing, Elias rode over, just like we had a hundred times before, except this time, Arkady said he was trespassing, and that none of the cattle on his property were ours. He wouldn't even let Elias look. Even so, Elias saw a few grown steers with fresh brands."

"You may not know this, Dex, but you brand cattle when they're calves— not when they're full grown," Agatha said.

"When the weather warmed up, near the end of Kravynth," Eli continued, "instead of a few head here and there, we started losing dozens at a time. Elias had the vaqueros keep a close eye on the area where our land butts up to Whitman's. A couple of weeks ago, some of the men saw Whitman's people knock down our fence and drive nearly a hundred head through. One of our men came and found Elias, and he rode out. He caught Arkady red-handed— literally. Our steers were bawling under the hot iron. He and Arkady had words, but there were more of Arkady's men than ours, so Elias left. We were going to go to the Council of Thanes."

"What would they do?" I asked.

"One thing the members of the Council can't stand is thieving. A few members would have come calling on Arkady and demanded to inspect his herds. They would have seen the overbranding, and Arkady would have been in serious trouble."

"What kind of trouble?" I asked.

"The last time a member was found guilty of stealing someone else's stock, the Council went to the Crown. The king took the man's holdings away and gave them to an honest relative—a cousin, I think. They also turned the man over to the Sylvarans for a brand on his cheek."

"Can the king do that?"

"Technically, all of this is his land," Eli said. "Our families were granted the use of it generations and generations ago, but we don't really own it."

"The law is clear," Julia said. "Thanes like us are stewards, not owners. We own the right to use it. The king at the time granted our family the use of the land as a reward for loyalty way back when, but we hold the land in trust. But if we fail, the Crown can step in. That is why … why we arranged Agatha's marriage."

"You were in danger of losing the land?"

"Yes," Eli said with a heavy sigh. "You were our last and only hope. But if I had known what a price you would pay, I would not have done it. And now, with Elias dead…"

"You still have me, Father. With Elias gone, can I not inherit?"

"Yes," he said hesitantly. "Of course you can," he added more firmly a moment later. "I just—you weren't—we didn't—"

"I understand, Father," Agatha said, patting his hand and giving him a kindly smile. "There is something else I haven't yet told you. We left the table before I'd properly finished my story."

"And what is that?" Julia asked.

"As his widow, I inherited Voss's estate. It is worth almost half a million dinars."

Eli and Julia both looked stunned.

"And there is quite a bit I glossed over regarding Dex," Agatha continued. "The best way to put it is that he helps people solve problems. It's how he's been making a living. He was working for Ugarte Trading when we met, trying to find out what happened to a shipment of spices from the Kryyder Islands. There is no one better suited to deal with Arkady Whitman than Dexter Falk."

"Are you a killer, Mr. Falk?" Eli asked, suddenly worried.

"I will defend myself to the best of my ability—"

"Which is considerable," Agatha interjected.

"But no one hires me to kill someone. I would not take the job if they did. In the situation at hand, if you asked for my help with Arkady, my goal would be to see that he faces justice. The problem we will face is that the only proof that he killed Elias will be if he confesses in front of witnesses. From what you've told me, the same holds true for his brother's and father's deaths. It seems to me that proving he stole your cattle should be easily accomplished. The consequences for that are still fairly dire."

"Aye, but it will leave that rat alive. None of us will ever be able to sleep soundly at night with him still drawing breath," Eli said. "But I'll accept whatever help you're willing to offer, Mr. Falk."

"What evidence was Elias going to present to the Council of Thanes?" I asked.

"It's in the study," Eli said. "I haven't touched it. He had a complete list of the animals that went missing, a sketch of Whitman's new brand, and written testimony from the vaqueros who were with him when he caught Arkady with the cattle."

"These testimonies?" I asked.

"Given to a priestess of Eldryne, who wrote them down," Julia said. "They bear her mark."

"Oh, very good," I said.

Magistrates would accept testimony given to a priestess of Eldryne, our goddess of wisdom, as being the truth. Much as Sylvaris occasionally granted me the gift of persuasion, Eldryne's servants could detect falsehood—always. Unlike Sylvaris, Eldryne did not play games with the gifts she granted. She was known for having no sense of humor.

33

"I think our best course of action will be for Agatha to present what Elias gathered to the Council of Thanes," I said. "I will accompany her for her protection. You and Julia need to stay here. Pull the vaqueros back to the house until we return to help keep you safe. Arkady has shown that he accepts no limits to his behavior."

"Why shouldn't I go?" Eli asked.

"Because I would feel the need to accompany you for your protection, leaving Agatha behind. I strongly prefer not to do that. Arkady might try to prevent us from reaching the Council, burn this place to the ground, or both. My guess is both. And I know Agatha will represent your interests well."

"It's a five-day ride to Corwig, and the road takes you past Whitman land. Arkady may spot you," Eli warned.

"Agatha, do you know the road?" I asked.

"Yes."

"Well enough to travel in the dark? From what you've told me, I doubt he keeps a watch. He's the one making trouble. He doesn't expect any to be coming for him. If we set off before sunrise, will we be past his place before daybreak?"

"Yes."

"Then we'll set off before dawn," I said.

"Take some of the men with you," Eli urged.

"Thank you, but no, sir. Keep your men here. Draw them back to the house to prevent Arkady from escalating things further. I don't know that he will, but better to be safe."

"Once you arrive in Corwig, it will take at least ten more days to gather enough of the Council to make a decision," Eli said.

"All the more reason to have your men close by. If Agatha is successful in presenting your case, what will be the next step the Council will take?"

"If Agatha is completely successful, they will forego sending a delegation to see for themselves," Eli said. "The Council will inform the king that Arkady is a thief and no longer can be considered an honorable vassal. The king will then strip the holding from Arkady and install a new person."

"Any idea who?"

"The last time something like this happened—many, many years ago, well before I was born—the king chose a relative of the former holder. Arkady has two male cousins, if I recall correctly."

"Yes," Julia confirmed. "Nikolai and Maxim. Maxim is the younger."

"I remember Maxim," Agatha said. "I met him when he came to visit back when we were children. He was a couple of years younger than Dmitri, but they could have almost passed for twins if they'd been the same age."

"Nikolai stands to inherit his branch of the family's lands," Eli said. "If the king strips Arkady of the land, but wants to keep it in the Whitman family, it will go to Maxim, unless there are other relatives I've forgotten. I don't know much about either young man. But that also means neither has a bad reputation, unlike Arkady."

"We'll leave before dawn," Agatha said. "Dex is right, Father. Pull the men back to the house."

"Have them keep watch through the night," I suggested. "If you have other neighbors who are friends, you might ask if they can spare some men. I hope this proves to be an unnecessary caution."

"Let's all hope that," Julia said.

"Let me write a letter, authorizing you to speak on my behalf," Eli said. "They would have listened to Elias without question, but some of them will have a problem dealing with a woman."

He disappeared into his study and returned with the letter. He dripped wax from one of the candles and embossed it with his signet ring below where he signed it. Agatha took it and put it with the rest of the material Elias had gathered.

We went to bed not long after. Her parents did not offer me a guest room. I reckoned that Agatha told her mother and father that we were intimate. Before turning in, I drank as much water as I could hold in order to have my bladder wake me before dawn.

Agatha wanted to be held, and I understood. Her anticipation of a happy homecoming had been smashed by the news of her brother's death—murder, we all assumed. Instead of a joyous reunion, we needed to embark immediately on an urgent errand to the Council of Thanes.

I wished I could be two places at once. There was no way I would allow Agatha to travel to Corwig by herself under the current circumstances. But I also feared for her parents. Arkady's actions demonstrated an escalation over time. The next step might be an attack on the house. Setting fire to it in the middle of the night would be my guess.

Agatha woke when I left the bed. We dressed together quickly and quietly. Our saddlebags were still packed, so that saved time. We headed downstairs and through the kitchen.

Sitting on the kitchen table was a bundle wrapped in cloth, along with a note. Martha had left some food for us—cheese and bread. I stowed it in my bags, and we headed for the stable.

Both Chester and Rufus knew us well enough that our arrival in the middle of the night did not spook them. We saddled them in the dark, working mostly by feel. After we climbed into the saddle, I let Agatha take the lead. She knew where she was going, and I did not.

The moon was a sliver, casting only faint light over the sea of grass that was the cortaderia. We rode in silence, Rufus keeping pace with Chester, with the only sound the soft clop of hooves on the dirt road. After about an hour, the sky began to lighten with the gray of false dawn.

"We're almost past Whitman lands," Agatha said quietly. "By the time the sun rises, they'll be behind us."

"How are you holding up?" I asked. "Things have certainly not turned out the way I thought they would."

"I'm still trying to wrap my head and heart around Elias being killed. It would be harder to accept if it had been an accident."

"All of you are convinced that Arkady killed him."

"You don't know Arkady. We do."

"Tell me."

"Arkady Whitman was always snake-mean," she said. "Dmitri once told me that their father caught Arkady mistreating their animals and beat his ass bloody."

"Did he stop?"

"Not according to Dmitri—he just made sure he didn't get caught again. All children like to play tricks on one another, all in good fun. Arkady wanted to hurt people. My father said Arkady was born with a forked tongue. There were a couple of the Whitman hands who were bad apples as well. Those were the two Arkady spent time with. Their father knew Arkady was trouble—how could he not?—but he tried to ignore him, hoping he would grow out of it. That clearly did not happen."

"Do you think he killed his brother and father as well?"

"I think it's completely believable. Arkady hated his brother. Dmitri was good in every way that Arkady was bad. When their father died, everyone knew Dmitri would inherit, and Arkady would get nothing. Dmitri would probably have allowed Arkady to stay on the property and would have supported him, but that wouldn't have been enough to satisfy him. Father is correct about the ringneck snakes in these parts. Getting a bite from one of them will hurt fiercely and might affect the area near the bite, but it wouldn't kill you if you got help. They're more of an annoyance than anything—like being stung by a hornet."

"If the sheriff has already visited, I don't think you'll be able to accuse Arkady of murder," I said.

"But with the material Elias gathered regarding Arkady stealing our stock and rebranding them, we won't need to," Agatha said. "For the Council of Thanes, all of whom depend on their herds for a living, stealing cattle is just as bad as murder. For anyone less than a Thane, it's a hanging offense."

We continued on in silence, as the sun rose behind us. I scanned the horizon often, but we saw no other riders until we encountered a group of three wagons approaching us. I gave Agatha some instructions while we were still out of earshot.

"Keep the brim of your hat pulled low and pretend to be disinterested."

"Where ya headed?" the man asked when he drew close.

"Altaden," I said, naming a town I knew was on the far side of Corwig. "You?"

"All the way to Lenoa. Thane always sends us this time of year. Who you going to see in Altaden?"

"I don't mean to be rude, but I'm a solicitor, and I can't really talk about my clients' business affairs," I explained in a kindly tone, but jerked my head slightly toward Agatha, as though to indicate that she was the client. "They pay me to keep my mouth shut."

"Oh. Gotcha," the man said with a slight grin. "No business of mine, anyway. Just making conversation."

"I know," I said with a smile. "And I hate to be stand-offish, but I need to act in the best interests of my clients."

We continued on our way. It didn't take too long before we lost sight of the wagons after cresting a low hill. Agatha looked at me and started to snicker.

"You are a talented liar, Dexter Falk."

"Well, someone as chatty as he was might share what he saw with the next people he meets," I said with a shrug of my shoulders. "If he tells one of Arkady's men that he saw a man and a woman heading to Corwig to summon the Council of Thanes, that might bring the kind of trouble we don't want. A man and a woman, whom he didn't get a good look at, traveling to Altaden on some unspecified business, won't mean anything. It helps that Arkady doesn't know you returned. If he did catch wind of that…"

"I understood all that," she said. "It's simply that your tone was perfect. You left that man feeling that, if I had not been present, you would have shared everything. As a result, he doesn't feel you're a self-righteous prig. In fact, he's probably laughing about how he put you in a spot."

"That was my idea. If I'd been rude, he would stew about it for miles, and it would stick in his memory. As it was, I was polite and slightly embarrassed— a perfectly normal and very human reaction. Chances are, he can't even recall clearly what I look like by now. If I'd upset him, his recollection would be much clearer."

"How do you know these things?"

"Some of it I learned while I was a boy in Meropan, some I picked up just from watching people and making mistakes."

"You're a lot more clever than I initially thought," she said with a smirk.

"You thought I was an oaf?"

"After giving me the side-eye all day, you stripped bare ass right in front of me in the rain. I thought you figured that one look at your manly form would have me swooning."

"Well, in my defense, you did come out and join me, as I recall. Of course, that was after you sat there and watched me as though you were at the theater. And I was very pleased that you did."

"To tease you further for your overconfidence. I planned to get you all worked up and then send you away."

"What changed your mind?"

"I'm not sure," she said. "I think it was because I recognized that you understood I was teasing you. Despite the temptation, you didn't try to escalate things."

"I was well aware that any number of people were watching us carefully from no great distance. If I tried to do something you didn't want, I suspected there would be four or five men with knives surrounding me in a heartbeat."

"At least four or five," she joked.

34

The remainder of our journey to Corwig was uneventful. When we encountered other travelers, we told the same story. I was a solicitor traveling to Altaden with my client on unspecified business. Agatha adopted an aloof, impatient pose to cut the conversation short.

Corwig was only a third the size of Lenoa or Tallesin in terms of people, but it sprawled over a low rise in the ground. The city center was not dissimilar, but the residential areas surrounding it sported plenty of green space. Agatha took us to the largest inn, in sight of the crown's administrative offices. The ground floor appeared to be made of fieldstone, with the upper stories of timber, sided with shake.

Arriving late in the day, we stabled Chester and Rufus. I tipped the groom a couple of quadrans to give both horses a thorough rubdown. Agatha handled the negotiation with the innkeeper, paying in advance for ten days but warning him that we might need to extend it to a full fortnight and possibly beyond. He seemed quite pleased by this.

He whistled for a boy, who came trotting out and shouldered our saddle bags. The youngster, no more than nine or ten years of age, took us to our room on the second floor. I gave him a quadrans for his assistance.

The room was well-appointed—a clear step up from the roadside accommodations we'd had on the way there. It featured a sumptuous feather bed that promised better nights of sleep than we'd enjoyed recently. When the boy left, Agatha flopped onto the mattress with a sigh.

"We made it," she said with a sigh, "and with Arkady none the wiser. We visit the Council chamber tomorrow. None of the thanes will be there, but there is a steward. He will take a look at what we've brought and then call a meeting of the thanes. Arkady will be summoned as well to answer the charges."

"What if he doesn't appear?"

"His absence will be construed as his response. The Council will decide without him or his testimony."

"How long will it take for the Council to gather?"

"More than half of the thanes reside within a ride of five days. Once they get at least half of the members, they convene, and their actions are binding. Given the seriousness of the accusation against Arkady, I imagine the Council will want more than a simple majority and will postpone the official meeting until the eighth or ninth day. That is why I told the innkeeper we might be here a fortnight. It might drag on for another couple of days after that."

"Don't you expect them to decide quickly?"

"I do. The material Elias gathered is damning. The eyewitness testimony, the truthfulness of which is attested to by a priestess of Eldryne, is unshakeable. After the Council decides, however, they inform the king. Getting a ruling from him might take a few days."

The following morning, after breakfast, we walked to the Council's office. The only person there was a wiry man, with a sun-leathered face, named Hargreaves. Agatha introduced herself and stated her business. Hargreaves immediately requested proof that she possessed the authority to negotiate on her father's behalf, although he did so apologetically.

"It's not so much for me, Lady Mountjoy, you see," he said. "Some of the thanes are a bit … prickly about certain matters."

"My father anticipated that. Here is his letter, with his seal affixed below his signature."

"Oh, that will do nicely," Hargreaves said with a reassuring smile after he scanned it. "Shut them right up, it will. Terribly sorry to hear about your brother. Only got to know him the last couple of years, but to know him was to like him. I knew the thane had a daughter, but thought I heard that she'd disappeared."

"I was away, but not disappeared exactly," Agatha said.

"Let me read what you brought. Take a seat, and I'll be with you as soon as I finish."

Agatha and I perched on the comfortable armchairs in what looked very much like the common room of a top-notch inn. I imagined the thanes socialized here when they gathered. If I looked in the next room, I would not have been surprised to see a keg of ale and a barrel of cider.

We listened as Hargreaves reviewed the material Elias had prepared. We could almost tell which piece Hargreaves was viewing based on the sounds he made. There were sharp intakes of breath, and then a low, soft whistle. I figured the whistle was when he saw the seal of the priestess of Eldryne on the witness accounts.

"I've seen enough, Lady Mountjoy," he called over. "There is ample reason to summon the Council. I will begin writing the letters immediately and send them by riders before the day is half over. You know I must inform Arkady Whitman of this, don't you?"

"I do," Agatha said. "My father has pulled the vaqueros back to the house and was hoping some of the neighbors would send some extra men over, in case Arkady tries something drastic."

"It would surprise exactly no one if he did," Hargreaves said. "But neither would his arrival in Corwig be too shocking. The man is unhinged. He might show up thinking he can somehow intimidate the other thanes. Maybe he plans to kill everyone? Every person who has heard is fairly certain he killed his brother and father. With the evidence you brought with you, they will add your brother to the list of his victims. But enough idle chitchat. I have letters to scribble, and riders to summon. It is a pleasure to meet you, Lady Mountjoy, although I wish circumstances were much happier. I will ask you one favor, though."

"Which is?"

"There is a temple of Eldryne here in Corwig. Take all your papers and have them copied by the staff and affix their seals. Bring me one set of the copies. I'll put them in our safe. You keep the originals, although ... where are you staying?"

"Barnaby's."

"Ask Barnaby to put your copies in his safe. There's no pressing urgency. It will take five days for the summons to reach Arkady, and five more for him to get to Corwig unless he rides through the night. But when he does get here—"

"He'll attempt to destroy the evidence against him," I said.

"Yes. Desperate men do desperate things, and I think we can all agree that Arkady has already shown what he is capable of doing," Hargreaves stated.

Hargreaves told us where to find the temple. On the way, we passed the temple of Sylvaris. We found Eldryne's temple, and a blue-robed priestess met with us. We asked them to make not one, but two copies of the documents. She asked Agatha to accompany her to the back, where some of the staff would begin the work of copying. I left Agatha there and returned to the temple of Sylvaris.

In my wide wanderings, I had not been to Corwig before. I took Hargreaves's warning to heart. Arkady might very well ride through the night to Corwig and attempt to destroy the evidence and kill the messenger. If that happened, I wanted to have assistance nearby.

The temple here was smaller than the ones in Lenoa, Eudus, or Tallesin, but those were cities built on trade—the province of Sylvaris. Corwig was the administrative center of the kingdom of Swardle, and the site of the royal court, but the trade that passed through was only a fraction of what those other cities handled. Still, though the temple was small, it was beautiful, surrounded by a beautifully manicured garden. No priests-militant, but gray-robed acolytes stood at the door. I felt the presence of Sylvaris's numen as I drew closer.

"Good day to you," I said. "My name is Dexter Falk, and I would like to see the head priest if it is convenient."

"May I ask in what regard?" one inquired.

"My business is my own, I'm afraid, but you can tell the head priest that I recently assisted Azar with some unpleasantness in Lenoa. He may have received dispatches about that recently."

"Would you like to come inside, out of the sun?" one asked politely while the other slipped away.

"It's still quite pleasant here," I said. "If this were a few hours later in the day, I would very much appreciate being invited in, but I will stay with you and enjoy the fresh air, if you don't mind."

A few minutes later, the other acolyte returned, accompanied by a striking-looking woman. If I had to guess, I would say she was roughly twenty years older than me, based on her gray hair, but her face was unlined and quite beautiful. I gave her a slight bow of respect.

"May I ask your name?"

"Dexter Falk, Your Grace."

"Well, if that doesn't beat all," she said with a smile. "Just yesterday, I read a missive from Azar regarding some trouble in Lenoa, and your name figured prominently in its resolution."

The acolytes were both impressed. What I had told them was the truth, verified by the head of their temple no less. The priestess beckoned me inside, and I followed her to the rear of the building.

We did not go to an office, but to some cushioned chairs on a veranda on the rear of the building. She offered me a glass of water, which I accepted. She then bade me sit.

"What in the name of all that's holy brings a personage such as yourself to Corwig?" she asked after she took her own seat. "My name is Leora, by the way. I won't have you continue to call me, 'Your Grace.' It would make me feel uncomfortable, given the assistance you provided us recently."

I explained the situation with Agatha, her family, her brother, and Arkady Whitman. Then I passed along Hargreaves's warning that Arkady might come to Corwig. Leora nodded thoughtfully.

"You want help nearby if that happens," she said before I had the chance to ask.

"Yes."

"And it will be at least eight or nine days before this Whitman fellow can get to Corwig?"

"Yes."

"Good. That gives me some time. We're a small temple, as I'm sure you noticed. We have only six priests-militant, and they are scattered all over the cortaderia. It will take me that long to send acolytes out and bring three or four of them back."

"What do your priests-militant do out on the plains?"

"It's an interesting thing about our god," she said. "According to the legends, his first recorded act was stealing his brother's cattle. Despite that, Sylvaris does not tolerate the theft of livestock by humans. Cut-purses, petty thieves, and the like, he looks out for. Reiving, he will not accept. The priests-militant ride in search of the small bands that can arise from time to time, preying on the herds of the thanes. The thanes support the temple generously as a result."

"I noticed it is very well-kept. The grounds are beautiful."

"Thank you. The donations from the thanes make it possible. Anyway, with the priests-militant so spread out, it will take time to bring them to Corwig. Where are you and Lady Mountjoy staying?"

"I believe it is known as Barnaby's."

"He is a good man, and a friend to us."

"I have decided to return to her parents' house. Arkady Whitman has already demonstrated that he will choose violence. I worry that Lord Mountjoy and his vaqueros will not be enough. If I do not return to Corwig before this Arkady fellow, please have the priests-militant protect Lady Agatha."

"Consider it done."

"There is one other favor I would like to ask, Leora. We are having copies of all our evidence made at the temple of Eldryne right now. One set will go to Hargreaves; we will ask the innkeeper to put the originals in his safe, and I would like to ask you to keep the other set of copies. It is probably more precaution than is necessary, but I will sleep better knowing that you hold a set. Arkady Whitman will know or suspect that the Council of Thanes will have copies, but he does not know of my connection with the temple of Sylvaris."

"We will keep them safe," she said, then smiled. "It is more precaution than necessary, but better to be overprepared. This Arkady is just one man."

"With his hired thugs. I have only been in Corwig a short time, but my sense is that violence is unknown here, due to the presence of the king. The local constabulary is probably not prepared for someone like him."

"That's a fair assessment, except you forget the thanes. None of them will travel to the city alone. Their men are hardened by the cortaderia. They will know how to respond to anything this man attempts. And with some of the priests-militant to help, you should be able to deal with him successfully."

35

“And after this is resolved, what then, Dexter?” Leora asked.

“I would like to see what happens with Agatha. I’ve never felt this way about any woman before.”

“I can see that. What if the god we both serve has other plans for you?”

“I hope he doesn’t, but I suppose he will make that known somehow.”

“I suppose he will,” Leora said with a smile.

Leora changed the subject deftly and dismissed me shortly after. When I left to return to find Agatha, I wondered what Leora was trying to tell me, or what she had been able to see. All she did was trouble me. I tried to put it out of my mind. Other issues were more pressing.

After finding Agatha at the temple of Eldryne, with the documents in hand, we returned to give a set to Leora and one to Hargreaves. He was busy writing the summons to the thanes, and we left him to it. The originals we took to the inn and gave to Barnaby to put in his safe.

“Expecting trouble, Lady Mountjoy?” he asked.

“Not for a week or more. Would you do us a favor, in addition to storing this information?”

He nodded.

“When a man named Arkady Whitman arrives in the city, in eight or nine days, please tell him you’re full and have no room for him.”

“I don’t recall meeting the man, but I’ve overheard some pretty unsavory talk about him from thanes who’ve visited. Please don’t get the impression I eavesdrop. It’s just that heated conversation is hard to unhear, if you get my meaning.”

"And what have you heard?" I asked.

"Speculation is that he killed his older brother and then his father. I haven't heard anything since. If there's even a whiff of truth to it, I don't want him under my roof. I'll gladly turn him away, even if he is a thane now."

"Thank you, Mr. Barnaby."

We left, hand-in-hand, and climbed the stairs to our room. Agatha loosened her hair. She flopped on the bed with a sigh.

"All we can do now is wait for the thanes to gather."

"And ready ourselves for Arkady, if he comes."

"Do you think he will?"

"I'm almost certain of it. Unfortunately, I think that will be the second thing he does."

"What will he do first?"

"Commit some act of violence toward your family. I am going to ride back to help your father and mother. Although I am reluctant to leave you here alone in the city, you are safe for now. The more I have thought about it, the more I feel I should start right away."

"Then I will come with—"

"You absolutely will not come with me," I stated firmly. "You must stay safe and present the case to the thanes when they arrive. I have no standing with them. As an outsider, and not a member of your family, I doubt they would even allow me the opportunity to speak."

"But I don't want you to go."

"And there is a large part of me that would love to stay here with you, but I'm afraid I must leave. You've sacrificed enough, Agatha. I will not allow your family to be taken from you. If I depart now, I may be able to catch up with the rider Hargreaves sent."

"I understand the logic, and I worry for my parents as well. Marco and the others are good men, but I sensed he was a bit frightened by the people Arkady has."

"Thank you for understanding," I said, then turned to return my clothes to my saddlebags.

It did not take long, as I had not unpacked when we arrived. When I finished, I turned around to see Agatha naked on the bed. She held her arms out to me.

"If you are going to leave, I want to give you a proper send-off," she said with a sly smile. "Something to entice you to hurry back, safe and sound."

"I would have hurried back regardless," I answered as I stripped off my clothes to join her, "but this is powerful incentive indeed."

Needless to say, I did not hurry my departure. I figured I could just ride later into the night to make up for it and would consider the time well spent. Eventually, reluctantly, I pulled myself away and dressed.

"You will come back to me?" she asked.

"Gods permitting," I said as I shouldered my saddlebag and left the room.

I headed to the stable and started saddling Rufus. The groom came to do it, but I waved him off, flipping him a quadrans anyway. I finished quickly and mounted. The twinge in my side was almost gone. Only the faintest reminder was still present.

For the next four days, I pushed Rufus as hard as I thought he could handle. We started early and rode into the night. I did not encounter the rider Hargreaves sent among the people we overtook.

Agatha had definitely sent me on my way with something to think about. She was never far from my mind as we traveled back to her family's home. Unfortunately, Leora's question troubled me.

"Who goes there?" came a voice from the dark just after I turned off the road well after dark on the fourth night after I set out, with a half-moon to guide me.

"Dexter Falk," I replied, reining Rufus in. "I was the one who rode to Corwig with Lady Agatha."

"What are you doing back here? Is she with you?"

"She is still in Corwig. The summons to call all the thanes to Council went out. Arkady would have just received his. I came to help in case he tries anything."

"Who can vouch that you are who you say?"

"Marco, the thane, Lady Julia, Gus, and Martha are the people I met."

"Come with me, then. We'll wake Marco up. Hand me the reins."

"Lead the way. I'm here to prevent trouble, not cause it."

The man led us toward the stable. The first person we saw that I recognized was Gus Polever. The man nudged him with his boot, and Gus woke, startled.

"This fella here says you know him."

"Aye," Gus said after squinting in the dark. "Sandy hair, tall drink of water, brought Miss Agatha home, then went with her to Corwig. Your name escapes me, mister. What're you doing back here?"

"Dexter Falk, Gus."

"That's it. Why're you back? Where's Miss Agatha?"

"Agatha is still in Corwig. We met with the steward of the Council, and he sent notices to all the thanes for a meeting. I tried to catch up with the messenger but wasn't able to. Arkady would have received a summons to answer to the Council earlier today, if I had to guess. He knows who is to blame for the summons. I reckon he'll lash out before he heads to Corwig."

"He'll come flaming hot, I reckon," Gus said. "We been keepin' watch since you left, pulled the herds back as much as we could. There are twenty of us, but Whitman has more and they ain't vaqueros so much as thugs on horseback. Neighbors on the far side of Whitman's have promised to send some men, but they hain't arrived yet. Neighbors to Whitman cain't spare a soul. He been raiding their herds, too. Not as bad as what he done to us, but enough that they won't spare a man. We can use you, for certain. Long as you woke me up, lemme take your horse. Looks like he's tired."

"He brought me from Corwig in less than four days, so I imagine he could use some rest and care," I said as I dismounted.

"You do that, boy?" Gus said, addressing Rufus and stroking his snout. "Knew we needed help, did ya? Good on ya. Come with old Gus and we'll give you nice rub and summat to eat."

"You want me to wake Marco, too, or just head up to the house?" the man with me asked.

"I'll just head up. Do you think anyone is still awake?"

"Martha is, by the light. Just give her a soft yoo-hoo so you don't startle her too bad and end up waking everyone."

I trudged up to the kitchen door and opened it softly, calling out quietly as instructed. Martha came bustling downstairs in a nightdress, carrying a candle. She approached slowly until she could see my face.

"Mr. Falk!" she exclaimed quietly. "What're you doing here? Is Miss Agatha—?"

"Agatha is still in Corwig. I came back because Arkady will have just received the summons from the Council, and I figure he'll do something reckless."

"You poor thing. You look just about done in. Should I wake the thane and Lady Julia?"

"I hate to disturb their sleep, but I have a feeling that will happen in the next few hours anyway. If you don't mind, Martha."

"I'll be right back," she said. "You go on and take a seat."

I saw a chair over by the kitchen table and went to it. No sooner did I plunk my butt down than the door opened again. I immediately jumped up.

"Mr. Falk?" came a voice in the dark.

"Is that Marco?" I asked.

"Aye. I heard you might be bringing trouble with you."

"The trouble was coming whether I did or not," I said. "I wanted to hurry back to lend a hand if I could."

"Aye. Tomas told me that Arkady would have just gotten notice from the Council. We should wake the thane and Lady Julia,"

"Martha just went to get them."

Sure enough, a couple of minutes later, we saw the light of Martha's candle from the back stairway. There was another light behind her. She entered the kitchen, then stepped aside and used her candle to start lighting lamps.

Before Eli and Julia had the chance to ask me the same questions I'd faced since my arrival, I told them why I was here before they had the chance. When I mentioned that Agatha was still in Corwig, I saw relief wash over Eli's face. He came over and sat at the table with me.

"You think he'll come for us? Or head to Corwig?" Eli asked.

"Of the two, I am almost certain he will pay us a visit tonight. Regarding Corwig and answering the Council's summons, I'm less sure of that. He may try to do both, but only if he leaves no survivors here."

"Aye," Eli said, nodding his head thoughtfully as Julia shuddered. "Just as you say. He'll know the reason for the summons came from us, so he'll want revenge. Of course, if he attacks us, he will lose his case with the Council when they hear of it. It won't matter if he kills all of us. They will figure it out. I wonder if he has thought that through. Probably not. And Agatha is far safer in Corwig than here. Marco, wake the men. I'm afraid no one gets any sleep tonight."

"You think he will move so soon?" Marco asked.

"I do," I responded. "I haven't met the man, but from everything you've told me, I think he started off just after he received the summons. The only reason for delay he has is that he wants to hit us after the moon sets. That will be any minute now."

"Then I'll go make sure everyone is alert."

"He's probably going to try to burn the buildings to the ground. Have the men pull buckets of water and bring them up here to the house. Make sure there are no animals in the barn. I don't think we'll be able to prevent losing that, but I want to save the house if we can. Once the moon sets, he'll be coming."

36

Marco did as I asked. Within a few minutes, the vaqueros were hauling buckets of water up to the house. Eli told them where to place them. Julia and Martha grabbed a couple of the men and moved all the furniture away from the windows.

They finished these tasks just before the moon dipped below the horizon. I looked around for Marco but couldn't find him. Just when I started to worry, he announced his presence behind me with a small cough.

"Sorry, Mr. Falk. I was taking care of a few last-minute surprises for our friends."

"Really? What?"

"I've strung some ropes between the house and some of the trees. They won't see 'em in the dark. It'll knock a few of 'em out of the saddle, mebbe break a neck or two. We kin hope."

"How high?"

"Won't bother us none, on foot. Them who's ridin', it'll catch 'em in the chops."

I chuckled softly. It was a clever ploy. Whitman and his people would probably never see the ropes. If they rode into them at any sort of speed, a broken neck was entirely possible. Even if the rider managed to avoid that fate, he'd be knocked to the ground unexpectedly and easy prey for Marco's vaqueros.

Marco went off to position his men. I was about to head after him when Eli came outside. He was holding a saber in his hand.

"Eli, my lord," I said politely, "I understand you want to defend your home and avenge your son's death, but we can't take the chance of you getting killed. Julia and Agatha will need your strength in the days to come. Your best place is inside, defending Julia, and directing any efforts against the fire, should it come to that."

"Mr. Falk, I am the Thane of Hessel, and I do as I please on these lands," he growled.

"I understand completely, my lord, but think of your wife and daughter. They've already lost Elias. Losing you would break them. If you are resolved to test yourself against men younger and fitter than you, who have no mercy in their souls, I cannot stop you. But if someone manages to get past the rest of us and makes it into the house, who will protect your wife?"

Eli glared at me defiantly, his grip on his saber tight enough that in the dim light from the window, I saw his knuckles go white. He clenched his jaw and tried to stare me down. I held my ground and returned his gaze with, I hoped, a kindly expression.

"Damn you, Falk. I want to make my stand. I don't want to hide with the women."

"Except this woman needs you, Eli," Julia said, appearing in the doorway behind him. "We have lost Elias, but Agatha has returned. She is the future of this holding, but she will need your guidance to help us recover after all this is over. You won't be able to provide it from beyond the grave."

"Keep your saber, my lord. As I said, if someone manages to get in the house, that is where to make your stand."

"Please, Eli?" Julia asked.

"Fine," he muttered grumpily. "I'll do it, but don't expect me to like it."

As they went back inside, I stepped off the porch toward the barn. The half-moon had set, and the night was extremely dark now. I heard someone hiss at me.

"Over here, Falk," Marco whispered from the corner of the house. "They're coming. See the torches?"

I peered into the darkness. Like fireflies, I saw at least a dozen torches bobbing along. I reckoned they were just under three miles away. At a canter, they would be upon us in roughly a quarter-hour.

"How many crossbows do we have?" I asked.

"A half dozen."

"Aim for the men with the torches first."

"They know."

It was less time than I thought before they drew close. They must have been coming at the gallop and not a canter. Their horses would be winded by the time they reached us, not that it mattered. They were probably figuring they could return to Whitman's at a leisurely pace once we were all dead.

The torches grew closer. There were fourteen of them. I could see no other riders, only those carrying the firebrands.

"The one in front is Whitman," Marco whispered to me.

I withdrew my rapier from the scabbard and prepared myself. For the first time, I got a look at Arkady Whitman in the glow of the torch he carried. Even at this distance, I could see that his face bore a sneering grin. My guess was that he had left immediately upon receiving the summons, judging from his expression.

"Rico's group to the barn, just like I said," Whitman shouted. "The rest of you with me to the house."

Marco's vaqueros might not have been soldiers, but they knew patience. They also knew the importance of making every shot count, as one didn't get a second chance when hunting the jaguars and panthers that preyed on their herds. I heard the twang of their crossbows then, and saw six of the seven men heading for the barn fall, their torches landing on the ground. The remaining rider only lasted two seconds more before something pulled him from the saddle.

I had no time to admire the efficiency of Marco's men. Whitman's group was almost upon us. If it had been me, I would have posted our crossbows by the house instead of the barn, but it was too late now.

Suddenly, one at a time, three of the seven men with Arkady were yanked from their saddles. They had not seen the ropes Marco had strung between the trees. Their horses continued, but the men were jerked backward, their torches flying into the dry grass.

Another man was pulled from the saddle, but not by one of Marco's ropes. As they drew next to the house, another man fell. I learned later that the vaqueros used their long whips with great effect.

That still left Arkady and another man. They pulled up short. The man with Arkady tossed his flaming firebrand onto the porch. Arkady aimed for a window. As he went to it, I came from my hiding place at a sprint.

I was a split second too late. With a crash of broken glass, his torch flew through the window just as I pulled him from the saddle. We both tumbled to the ground, with him landing on top of me and knocking my wind out.

He was on his feet first, a wicked-looking long knife in his hand. My rapier was somewhere on the ground. Bent over, trying to breathe, my first concern was Arkady, who slashed at me viciously. I dodged, but he slashed backhanded deep into my left arm, which I had thrown up as a defense. He followed that with a punch that caught the side of my head and knocked me over.

I rolled to the side just as he pounced to finish me off. I kept rolling and bumped into the hilt of my rapier. Grabbing it, I came to my knees, just as Arkady lunged at me again. He ran onto my outstretched blade, which entered just below the ribcage on an upward path.

His eyes showed furious disbelief. Rage and pain were mixed in the expression I saw in the light from the torch that landed on the porch. His knees gave way, and I needed to tug my arm back quickly to prevent him from dragging my sword with him as he fell.

I stood, just now recovering my ability to breathe freely. My first worry was the man who rode with Arkady to the house, but I did not see him. Already, Marco's men were running toward us, preparing to fight the fire that had already begun to spread. Then I allowed myself to assess the gash in my forearm. Even in the dim light, I could see he'd cut deep, possibly to the bone.

The flames were licking greedily at the dry wood siding of the house. Already, the fire had gained a purchase. I stood, holding my bloody rapier, as men came past, reaching the buckets we had already placed by the house. Stooping, I wiped the blood off on Arkady's shirt, then sheathed my blade.

It was then that I remembered the torch he had thrown through the window. I headed for the door, feeling weaker with every step. Before I reached it, Eli came striding out. He stopped me with an outstretched hand on my shoulder.

"Nothing to worry about inside," he said. "Julia and I took care of it. The precautions we took paid off."

He headed around to where the others had doused the fire on the porch. It was well and truly out, but a man stood by with a full bucket of water, just in case. We heard Marco calling to the men to put out the grass fires that had started from the fallen torches.

"Six of 'em are still alive," Marco said, appearing from the darkness. "We got 'em tied up like calves for branding. What do you want to do with 'em?"

"I suppose that's good enough for now," Eli said. "Have the men keep a close watch on them. We need to hold them until the sheriff gets here. Come morning, we need to send a rider for him."

"Aye."

"In the morning, have the prisoners start digging graves. We can't bury the bodies until after the sheriff's visit, though."

"Aye. Where do you wanna keep 'em? They'll start to stink real quick."

"By the manure pile," Eli said with a smile. "The men did a great job tonight, Marco. We owe you our lives."

"Truth be told, Eli, it turned out to be a lotta fun. It sure was nice gettin' some of our own back, after what these fellas done to us and to Mr. Elias. Mr. Falk, I saw you done for Arkady."

"I did."

"Good."

"Unfortunately, that means you need to stay until the sheriff comes," Eli remarked.

"We got plenty a witnesses who kin say it were self-defense," Marco said.

"Even so, Mr. Falk needs to stay until the sheriff hears what happened. Otherwise, it looks bad. Mr. Falk doesn't need any taint of guilt to follow him," Eli stated.

"Mr. Falk, pardon my sayin' so, but you don't look so good," Marco commented.

It was at that moment that I collapsed. What happened after that, I wasn't awake to experience. When I woke, I could smell Agatha on the bedclothes.

They'd carried me upstairs and put me in her bed, the one we'd shared before heading to Corwig. As pleasant as the lingering smell of her hair was on the pillow, it was overwhelmed by the burning I felt in my arm. I raised it up to find it heavily bandaged, with spots of blood having soaked through the dressing.

It was day, but not a bright sunny one. I could hear the patter of rain outside the open window. It made me realize I was thirsty. I struggled to lift myself with only my right arm to help, finding I was as weak as a newborn kitten.

"What do you think you're doin' Mr. Falk?" Martha said, entering the room at that moment.

"I'm thirsty," I croaked.

"Then I'll fetch you some water. Let me prop you up first, but you're not to leave that bed until I say so."

Martha helped me sit up and fluffed some pillows behind me. She was surprisingly strong. When she was satisfied that I was comfortable, she bustled out. I could hear her talking to someone.

When she returned, Julia came with her. It was then that I realized I was naked under the sheet. I clutched it and drew it up higher as Martha handed me a glass of water.

"Gave us a bit of a scare, Mr. Falk," Julia said. "We thought we'd lost you for a bit."

37

"What happened?" I asked.

"After you fell down, they brought you into the kitchen," Martha said. "That cut is a nasty one—clear to the bone—but it missed the artery or we wouldn't be talkin' right now."

"Martha stitched you up," Julia said. "And Marco and some of the men brought you up here."

"Is everything under control?"

"I'll say," Martha said. "We killed eight of those criminals, including Arkady Whitman, and have the other six trussed up so tight they can hardly breathe. We have a couple of fellas keepin' an eye on 'em."

"We've sent a rider to fetch the sheriff, and another man to Corwig to let Agatha and the thanes know what happened," Julia added, as Martha departed.

"Where is Eli?"

"He took Marco and some of the men to the Whitman place to begin reclaiming the cattle they stole."

"What if they run into—?"

"Can't be more than eight or nine left," Julia said. "Eli, Marco, and the boys will outnumber them. Besides, when those thugs learn that Arkady is dead, they will probably take off. They weren't true vaqueros—more like highwaymen. If they know the sheriff is coming, and Arkady isn't there to speak for them, they'll probably decide there are greener pastures elsewhere."

"Is there much damage to the house?"

"We'll need to replace some of the siding and a few floorboards on the porch, but that will be easily remedied. The barn is untouched, and the house still stands, thanks to you."

"How is Eli? He was mighty upset when I shooed him into the house last night."

"He got over it pretty quick," Julia said with a laugh. "When that torch crashed through the window, he was right there. Doused it with a bucket before it had a chance to do any damage. And this morning, he seems more alive than he has since Elias was killed. With Agatha back and Arkady dealt with, we have hope again. Eli woke up this morning with things to do and a sense of purpose. I thank you for that."

Martha came bustling in, bearing a bowl of something that smelled like beef. When she placed it carefully in my lap, I saw it was a stew. She handed me a spoon.

"You need to eat up, Mr. Falk, get your strength back. You lost a lot of blood."

"Is that why I'm not wearing anything?"

"The clothes you were wearing got soaked," she said. "The shirt's a loss. I'm hopin' I can save the breeches and jacket. Your boots were covered, too. It took some time to clean them. Now, eat, or I'll start to feed you like a child."

"Yes, ma'am."

When the first spoonful hit my mouth, my hunger woke up. I realized I was starving, having not eaten since midday the day before. In a matter of moments, I'd finished the entire bowl.

"Good. I'll fetch more after I look at your dressing."

Martha came over and unwrapped the bandages on my forearm. They grew bloodier the further she went. The last bit was uncomfortable as the blood glued the fabric to my skin, and pulling the cloth away reopened the edges of the wound.

"Sit tight, Mr. Falk. I need to wash this."

Martha bustled away, taking my empty bowl and spoon with her. Julia pulled up a chair on my right. She reached out and took my hand in hers.

"You gave us a scare, Mr. Falk, when you collapsed like that. Eli was worried that you were done for, but your breathing was strong and steady. Martha stitched you up. It isn't the first time she's needed to do that for one of the men."

"Well, I'm grateful."

"Not half as much as we are. First, you free Agatha and bring her back to us, then you free us from Arkady Whitman. All I can figure is that the gods sent you to help our family in a time of great need."

Martha returned with two steaming bowls. One was more stew, which she placed in my lap again. The other was clean water just off the boil. She dipped a clean cloth into it and then began gently dabbing around the stitches she'd sewn. The water quickly grew pink as she rinsed the cloth after each pass.

The wound itself was ugly—a long, straight slash right down the middle of the top of my forearm. It was stitched tight with thick black thread, and fresh blood was welling up along the edges. Martha finished cleaning up the dried blood and then started wrapping my forearm again with a fresh bandage. Julia departed while she was ministering to me.

"You're lucky," she said. "The cut managed to miss the arteries and veins. A little bit to one side or the other, and we wouldn't be talkin' right now. You'd be standin' in front of Thalorix. I reckon what you did for this family would weigh pretty good in your favor with him."

"Thank you, Martha, for the stitches and the stew."

"You can thank me best by stayin' put, Mr. Falk. Don't try to get out of bed without hollerin' for help. You'll like to pitch face forward if'n you do, and you're too heavy so I'd just leave you lie on the floor."

"Yes, ma'am."

"You need a shave, too. I'll be back in a jiffy to scrape those whiskers from your face. You're better lookin' without the beard."

"So I've been told."

After Martha shaved me, I fell asleep to the sound of the rain outside. I woke to the sound of someone entering the room. Looking up, it was Eli.

"How are you feeling, Mr. Falk?"

"I would feel much better if you would call me Dexter, Eli."

"Fair enough. It's just … we're greatly in your debt."

"You don't owe me a thing, Eli."

"I'm afraid we'll have to differ, son."

"Lady Julia said you rode over to the Whitman place today. How did that go?"

"Well, good and bad. The good part was that the ruffians Arkady brought on scattered like leaves in the wind when Marco told them that Arkady was dead, and the folks who attacked us last night were either dead or waiting on the sheriff. I think they decided not to wait on his arrival."

"And the bad?"

"That damned Arkady…" He spat, then paused and collected himself. "We went out looking for overbrands. There were plenty. We came back with over a hundred head that he'd stolen from us, and we only saw a portion of their herds. It'll take a couple of weeks to sort it all out. I sent men to Whitman's other neighbors to let them know that no one was watching their stock, so they'll need to keep an eye on things."

"How long until the sheriff arrives?"

"Days. Depends on where he is and how quick our man finds him. You're not going anywhere soon, regardless, Dexter. The amount of blood you lost is going to keep you in that bed for at least a few days, and you won't be ready to do much for at least another week after that."

"Agatha should be returning from Corwig about then."

"Yes, she will. Of course, the whole problem resolved itself, without the thanes needing to weigh in, thanks to you. I'll be interested to see who the king chooses. Maxim Whitman would be my choice. He and his brother Nikolai are good men, like their cousin Dmitri was. Don't know how Arkady came from the same family."

It was another three days before Martha allowed me out of bed. She insisted that I take a bath. It was only after much pleading that I convinced her I didn't need her assistance.

When I finished, she wrapped a fresh dressing on my arm, which was now solidly scabbed over. I then dressed for the first time in days, and was allowed downstairs, but only once one of the men came to prevent me from falling. While I was weak, I wasn't wobbly, and I made it without difficulty.

After that, it was waiting on the sheriff's arrival. I spent my time on the porch enjoying the late-summer weather. Eli and the men headed out every morning to the Whitman place, culling their cattle from the Whitman herds. By the time they declared themselves satisfied, they'd retrieved nearly three hundred head.

Yet day by day, my thoughts grew muddier. When Agatha and I rode to Corwig, I was certain that I knew my future—with her. But waiting for the sheriff and Agatha's return, doubt started to creep in.

The cortaderia was not my world. Eli and Julia could not be any kinder to me or more grateful, but I sensed they still considered me an outsider. I'd already felt that in Corwig when we met with the steward Hargreaves. Agatha belonged here and was accepted. I was from somewhere else. Twenty years from now, I felt they would still consider me a stranger. I tried to talk myself out of these feelings, but they kept returning.

The sheriff's visit, ten days after Arkady's attack, was anticlimactic. It took only a few hours. He questioned everyone else before he got around to me.

"Let me see the wound they said you took," he asked.

Martha overheard and scurried out of the kitchen to do that. Sensing the sheriff's impatience, she hurried. He waited until she finished and went back inside before he spoke.

"They said it was a fair fight, and you acted in self-defense. From what I see here, I believe it. That the way you see it, Mr. Falk?" he asked while he peered at my forearm.

"Yes, sheriff."

"Well, don't expect me to be grateful," he said gruffly. "It's no different from killing a poisonous snake. Has to be done. No thanks accrue. You're free to go whenever, Mr. Falk. The law has no interest in you."

The sheriff's comment plucked the string inside me of my feelings of being an outsider. He assumed I would be moving on soon. After he left, and after Martha rebandaged my arm, I stayed on the porch, chewing on my thoughts. I remembered the priestess Leora's cryptic question and wondered what she knew, or what Azar might have told her in his letter.

"What if the god we both serve has other plans for you?" Leora had asked.

At the time, I was consumed with the problem of Arkady Whitman. I disregarded the question; not entirely, since it bothered me a bit on the ride back, but I'd shoved it to the back of my mind. Now the seed of doubt she'd planted was taking root. I'd forgotten about the letter Azar had given me. I remembered it now, buried in the bottom of my saddlebag.

He'd said I would know when to read it. It wasn't now. That was about the only thing I was sure of—that, and my feelings for Agatha. With the sheriff's visit behind us, her return was the next event on my calendar.

38

Three days after the sheriff's visit, I was again on the porch, waiting and watching for Agatha's arrival. My strength had returned, and Martha had pulled the stitches from my arm. Eli had invited me to ride with him that morning, and we'd just returned.

I saw her from a distance, but she was not alone. A man with dark brown hair rode next to her. They appeared to be in conversation. In that instant, a dreadful realization swept over me. I felt the tingle of Sylvaris's presence on the back of my neck.

Even though I could not make out the man's features yet, I knew he and Agatha were meant to be together. The certainty of it hit me like a punch to the gut. Sylvaris confirmed it. Saliva filled my mouth, and I felt briefly that I might be sick. I swallowed repeatedly, and the nausea passed, but the inevitability of what I'd felt remained.

Agatha rode with the easy grace I admired so, her blonde hair catching the sun's rays. The man beside her was tall and broad-shouldered, just like me. He laughed at something she said, and she tilted her head back and joined him, the sound of her laughter carrying to me on the breeze.

"Dex!" she cried when she turned and noticed me.

She nudged Chester forward in a canter, leaving the man behind. She stopped short of the porch and slid from the saddle, running to me. She threw her arms around my neck and kissed me. For a brief moment, my doubts fled, only to return when she released me.

"Dex, allow me to introduce Maxim Whitman," she said, gesturing to her riding partner, who had dismounted and was approaching on foot. "He accompanied me from Corwig. Max, this is Dex."

"Agatha told me you'd be here," he said, offering his hand.

His grip was dry and firm. His hand was callused from work. The smile on his face was genuine, and, as much as part of me wanted to hate him, another part did not and could not.

"Max? Or Maxim?" I asked.

"Max, if I'm allowed to call you Dex."

I nodded, with a smile on my face that I did not feel.

"We heard the story from the man you sent. The Council had already made its decision, but you cleaned up what might have been messy. Arkady was a blight on our family name. We have no doubt that he killed his father and brother, and Elias as well."

"Has the king—?"

"That's why we didn't arrive yesterday," Maxim said. "The king decreed that I should take over. My brother Nikolai is slightly upset. I'll have more land and a larger herd than he inherited from our father."

"I brought him here because we were worried that some of the roustabouts Arkady brought on might still be lingering around. Plus, there's no telling what sort of condition the place is in right now. I have a bad feeling that it's a mess."

"Plus, I don't have any help at the moment," he said. "Nikolai is sending a few men to help me get started, but I'll need to hire my own hands quickly."

Eli and Julia appeared then, taking the burden of conversation away from me. The four of them formed a tight little group, with me watching from a few paces away. They didn't intend to slight me—I knew that—but it reinforced my doubts and fears.

Martha came out with a pitcher of water, and oohed and aahed over how much Max had grown since she'd last seen him years before. They pulled chairs together to sit. I took one on the end.

Max, Eli, and Agatha were talking about cattle, grazing, fences, and such. I had nothing that I could contribute to the conversation. At one point, Julia caught my eye and gave me a sympathetic smile. Even she was able to take a meaningful part in the discussion.

Martha called us to dinner after a while. She seated Max next to Eli. I was next to Agatha, the furthest from the head of the table. Again, I knew they were not intending anything, but it played into the thoughts that had been plaguing me.

After dinner, the conversation continued. They discussed the rest of the Whitman clan and their reaction to what Arkady had done. This was another matter where I had nothing to add. After waiting a decent interval, I excused myself, claiming I was still feeling the aftereffect of my wound, and went to bed.

Lying there, I tried to sort out my feelings. I wasn't jealous; I was sad. I'm like most people—I take no pleasure in admitting to myself that I was wrong. And in this case, I'd believed the happy dream of a future with Agatha.

When she came to bed, for the first time, she did not curl herself against me. She stayed on her side of the bed and was still there when I woke. I don't think she did it consciously, but I took it as another sign. In the morning, I managed to slip out of bed without waking her, got dressed, and headed downstairs.

When the others were awake, and Martha put breakfast in front of us, I learned what they discussed after I went to bed the night before. Max and Agatha were going to head to the Whitman place and assess its condition. They would take ten of the men with them, just in case some of Arkady's people had circled back.

It was nearly a full day's ride to the Whitman house. I had no desire to join them. In fact, my absence might help Agatha and Max grow closer. It seemed inevitable to me now. Again, Sylvaris made his presence felt to me.

"What's wrong?" Agatha hissed at me after pulling me aside following breakfast. "Why won't you come with us?"

"Agatha," I said, thinking of my words carefully before I let them pass my lips, "you and Max … you both belong here. You have known him since you were children. He comes from the same world you do. That he will need your help, I have no doubt. Me? When you talk of herds and head, and calving and such, I understand what you're discussing, but I don't know the slightest bit about it. I'm just an outsider."

"That's nonsense," she spluttered, though I thought I detected the slightest bit of doubt—or recognition of the accuracy of my statement—in the corners of her eyes. "You've earned a place here. You saved my parents, the house … you killed Arkady for us. We owe you—"

"Nothing," I said calmly with a smile. "It's as the sheriff said, killing a poisonous snake isn't any sort of noble deed. It's just doing what needed doing. And it's done."

"So—what? You're going to leave me? I love you, Dex!"

"I love you, Agatha. I love you enough to realize that … that this isn't my world."

"What are you saying?" she demanded, although I think she already knew the answer, as I saw tears welling in her eyes.

"I'm saying that I need to do what must be done," I responded quietly, holding her gaze, "before it becomes obvious to you that I'm not the man you're meant to be with. If I leave now, you may hate me for a while, but in time, you'll remember me somewhat fondly, I hope."

"But—you saved me, Dex!" she pleaded. "You can't just leave."

The tears were spilling from her eyes now, but she had listened to me. They weren't just tears that I was planning to leave. She was also acknowledging that I might be right but did not want to admit it to herself. Her blue eyes, brimming with tears, had a flicker of uncertainty. I wondered if Sylvaris was affecting her as well.

"Agatha," I said softly, using my thumbs to clear the tears from her cheeks, "I'm not leaving because I don't love you. It's because I do love you that I must go. The cortaderia—the thanes, the herds, the vaqueros, the horses—it's what you dreamed of returning to."

"But you could make it work. You will learn. Father already knows he owes you—"

"But I will always be a stranger here, Agatha. When I saw you riding up with Max, it made me sick to my stomach. Not from jealousy—you gave me no reason to feel that—but because I saw that you were meant to be with him. Don't ask me how I know, I just do."

"There's nothing between us," she protested. "I knew him a little bit from when we were children, that's all."

"Max is a part of this land in a way that I will never be. He understands it from his upbringing. When the two of you were speaking about it last night and this morning, it was almost as though you were using a different language that I did not understand."

"But you will, eventually," she said.

"There's more to it than that, Agatha," I confessed. "When we went to Corwig, and I met the priestess, she hinted that Sylvaris had other plans for me. I didn't understand what she meant, but as I was waiting for you to return, I was troubled more and more. I do love you, Agatha, and all I want is for you to be happy for the rest of your life. The gods know you've earned that. It has been an unpleasant disappointment to realize that I am not meant to be a part of it."

"Go then," she said bitterly, "if that's what you want."

"It's not at all what I want, Agatha. It is what must be."

She turned away from me and headed outside. Max was there, already in the saddle, holding Chester's reins. Agatha mounted her horse and turned him away. She led the small procession back to the Whitman place. I watched her go, but she did not turn her head back.

After climbing the stairs, I quickly packed my belongings in my saddlebags and threw them over my shoulder. Eli and Julia were coming into the house as I came down the stairs. They gave me a puzzled look.

"I thought you weren't going with them?" Eli inquired.

"I'm not," I said with a rueful smile.

"You're leaving?" Julia asked plaintively.

"I am. Thank you for your hospitality."

"Does Agatha know?" Eli asked.

"Yes. We talked. She will probably hate me for a bit. I already hate myself, but I can't stay."

Eli and Julia shared a glance, the kind of look a long-married couple uses to communicate shared thoughts. I read from that look that they'd considered some of the things that bothered me. They felt they owed me a great debt, but I was not from their world.

"Dexter, we owe you for returning our daughter to us when we had nothing left in our lives except despair. Then you put yourself in between us and a killer," Eli said.

"But…" I offered.

"But … you might have your head squarely on your shoulders," he said with a shrug. "We've both noted you sitting on the porch these last few days, looking like storm clouds were swirling around your head, getting darker every day."

"The truth of it is," Julia added, "it was clear to both of us that this isn't home for you. I don't know where that is, and you might be one of those folks who never has one."

"You might be right, Julia," I said with a sigh. "I just want Agatha to be happy. I do love your daughter, and I hope that one day she realizes that it is because I love her that I'm leaving."

"You're right that she will probably hate you for a time," Julia said. "And, in a way, it's a kindness. It will help her get over the loss much quicker. But in time, she'll realize what a difficult thing you did. If she doesn't, I'll educate her."

"We'll always think well of you, Dex," Eli said, offering me his hand.

"I'm happy I was able to help."

"Be safe, Dex," Julia said, giving me a quick hug. "You'll always be welcome here—but you ought to wait a couple of years before you visit again."

I headed outside. Gus was just finishing saddling Rufus. I wondered if he had been listening to my conversation with Agatha or her parents, or whether Martha had alerted him. It could be that he simply knew it was time. I preferred to think that.

"Thank you, Gus."

"It's been a pleasure, Mr. Falk. Ride safe now."

39

I headed back toward Lenoa. It's not that I had any business there, but going there first was the easiest path back to Tallesin. As I rode away from Agatha's home, I sensed a feeling of sympathy from Sylvaris. I shook my head angrily. I was not happy with the god I served just now. When I reached the inn that night and went to my room, the letter Azar had given me somehow was now at the very top when I opened my saddlebag.

Dex—

If you are reading this when you are meant to, you have just made the painful decision to leave Agatha. I'm sorry. Sylvaris is not known for sharing the future—that is generally Eldryne's province—but he does provide me glimpses from time to time. I can tell you that the difficult choice you made will ensure that Agatha leads a happy and full life.

You may be feeling some resentment that I did not tell you back in Lenoa. That is because it was a choice you would have to make, at the appropriate time. I apologize, old friend.

Years ago, you asked me if you were meant for the priesthood, and I told you that Sylvaris had other plans for you. I can share with you that you have been doing exactly what the god wants, even though it is not given for you to understand what his desires are. Perhaps, many years from now, you will chart the course of your life, and things will become more apparent.

Other challenges, and other loves, await. They will find you, don't worry. Sylvaris will not waste your time on a ridiculous quest for meaning, the way some of the other gods do to their people. He does like his jokes, but not of that variety.

Someday, there will be a quiet hearth and a peaceful home for you. I'm afraid you have more miles to travel before you reach it. Do not lose heart. Enjoy the journey for the adventures it will bring.

Azar

P.S. Keep the horse she gave you. I know you have avoided owning one up to now. He is meant to be with you.

My feelings upon reading this were quite mixed, let me tell you. On the one hand, I was angry. Azar had known that Agatha and I were not meant to share a future. On the other hand, I felt relieved that I had made the correct decision, as unpleasant as it was.

Over dinner that night, I chewed on the words in that note as much as I did my food. I tried to think of things as objectively as possible. After returning to my room, I stared at the ceiling for hours. Eventually, I accepted that foreknowledge would have lessened my enjoyment of being with Agatha. I might not have stayed to help with Arkady, although I hoped I was noble enough of character that I would have. If I'd known we would part, perhaps I would hurt less now, but I would not have enjoyed myself as much along the way.

These conflicting emotions left me in a bittersweet frame of mind. Eventually, I gave up trying to figure it out. Azar had told me that I wasn't meant to understand. I decided to take him at his word.

ABOUT THE AUTHOR

John Spearman has been a Fortune 500 sales and marketing executive, a Latin teacher and coach at a prestigious New England boarding school, and an award-winning author. He lives in coastal Maine with his wife and their dogs.

If you enjoyed reading this book, please consider leaving a positive review on Amazon.com or Goodreads.com. It will help other readers like you find books they might enjoy. To learn more about the author's different works, please visit www.johnjspearman.com.